CW00664281

MERSEYSIDE POLICE MISSING PERS(

DATE:

8th September 2010

NAME:

Ruth Jennifer Anderson

D.O.B

4th May 1987

ADDRESS:

Flat 1, 149 St John's Road, Waterloo, L22 9QE

ATTENDING OFFICERS:

489 DC M Atkinson & 637 PC I Bassey

NEXT OF KIN:

Mr Jerome Anderson, 43 Highgrove, Solihull, Birmingham, B12 7JP

OCCUPATION:

Teaching Assistant, St Michaels High School, St Michaels Road, Crosby
L23 7UL

I

Where the fuck are you? - Detective Inspector Martin Atkinson asked himself. He put the file back in the cabinet. It was the only one marked "You Can't Win Them All". There were many others that, in the course of his career, could have been placed alongside it. But this was the first case he'd ever been in charge of as a fresh-faced Detective Constable. He hadn't been able to solve his first ever case. How shit was that?

*

A young teaching assistant, Ruth Anderson, had not turned up for work at the start of the new school year. After a couple of days there had been no contact and her colleagues had become worried about her. She had always phoned school in the past to let them know if she wasn't coming in. The school tried to contact her, but her phone went straight to voice mail. Ben Smart, the teacher that Ruth supported, was the first to go to her flat. He had no luck knocking on the door. He asked in the Copper Kettle, the café under the flat, if anyone had seen Ruth. No-one could remember seeing her since the end of July, when school had finished. The next day Smart expressed his concerns to the Deputy Head and, after consultation with the Head, it was decided to contact the police. PC Irene Bassey was the first officer to go to the flat. Like Smart, she had no joy from knocking on the door or talking to the staff in the café.

After a little research Bassey was able to contact Ruth's landlord, Mike Cooksey a local butcher, whose shop was just a few doors away. He came as quickly as he could and opened the door on the street that led to the flat. Inside was a flight of stairs and a narrow passageway.

'Where does that go?' Bassey enquired.

'Out to the back yard that's shared with the tea shop and then into the back jigger.'

Bassey thanked him for his help and took the key to the flat door. She put on a pair of blue nitryl gloves and walked up the stairs. Cooksey started to follow her, she turned and looked at him and shook her head. He shrugged and went back to his shop. As Bassey put the key in the lock and tried to turn it the door gently swung open, it was unlocked. Not knowing what she might see when she went into the flat, she took a deep breath and entered with some trepidation.

Just inside the door was a small entrance hall, the laminate floor looked new and clean. There were two doors to the left and one directly in front of her. The third wall had a large mirror and three coat hooks. A Nike hoodie hung from the middle hook, the other two were empty. There was a very faint smell of bleach in the air.

She carefully pushed open the first door on the left. She could see an old-fashioned matching avocado bath, shower, basin and toilet. On the wall was an open fronted cabinet which held Elvive Nourishing shampoo, Sainsbury's paracetamol, Rimmel nail polish remover and a packet of birth control pills. In fact, all the bits and pieces that you would expect a 23-year-old woman to have in her bathroom. On the shelf above the sink was a small glass tumbler containing two toothbrushes, a pink one quite well worn and a blue one, much less so. Next to the tumbler was a bottle of Oxylyse bleach, not a brand she'd heard of. The lid to the bottle was not properly secured – that accounted for the slight whiff of bleach when coming through the front door. There was a towel rail to the right of the sink with a neatly folded hand towel on it, no sign of a bath towel.

The second room was the bedroom, a very large bedroom. It contained a double bed, a double wardrobe, two chests of drawers, a dressing table and two bedside tables. All of which looked quite new. IKEA perhaps? The walls were painted a relaxing apple green colour with a matching roman blind covering the window. This was better furnished than her place. There was nothing at all out of place in the whole room. No pile of dirty clothes, no stray knickers or tights, no ironing waiting to be put away - nothing. Why couldn't she be this tidy? But there was no corpse or sign of a struggle either. So, anything unpleasant would now be behind the third door.

Bassey steeled herself and pushed the door open. Inside, was a well-proportioned living room leading through an archway to a small kitchen/diner. Again, there was no body and nothing looked out of place. Deffo tidier than her place. The whole flat looked as though the occupant had just stepped out after a very busy day of cleaning and tidying.

'Control, this is 637 Bassey. I've gained entrance to the flat at 149 St John's Road. No sign of the occupant or a disturbance.'

'637 Bassey, this is Control. Sit tight, we'll have someone round to assist as soon as possible. And don't touch anything!'

'OK. Bassey out.' She kicked the wall. Did they think she was some kind of idiot?

The assistance arrived about thirty minutes later, he was scruffy and looked not much older than Bassey. His shoes hadn't seen any Kiwi or Cherry Blossom for quite a while and his suit looked like one that his mother had bought him to grow into. Bassey was slumped against the wall with her hands in her pockets, in the street outside the door leading to the flat. She'd seen him around the station but they'd never spoken.

'I hope you haven't touched anything,' he said as he pulled on a pair of nitryl gloves, rubbing his shoes on the backs of his trouser legs.

'Do you think I'm a fucking idiot as well!' She straightened up and pulled her blue covered hands from her pockets.

The young detective looked perplexed.

*

It hadn't been a good start, thought Atkinson with a wry smile. He felt rather than saw someone standing in the doorway to his office.

'DCI wants to see you Ron.'

'OK, Shirl, I'm on my way.'

Detective Sergeant Irene Bassey turned from the office door smiling and remembering the first time Atkinson had called her Shirley. It had been 8 years ago, inside that flat in St John's Road. Since then she'd followed his career path throughout their time together at Copy Lane police station. Always one rank behind. That niggled her a little bit, but there was nothing she could do about it, at the moment at least. They made a good team though, and she enjoyed working with him. Life could be worse.

II

They climbed the stairs together, him in front and Bassey behind. He was over six feet tall, medium build and towered over Bassey's five feet six.

'I'm Detective Constable Martin Atkinson,' he said over his shoulder, 'so, what's your name?'

'Bassey, Irene Bassey. So, why'd they send you then?'

'No one else available. Big shout in Kirkby, someone had to stay and look after the shop,' he sounded disappointed. Stopping halfway up the stairs he turned to look at her. He gazed down at her for a few seconds with pursed lips, deep in thought.

'Every great detective has a side kick,' he suddenly said, 'someone who they can bounce ideas off, someone who makes them look clever. Holmes has Watson, Batman has Robin, Cagney has Lacey and Ant has Dec,' he smiled. 'It looks like you're going to fill that role today.' There was a short pause before Atkinson continued. 'Bassey eh? Atkinson and Bassey doesn't have a great ring to it. Neither does Martin and Irene. I know! How about I call you Shirley? Martin and Shirley? We'll sound just like that guy from Spandau Ballet and his wife. What d'you think?'

Wanker! That's what I'm thinking. 'How original,' Bassey said, wondering when he was going to pull out the oversized magnifying glass and deer stalker to prove he was the detective. 'I think I'll call you Big Ron, just to piss you off.'

III

Big Ron. She'd stopped calling him 'Big' after she found out that the ex-football manager turned pundit, had got into trouble making a racist comment about a Chelsea player on an open microphone that he thought had been turned off. Martin Atkinson may not be Sherlock Holmes, but even he wouldn't have been so foolish as to do something like that. Methodical is probably the best way to describe Atkinson, follow the marked route and no deviation. He makes lists for fucks sake!

He'd obviously been looking at that file again. He'd been going back again and again to that case for eight years and was no closer to solving it now than they had been at the beginning. Why didn't he just forget about it? Bassey knew the answer to that. She couldn't forget about it, so why should he? It haunted both of them.

*

Atkinson stopped at the top of the stairs, stooped down and examined the lock to the flat door.

'No sign of forced entry,' he observed.

'Well, there wouldn't be,' grinned Bassey. 'It was unlocked.'

They both went inside and stood in the small entrance hall. They could see into all the rooms as Bassey had left the doors open after her initial visit.

'All looks very neat and tidy. Is that bleach I can smell?' Bassey nodded. 'Did you find anything? Did you have a root about?'

'I just had a quick looksee to make sure there were no bodies lying about anywhere. I didn't touch or move anything. You know, being just a lowly PC, I thought I'd wait for someone in a suit with more experience and needing a sidekick to do all that.'

'OK,' Atkinson said, either ignoring or missing the multiple layers of sarcasm. 'You have a good look in the bedroom. Leave no sheet unturned.'

'Had we better not call in the Scene of Crime team?'

'It's not a crime scene Shirley. At the moment it's an empty flat. We'll get SOC when and if we need them.'

'OK, what am I looking for then?'

'I've no idea until we find it, and then I'll know. Plus, if you keep asking questions like that you'll always be in uniform and always be a sidekick.'

*

They'd both known it when they'd found it.

IV

Atkinson stood outside Detective Chief Inspector Mitchell's office looking at the wall next to the door. Here was the DCI's traffic light system. Mitchell had rescued it from the Headmaster's Study of his old school when it had been demolished in the late nineties. It was a very simple and effective device. A visitor would push the button at the bottom of the traffic lights. If the red light flashed it meant - I'm busy, go away and come back later. If the amber light flashed it meant – I'm busy, but I'll only be a couple of minutes, please wait. And if the green light flashed it meant – come right in.

Atkinson was sure that errant pupils had always hoped, or prayed, for the red light. He though always hoped for the green one, which is what he got. Before he opened the door and stepped inside, he gave his shoes a quick rub on the back of his trouser legs.

Reg Mitchell was not an impressive looking man. He was short and squat and looked every one of his 53 years. He'd started his career in Cornwall where he'd investigated fish market fraud, then tractor theft in Somerset, rape and murder in Birmingham and sheep rustling in North Wales, before arriving at Copy Lane. He'd taken over CID three years ago, when Atkinson had still been a DS. When Mitchell spoke, he spoke with a depth of experience few other policemen could match, so his input was always welcomed.

'Sit down Martin,' Mitchell said pointing towards a chair. 'Something has turned up in Bootle that I thought you might be interested in. A newsagent's on Bedford Road hasn't been open for the last 7 or 8 days. Locals and regular customers have been getting a little upset, he'd never said he was going away, and they've been having to walk a little further to get their Daily Mirrors and Lambert & Butlers. Someone contacted us and a PC went to have a look. He called for backup and they made a forced entry into the premises. Everywhere was clean and tidy. There was no sign of the newsagent, no sign of a struggle, nothing. I'd like you and Bassey to go and take a look.' Atkinson looked questioningly at Mitchell. 'I know he's not been missing for the same length of time, but I thought that there are similarities to that old case of yours that you keep going over. The missing young girl, Ruth Anderson wasn't it?'

Atkinson looked at Mitchell with surprise. 'How do you know about that case sir? It was well before your time here.'

'Eyes and ears everywhere me. Look, I know you want to find out what happened to that young girl, even after all this time it's still bugging you. This newsagent thing may just be a case of a man pissing off on holiday and not telling anyone. But I know that if you don't go and have a look …. So off you go, have a look and keep me informed.'

*

Bassey set to work in the bedroom. She started by emptying everything out of the wardrobe and putting it onto the bed. She then climbed in and inspected the interior of the wardrobe. But there was no note stuck to the back wall and no secret compartments. Bassey had been joking earlier about having a quick look to make sure there were no bodies in the flat. But she was secretly relieved to find that there wasn't one propped up in the back of the wardrobe. She climbed out and started to look through the pile of clothes and handbags on the bed. There was quite a lot and most of it was high quality and expensive. How did a teaching assistant afford clothes like this? Stella frigging McCartney for fucks sake! Rich parents? Rich boyfriend? Sugar daddy? Big credit card bill? She found nothing in any of the pockets of the jackets and trousers. The designer handbags were all empty. Anderson must be one of those women who moves everything into the bag she's using. Bloody weirdo!

Bassey was going to start on the two chests of drawers next, when she remembered Atkinson's joke about leaving no sheet unturned. She carefully replaced all the clothes and bags in the wardrobe. Then she began systematically stripping the bed. She made sure that pillow slips contained nothing more than pillows and that the duvet cover held nothing more than the duvet. She pulled off the sheet, the mattress cover and the memory foam topper. This left just the mattress itself. This she upended so that she could study the underside. Nothing. Through the wooden slats of the bed she could see through to the floor. What sort of person lived in this flat? There was nothing at all under the bed! No lost socks or knickers, no storage boxes of winter clothes – nothing that in Bassey's opinion a normal person would have tucked under their bed.

While Bassey searched vainly in the bedroom Atkinson was looking in the kitchen/diner. He wasn't as thorough or conscientious in his search as Bassey. He was after all CID, not a lowly plod! It was pure accident that Atkinson found the one thing that turned the empty flat into a possible crime scene. As he looked along the kitchen window ledge above the sink, he managed to nudge the knife block, causing it to topple.

'Shit!' he said as he tried to stop the block from falling. He wasn't quite quick enough and two of the five knives it held fell out and onto the empty draining board. He righted the knife

block and returned the bread knife to its allocated slot. As he picked up the second knife, a very sharp six-inch chef knife, he noticed red brown staining on the blade.

'Shirley! Shirley!' he shouted 'I think I've found something!'

'What is it?' Bassey asked as she hurried into the room. Atkinson held out the knife blade. 'Oh, we'd better get SOC then hadn't we?'

Scene of Crime arrived very quickly. They put up the yellow 'Crime Scene Do Not Cross' tape around the street door, and posted a young PC next to it. They then, dressed in their white Tyvek plastic suits, overshoes and gloves, went up into the flat. Atkinson and Bassey sat in Atkinson's car and waited. Once they were fed up with waiting in the car, they moved into the café below the flat. They were on their fourth cup of coffee when Dave Venables, the senior SOC officer, found them.

'Clean as a whistle and I mean clean. It looks like someone has done a really deep and thorough clean recently. Luminol showed up no blood traces whatsoever. There's nothing up there of interest except for that knife. We'll get the blood on the blade checked out, if it is blood that is. And if it is, all we'll really be able to give you is the blood group. We won't be able to match it to your missing girl unless we have a sample of her blood. We've also lifted a few sets of prints which we'll run through the database. Doubt if we'll find anything there either. Sorry.'

The SOC officer's prediction proved to be right. It was blood on the knife blade. It was O positive, the world's most common blood group. Ruth's medical records told them that her blood group was also O positive, but without a sample of her blood to match other markers with, it was impossible to say if the blood was hers or not. The fingerprints were also a dead end. No matches were found on the database.

V

The Chief Super had told Bassey that she could work the Anderson case with Atkinson. It would be good experience for her, and for him. Also joy of joys, she could wear plain clothes for the duration of the investigation. Bassey desperately wanted to join CID, and she knew that if this went right it would almost guarantee her the switch.

As the more experienced officer Atkinson took the lead role. He decided that they should go and talk to the Headteacher of Ruth's school. They parked in the street and walked up the crumbling path that lead to Reception. The building dated from the 1960's and showed it's age. They had not phoned ahead, but once she'd established who they were, the receptionist took them straight to the Head's study. Why do Heads always have studies and not offices? They were shown straight in.

The walls were stark white, their only adornment a blow-up of the school timetable. The Head's desk was in front of a window directly opposite the door. A large bookcase was against one wall and a cupboard against the other. Two visitors' chairs occupied the centre of the huge floor space.   It reminded Atkinson of the stories his father used to tell about his visits to the Head's study –

"It was a huge room, on the left wall was a large fireplace, on the right wall there was a cupboard and the boss, Sweep as we called him, sat directly in front of you, at his desk in front of the window. He always looked as if he was just a shadow. 'And why have you come to see me Atkinson?' he would ask, even though he knew the reason well enough. He just wanted you to cough again for what you'd done. 'I'm afraid that this little misdemeanour can only be rectified by six of the best.' He would then come out from behind the desk and open the cupboard doors. There hanging from a rack on the back of each door were a selection of canes, running from left to right by decreasing thickness. The far left one was as thick as a working man's thumb and the far right one was thin and very whippy. The Boss would then ask you to choose which cane you wanted to be beaten with. Veterans of this sadistic little ceremony said it didn't matter which one you chose, they all hurt the same. And it was rumoured that one poor lad had had the opportunity to try them all. Once the instrument of choice had been unhooked from the rack, the Boss would give it a few practice swings so that you could hear it whistle through the air. 'Go and bend over with your head in the fireplace please, and remove your blazer.' Oh yes, this was a beating on the arse and

he didn't want the material of your blazer softening the blows. You would position yourself over by the fireplace, backside pointing towards the cupboard and head just inside the opening. Looking backwards through your legs you could see everything that happened. Sweep would stand in front of the cupboard with the cane in his raised right hand and his left hand pointing at the target. He would launch himself across the room and smack the cane with all the force he could muster on your arse. You would see him coming, you would hear the cane whistle and then you would feel excruciating pain either on your backside or the top of your legs. His aim wasn't always that good. What happened next was the killer though. Remember, you're bent over in the fireplace. No matter how hard you tried you could never stop yourself from straightening up once you'd been hit. This meant BOSH! You smacked the top of your head on the underside of the fireplace. This naturally quite often caused a little fall of soot onto your head and shoulders. So, it was always easy to tell who had been playing Sooty to the boss' Sweep."

- *He often wondered if it was true. Did the bookcase hide a fireplace? Was the cupboard an arsenal of canes?*

There seemed to be nothing personal on the desk, no obvious evidence of a life outside. This was an office, an administrative centre. It could almost have been an interrogation room. Atkinson wondered if the chairs were screwed down.

Charles Clarke BA(Hons), MA, PGCE - as it said on door - was sitting with the light behind him. He looked like the shadow in Atkinson's fathers' story. The shadow stood up and came around to shake hands and introduce himself, and then leaned back on his desk. He was a thin man, about 6 feet tall with thinning hair in the style of Bobby Charlton and round John Lennon glasses. He wore a light grey suit with a silver heart shaped pin on the left lapel. Atkinson estimated him to be in his late forties. He didn't offer the two police officers a seat.

'I suppose you're here about poor Miss Anderson,' he said after the introductions. 'The staff are all in a terrible state of shock about her disappearance. Is there any news yet?'

'No, I'm afraid not,' Atkinson replied, rubbing his shoes on his trousers. 'We're just trying to build up a picture of her and her movements. Did she have any particular friends among the staff? Someone she was particularly close to?'

'No, I don't think so. She'd only been with us since Christmas, when we opened the new Unit.'

'Unit?' Bassey asked.

'It's where we put the young people who have, shall we say, problems following the rules. But I'll let Mr Smart, the teacher in charge, tell you all about that.'

'OK, thanks. But did she appear to be any different at the end of last term? Worried for example?' Bassey continued.

'Again, Mr Smart is the one who could tell you more than me, he probably knew Miss Anderson better than anyone else. Shall we go down and see him?'

'After you Headmaster.'

The Head walked with long, quick strides which Atkinson easily matched, but Bassey had to occasionally break into a trot to keep up. As they reached the main corridor, they both noted large green slime covered glass domes in the ceiling and panels of internal windows for each classroom set about six feet from the floor. Obviously, an attempt to get more natural light. The Head kept up his manic pace looking straight ahead, even Atkinson had to scuttle a little to keep up.

'I understand the windows,' whispered Bassey 'but what's with the benches?' Atkinson shrugged. Beneath every set of windows was an old-fashioned gym bench. The sort of bench that anyone who had ever done Primary School PE would recognise.

'Well I don't suppose they're there for the kids to sit on and encourage dawdling to class.'

The Head suddenly stopped outside, what Atkinson presumed to be a classroom door. There were no windows in the walls here though. Screwed to the door was a sign that read in large gold letters: Learning Support Centre. Beneath this was a handwritten sign saying, Welcome To The Last Chance Saloon. Next to the door was a display board, also labelled, filled with examples of pupil's work. And even a cursory glance told Atkinson it was work of a very high quality. It wasn't there to boost the inmate's self-esteem; it was an advertisement to the rest of the school. This was a room on the defensive. You didn't have to be paranoid to work here, but it looked like it might help.

Clarke pushed open the door without knocking and beckoned the two police officers to follow him. Inside Atkinson saw a man in his late twenties, early thirties, talking to a group of eight boys.

'Mr Smart,' Clark said abruptly, giving the teacher no time to acknowledge their presence or complete what he was saying. 'These police officers would like to talk to you. I'll find someone to look after the Unit, so you can talk in the staffroom.' With this he turned on his heel and walked out of the room.

'Come in and sit down for a minute while I sort out something for these reprobates to do while I'm away. You should be safe over there in the quiet corner.' Smart smiled and pointed to two comfortable armchairs next to a bulging book case. They walked over but remained standing As Atkinson rubbed his shoes on his trouser legs eight pairs of eyes watched their every move.

'We now know how Mr Clarke runs his school,' Atkinson said quietly to Bassey, who nodded in agreement. They took the time while they were waiting to look around the room. Every wall contained more examples of pupil's written work, photographs and drawings. The back wall though, next to where they were standing, was the only one that had any space left on it. It was partially covered with small wooden shields, each with a different coat of arms and motto.

'OK folks,' they heard Smart say. 'While I'm away, what I want you to do is push two tables almost together so that they are at least a foot apart. Then, working in pairs, I want you to use the Lego to build a bridge to span the distance between the tables. The pair who build the bridge that will hold the most weight before it collapses will win the usual prize. Now according to my calculations, the only person PC will find in the staff room is Miss Carter. So be nice to her. You know she's terrified about coming in here.' He smiled as he said this. 'What you've got to do will see you through to lunch time and, I should be back for this afternoon's lessons.' He looked at Atkinson and Bassey for confirmation, they both nodded. 'Now remember, if I can't get a twelve-inch ruler between the desks your bridge is disqualified. And if you do finish and there's still time until lunch, just sit quietly and do some reading.'

'Ah sir! Do we have to?' said one of the boys.

'Yes, we do Joe,' Joe looked crestfallen, as did most of his classmates. 'Just read OK? No messing about and upsetting Miss Carter. Right get started on these bridges so that when she arrives, she will be impressed by your industriousness.'

'Is that a real word sir?'

'It is now.'

'Don't worry Mr Smart we've just got a couple of questions for you and they can wait until we get to somewhere more private,' Atkinson said as Smart joined them.

'Good plan, these buggers have eyes like hawks and ears like elephants.'

'We heard that sir.' Smart shrugged and smiled.

'PC? I know who you mean, but why?'

'Well, you've met Charles Clarke, our much beloved Headmaster. And I'm sure you've formulated an opinion of him very similar to the one the staff, and most of the pupils, have. PC stands for "Proper Charlie". Because that's what he is, a Proper Charlie. As he proved just now by bursting in here and announcing that you two are police officers.'

'Oh, I'm PC Bassey and this is DC Atkinson,' Bassey said realising they hadn't introduced themselves.

'Pleased to meet you. A better, more professional Head would have asked me to step into the corridor for a moment. The man shouldn't be in charge of an empty biscuit tin, let alone a school. He has no manners, no leadership qualities and is totally paranoid. You've seen the benches in the corridors? I'm sure, as detectives you've worked out that they're for him to stand on so he can see into the classrooms.' Atkinson and Bassey nodded knowingly – so that's what they're for. 'If he wants to know what's going on in a classroom all he has to do is knock on the door and go in, he's the Head for God's sake!

'I've covered the odd lesson in one of those rooms and the kids are constantly looking up to the corridor windows to see if he's watching them. He's got the whole place on edge. This is the only room that he doesn't look into and that's mainly because there are no windows. But also, because he has no interest in us. He doesn't think we can help his league tables.'

'And who are us?' queried Bassey.

'We, are the Learning Support Centre,' Smart announced spreading his arms expansively. 'It used to be known as "The Unit". And it's still called that by many of the staff and most of the pupils. It used to be an isolation room where "naughty" kids were sent, supposedly to sit in silence in horrible little cubicles and do meaningless work to fill the time. It was a horrible place, the kids hated it and so did the staff who had to take it in turns to supervise them. Noise and bedlam were common, even violence sometimes.

'Then, about four years ago the school decided to employ someone specifically to take charge. And this is where I come in. I told them at my interview, that my idea was to run a therapeutic area where young people could learn to deal with their emotions and fit in better within the school. I also said that if they were looking for someone to run a sin bin then I wasn't their man,' he shrugged. 'They still gave me the job. When I started we weren't in this nice room. We were out at the back of the school, away from everyone in a building that used to be the old ROSLA Unit.'

'ROSLA Unit?'

'ROSLA, Raising of School Leaving Age. Back in 1972 the school leaving age was raised from 15 to 16. Many schools had nowhere to put these extra pupils who were now going to *stay on in school for another year. So, they built extra accommodation to hold them. Quite often this accommodation was not physically attached to the main school, and was known as the ROSLA Unit. The out buildings at the back were this school's ROSLA Unit. So that's where we were. Out back, away from everyone.'*

Atkinson and Bassey nodded. 1972, well before their time at school.

'I ditched the cubicles, changed the name and put criteria in place for pupils to reach before I accepted them. That stopped staff just sending me kids they were having trouble with in a lesson. There had to be meetings with the parents or carers and targets for pupils to achieve to get back into the main school. I made entry into the Centre a managed option, not a prison sentence.

'That's what I decided to call the Unit when I started, the Learning Support Centre. It sounds friendlier and less threatening. And as you can see it's become a quite a nice, relaxed learning environment. We keep the pupils up to date with their Maths and English, and do a lot to develop emotional intelligence - team work, sharing ideas and just basically getting along together. Like this with the bridge building.'

'Sounds like you've got a good place here.' Atkinson interjected. Smart obviously liked to talk and he wanted to keep him going, it may prove useful when he asked more important questions.

'We only keep pupils until they've achieved their agreed targets and then we start feeding them back into the main school, usually starting with one or two lessons a day and building up from there. Many of them still pop in, after release, to make sure that their family crest' – *he gestured proudly* – *'is still on the wall.'*

A woman in her early thirties entered the room. She was wearing a blue tracksuit and her long blonde hair was tied in a pony tail. PE thought Bassey. From what she could remember, PE teachers were terrifying, never terrified. The boys all looked up at the new arrival, recognised who it was, and continued with their bridge building. Presumably she was a regular visitor and they all felt comfortable with her.

She looked at Smart, 'OK Ben, you take your guests down to the staff room, we'll be alright. I've put fresh coffee on.'

'Thanks,' Smart said. He turned to look at his class 'Remember. If I can't fit my twelve inches between the desks you're disqualified.' All eight boys groaned loudly. It was obviously the sort of remark they were used to hearing, but Atkinson noticed that Miss Carter started to blush slightly. Something going on there? Smart did seem to know her timetable very well.

Smart arse and Proper Charlie, they served each other well. But all Atkinson had found out about Ruth Anderson so far was that she was a bloody saint to put up with the pair of them for 6 months. He hoped for better luck in the staffroom. Thank Christ Bassey hadn't asked Smart to explain "the usual prize" or any other of his motivational wheezes.

VI

Atkinson eased the car to a halt opposite the newsagent's shop. He looked over at the signage running above the window and door. **B SMART NEWSAGENTS**

'They've missed out the "e"' he said to Bassey as they climbed out of the car. They crossed over the road and Atkinson realised there was no missing "e". There above the door was written: ***Proprietor B Smart***

'Look at that," he said pointing, 'ring a bell?'

'That's the same name as that teacher who worked with Ruth Anderson. A coincidence?'

'I don't believe in coincidences, do you?' Bassey shook her head. 'And I don't think Mitchell does either.' Atkinson pulled on nitryl gloves and ducked under the yellow police tape. Bassey quickly followed him.

'SOC?' Atkinson asked the PC standing by the tape.

'Not yet sir. Waiting for you to say yes or no.'

It was like stepping onto a film set from the 60's - a real old-fashioned newsagents. There were shelves full of magazines, including the usual top shelf suspects. Beneath the shelves were piles of the different daily newspapers, they were all there except The Sun, obviously. And all out of date now. Surely newspapers were delivered every day, what had happened to the last weeks' worth? Atkinson was sure that wholesalers dumped the days papers on the front step at some ungodly hour of the morning. What had happened to those papers? It had been a week before anyone had raised an alarm. Even the dimmest van driver would have seen yesterday's papers still on the step. Maybe Smart had just gone away and cancelled his deliveries. Or, maybe someone else had cancelled them.

A quick look around the shop told them absolutely nothing. Everything seemed to be in its allotted space. The tobacco shelves were almost stocked to capacity, the till had at least £85 in it. Nothing seemed to be amiss or out of place. Maybe the flat upstairs might tell them something. As they climbed the stairs Bassey looked at Atkinson and said 'Ron, do you really think this is the same Smart?'

Atkinson didn't reply, he'd been doing this job too long. Pushing open the door to the flat his suspicions were proved right immediately. There on the wall of the small entrance hall was a photograph of Ben Smart. It looked like it had been taken on a night out, as he was obviously sitting in a pub looking a little the worse for wear. Sitting next to him on his right, smiling for the camera, was Ruth Anderson. On his left was another face Atkinson recognised from the past – Miss Carter.

There was nothing disturbed in the flat. It looked as if Smart had just tidied round and nipped out for a minute. Ruth Anderson's flat had been exactly the same, even down to the smell of bleach, only the smell here was stronger. Maybe he had just gone away for a few days. But why not tell anyone? Most shop owners put up some kind of notice if they were going to be shut for a while.

Atkinson followed Bassey into the kitchen. As soon as he was through the door, he had a feeling, not a feeling of déjà vu exactly, but definitely something. 'There's something about this kitchen Shirl. I can't put my finger on it, but there's something.' Atkinson stood in the middle of the room and looked around. He had turned slowly round on the spot three times before he stopped and stared at the kitchen window. There it was. On the windowsill. A knife block. He walked over and carefully began to take the knives out, one at a time. Bassey watched him as, he slowly pulled the last knife from the block, he'd left the chef's knife until last. He showed her the blade. There were dark red/brown stains on it. Dried blood?

'Better give SOC a ring Shirl.'

Dave Venables and his team arrived thirty minutes later. Dave said that he would let them know as soon as possible if the stain on the knife was blood. Atkinson and Bassey left the SOC team to get on and went outside to plan their next move.

'I suppose we'd better talk to some of the locals,' Atkinson said. 'Let's start with the butchers over the road there.'

The weather-beaten sign above the shop read **Fred Lowe Master Butcher**. Atkinson rubbed his shoes on his trouser legs, as Bassey opened the door. To Bassey it looked like every other butcher's shop she had ever been in. The window displayed pieces of lamb, joints of beef and cuts of pork. A glass covered counter inside displaying various other cuts of meat, sausages, mince, offal, bacon and something that looked like – faggots? Behind the counter stood a portly man of about 50, in a bloodstained white apron, with a stub of pencil behind his right ear. There was a wide shelf behind him that held two large chopping blocks, an old-fashioned till and a telephone. There was another room off to the left that obviously contained the freezers.

'Good afternoon folks, what can I get you?'

Bassey opened her bag and pulled out her warrant card. 'DS Bassey and this is DI Atkinson. Are you Mr Lowe?'

'Yes, that's me. What can I do for you?' Before either Atkinson or Bassey could speak the phone on the back shelf rang. 'Excuse me. Hello? Oh, hello Mrs Davies,' Lowe listened intently for a short while. 'OK Mrs Davies I'll get Artie to pop them round to you. Save you coming back. Bye.' He put the phone down and called out 'Artie! Artie! Mrs Davies has left her pork chops. Have you seen them?'

'I wondered whose they were. They were on the side by the sink,' came a voice from the back room.

'She was in earlier and asked if she could use the toilet,' Lowe explained to the two police officers. 'She's 86, you can't really say no, can you? Dozy mare must have put her chops down and forgot to pick them up.' Then calling into the back room, 'I said you'd pop them over for her, save her coming back.'

'OK, no problem.'

Atkinson and Bassey watched as Artie came into the front of the shop. He looked to be in his early twenties, about six feet tall and was wearing a leather jacket and a full-face motorcycle helmet. All you could really tell about his face was that he had one of those fashionable hipster beards and that he wore glasses with blue lenses. In his hands he carried a white polythene bag, obviously the pork chops. He exited through the shop door and climbed onto a Yamaha XSR700 motorcycle which was parked outside the shop. He turned the key and the 700cc engine burst into life, he knocked it into first gear and set off down the road.

'Won't see him for at least an hour now,' the butcher said. 'He's got a real soft spot for Mrs Davies. He'll have a cup of tea and chat, and then probably take her dog for a quick walk. He's a lovely lad. Now, why have you two come to see me? It's about Ben isn't it?'

'Yes. Did you know him well?' Atkinson asked.

'As well as anybody, I suppose. He bought the newsagents about five years ago from Jim Rowan when he retired. Fitted in really well. The folk round here sometimes need a little help with the day to day things. You know the sort of thing – I'll undercharge them for the mince, or put a few more sausages in the bag after they've been weighed. That sort of thing. Not for everyone, you understand, only for those who need it. Ben was the same. He made sure that the really needy kids didn't go without a few sweets or the occasional comic.'

'Do you know where he's gone?'

'No, I'm afraid I don't. I didn't know he'd disappeared until yesterday. I've been away for a couple of weeks in Spain with the wife. He was here when we went away. I know, because he drove us to the airport. He was supposed to pick us up when we got back, but he never showed. I rang him a couple of times and got no answer. Thought he'd got the day mixed up, or more likely I had. It wasn't until I got back in the shop yesterday that I found out he was missing.'

'Did you close the shop up when you were away?'

'No, I can't afford to do that. I left Artie, Artie Miller, my assistant in charge. He's a good lad and knows how things should be done. I knew the shop was in safe hands.'

The shop door opened and a very thin middle-aged woman came in. She looked at the two police officers, immediately dismissed them with a sniff and turned her full attention to the butcher.

'Good to see you back Fred. Enjoy your holiday? Isn't it terrible about Mr Smart? What do you think's happened to him?' she rattled off the questions without giving the butcher a chance to answer. 'And these buggers are going around with lead boots on,' inclining her head towards Atkinson and Bassey. 'Neither use nor ornament!'

'We had a great time thanks Miss Round. And yes, it is terrible about Ben. Now what can I do for you?'

'While you were away, Artie made some wonderful faggots. Have you got any left?'

'There's these ones in the tray. I didn't make them so Artie must have done. Unless it was the faggot fairy. How many do you want?'

'I'll take all those on the tray,' she said, ignoring the butcher's attempt at humour. Lowe looked surprised as he started to count out the faggots.

'There's a dozen here Miss Round, are you sure you want them all?'

'Yes, please Fred. I'll have a couple for my tea tonight and freeze the rest.'

'We make faggots fresh every week you know, you don't have to freeze them. Have you ever come in and not seen any?'

Miss Round looked at the butcher like he was soft in the head. 'Yes, but these are Artie's. You'll be back making the faggots now. There may never be any of these again.'

The butcher took the comments with a shake of his head and put the faggots into a bag. He took the pencil stub from behind his ear and worked out the cost on a piece of paper. 'That'll be £8.40 please.'

Miss Round counted out the exact money onto the top of the display counter. Put the faggots into her shopping bag and started to leave the shop. She stopped and turned at the door, looked Atkinson up and down in a very deliberate manner, and said, 'It's about time you lot pulled your fingers out.' With a shake of her head she left the shop.

'I didn't know Artie could make faggots. OK, where were we? Oh yes. I came back in yesterday and was surprised to find that Ben had gone missing. It did explain though why he hadn't turned up at the airport. He never said anything about going away anywhere. In the past he's always arranged for someone to come in and look after the shop, he's never just closed up totally. He's like me, neither of us can afford to do that. Customers are fickle, they quickly find somewhere else to get their sausages and newspapers.' Lowe paused for a couple of seconds and then asked the question both Atkinson and Bassey were asking themselves. 'Has something happened to him?'

VII

Atkinson and Bassey settled themselves into the staff room while Smart busied himself in the small kitchen. After a couple of minutes, he came out carrying a tray with three steaming mugs, a carton of milk and a sugar bowl.

'Sorry, we haven't got any biscuits.'

'No problem,' Atkinson said pouring milk into a cup and adding three heaped spoons of sugar. Bassey and Smart drank theirs as it came, black and unsweetened.

'Have you found Ruth yet?' Smart asked blowing across the top of his mug.

'No, I'm afraid not,' Atkinson answered.

'Do you think she's dead?' Smart's voice had a slight tremor to it.

'We can't really answer that question. We hope not, we haven't found a body.'

'You left out the "yet",' added Smart ruefully.

'We have to assume that Ruth is still alive. You may think differently,' Bassey paused a moment. 'Or know differently?'

Smart sat forward in his seat and gave Bassey a long hard stare. 'Do you really think that I'd be capable of killing a friend and colleague?'

'Unfortunately, Ben, I can call you Ben?' cut in Atkinson 'Our job is to look at all the possibilities. As you probably know, most people who are murdered know their killer. So, in a case like this it makes sense to start close to home. It doesn't mean that we think you killed Ruth, or had anything to do with her disappearance. But we have to ask the questions. You do understand that, don't you?'

Smart settled back in his chair, 'Yes, I'm sorry. You're only doing your job. What do you need to know?'

Bassey let Atkinson take the lead. 'First off Ben, can you tell us a little bit about Ruth?'

'Well, she joined us here at school after the Christmas break. The boss asked me if I'd like her to be the teaching assistant in the Centre. Of course, I said yes. I didn't have a TA at the time, he'd promised me one for ages and I've always thought that they are a very important part of what goes on in places like the Centre. She's very good with the kids, who all love her. Also, she's an adult witness in the event of something untoward happening.'

'Something untoward? A witness?' Atkinson queried.

'You know, if one the pupils makes an accusation of some kind against me. I've had it happen in a previous school. A pupil accused me of strangling him with his tie until he

became unconscious. Can you believe that? It was my TA who helped sort it all out with the police.'

Bassey made a mental note to see if she could find out anything more about the incident, as Smart seemed, for once, unwilling to expand. *'Are you and Ruth close?'*

'In a romantic way do you mean? No, we became good friends, but nothing more. When you work so closely together in an environment like the Centre you either become good friends or get on each other's nerves. She does obviously have someone in her life, but I've no idea who. He's very generous though. Always buying her expensive clothes and handbags and that sort of stuff.'

The Sugar Daddy.

'Can you tell us the last time you saw Ruth?'

'It was the last day of the Summer Term. Most of the staff were going into Crosby for a few drinks after school. We'd done about three of the pubs, the Birkey, the Crow's Nest and Stamps, I think, things are a little hazy. I do remember though, it was about seven o'clock when Ruth came up to me, gave me a peck on the cheek, said she had to go and that she'd see me in September. I told her to have a good break, and that was the last time I saw her. I tried to get her to stay a little longer, but she said she definitely had to go. If I'd tried harder to get her to stay, I suppose she might still be here today. I got the impression she had someone to meet. Maybe the person who killed her? If she is dead. Funny though, how I can remember her leaving, but the rest of the night is mainly a blank.' Smart took a large gulp of coffee before continuing.

'When she didn't turn up on the first day back in September, I really thought nothing about it, just assumed she was unwell. It was only after a couple of days and there had been no contact from her that I began to worry. So, I went around to her flat in St John's Road. I rang the bell, but got no answer. I then went into the café beneath the flat and asked in there if anyone had seen her. No one could remember seeing her since the end of July, just after school had broken up. But as they said it's not their job to clock people in and out. I was really starting to get worried then. When I came into school the following day, I spoke to Bill Whitehouse, he's the Deputy Head, about my misgivings. He agreed with me that something could very well be amiss, so we informed the Head. Even he thought it strange that Ruth hadn't contacted school about her absence, and had not really been seen since the end of last term. That's when we contacted you guys.'

VIII

Atkinson looked at the butcher for a couple of seconds before he spoke, 'We're not sure at the moment, Fred. I can call you Fred? He may have just gone away for a while without telling anyone. There's no law against that. He appears to have cancelled his deliveries, so it could well be a planned break. Has he got any family that you know of who could have called him away? A family emergency or something like that?'

'None that I know of. She's not family, but he did keep in contact with one of the teachers he used to work with. She's the one who usually comes to look after the shop when he's away. He always went away in the school holidays; I suppose old habits die hard. She might know something. Now what's that lasses name?' Lowe stopped talking and was deep in thought for a few seconds. 'Carter, Jan Carter. That's it.'

Atkinson and Bassey looked at each other. 'Do you know where she lives?'

'No, I'm afraid not. Not exactly anyway, I'm pretty sure it's Aigburth or somewhere like that. I know it's south of town.'

'Thanks for that Fred. Is there anything else you think of, that we might need to know?' The butcher shook his head slowly. 'We'll have to come back and have a few words with Artie, as he was here when Mr Smart disappeared, so if you think of anything...' Atkinson trailed off. He and Bassey turned and left the shop, just as the next customer was coming in. Busy little place.

On the drive back to the station it was Bassey who broke the silence. 'This is not a coincidence is it?'

Atkinson shook his head. 'I think we should have a chat with Miss Carter if we can find her.'

'Shouldn't be too hard, Aigburth's not that big a place. Can't be more than 100,000 people living there. South side of Liverpool? Maybe another 200,000.' groaned Bassey. Despite Bassey's misgivings it turned out to be surprisingly easy to track down Miss Carter. One phone call revealed that she still taught at St Michaels. The school was also able to supply an address when Bassey went in person to prove she was who she said she was – 70 Kenmere Road, Wavertree. Not exactly Aigburth, but close.

As she arrived in work the next morning, Bassey saw Atkinson about to go into the DCI's office. Obviously going to bring him up to date. She watched as the traffic light went green and he rubbed his shoes on the back of his trousers and went in. Why doesn't he just polish them? She'd just sat down at her desk and turned on her computer when the phone in Atkinson's office rang. She knew he'd be a while with the DCI so, she went into the office to answer it. Bassey listened for a couple of minutes and then said 'Thanks Dave, I'll tell him.'

Bassey was like a cat on hot bricks waiting for Atkinson to return to the CID suite. 'Ron!' she called as he entered the room. She waved him over and he sat in the chair opposite hers. 'Just had a phone call from SOC. Dave Venables says they found nothing in the flat, it was forensically clean. But it was blood on the knife.' Atkinson nodded slowly; this is what he'd been expecting. He started to get up from the chair. 'That's not all though Ron. The blood on the knife exactly matches the blood that was on the knife in Ruth Andersons flat,' Atkinson crashed back down into the chair.

'That's bloody amazing! This gives us another little piece of the puzzle, but opens up yet another volume of unanswered questions. Two missing people, two knives with the same blood and eight years between the incidents. What the fuck's going on Shirley? Do you think they're dead? And if so, who killed them? I had Smart in the frame for murdering Ruth. Looks like I might have got that wrong – big style!'

'I think that they're both dead,' Bassey ventured. 'But, without bodies we can't say for sure. Is the blood on the new knife Smarts? He could have killed Ruth, and cut himself at home while cooking. You can't rule him out yet. Or, they could have both been killed by a third party. But why leave blood on the knives? Everywhere else in both scenes was spotless. No forensics at all.'

'I agree with you about them being dead, but as I said Shirl, more unanswered questions. I think that there's a third party involved here. Smart killing Ruth and then getting killed himself? Just seems a little improbable to me. OK let's see if we can find some answers to some of these questions. Now Miss Carter, do we visit her at school or at home do you think?'

'I think she'll be more relaxed at home, but that means we'll have to wait until at least four or five o'clock before we can see her. Possibly even later.'

'OK, school it is. Grab your coat it looks like it's starting to rain.'

It was only a ten-minute drive from Copy Lane to the school, but long enough to pose some more questions, but of a different kind. Bassey turned on the car radio, and soon both detectives were singing along. 'That was "Me and Bobby McGee" by the great Kris Kristofferson,' announced the DJ, 'first released in 1970. It doesn't matter how old a song is, class is still class.' Bassey looked at Atkinson, how did she know that song well enough to sing along? He obviously knew it as well. Who was Kris Kristofferson? 1970? She hadn't even been born! More unanswered questions, but at least these had nothing to do with the case and provided a little respite.

Atkinson parked the car on the street outside the school, the building still looked as though it needed some TLC. He opened the front door and followed Bassey inside. The receptionist looked familiar to Atkinson; possibly she was the same one as eight years ago? She didn't appear to recognise them and after a quick phone call to the Head, quickly ushered them into the Head's study. Nothing seemed to have changed. Charles Clarke BA(Hons), MA, PGCE was still in charge. He looked exactly the same, as he had, eight years ago, except for the hair. He'd moved from a Bobby Charlton to more of an Alan Shearer, with his hair now close cropped to his head. He still wore John Lennon glasses and sat in front of the window in a room with two chairs in what, Atkinson suspected, was exactly the same place as last time. Maybe they were actually screwed down.

'Please, come in. What can I do for you? Haven't we met before?' he asked. The expression on Clarke's face showed that he was deep in thought, trying to recall their past meeting. A blind man would have been able to tell he was thinking.

'Yes, we have,' Bassey replied. 'We spoke to you about one of your teaching assistants a few years ago.' She stayed deliberately vague to see how much Clarke remembered.

'Oh, yes. That's it, you're the officers who were investigating Miss Anderson's disappearance. Have you found her? Is there any news?'

Atkinson studied the Head. You recognised us, but why the - I'll have to think hard about this face? - How often do the police come calling to the school to investigate a member of staff disappearing?

'No, I'm afraid there's nothing new to report about Ruth,' Bassey continued, before Atkinson could say anything. 'But we're actually here to see you about another matter. Ben Smart, he ran the Learning Support Centre at the time Ruth disappeared.'

'Oh, he doesn't work here anymore,' Clarke answered curtly. 'He left us about six or seven years ago.'

'Yes, we know,' Atkinson said. 'Mr Smart himself has now gone missing. What we'd like to do, is have a word with Miss Carter. If we may? From what we've been told she's still in contact with Mr Smart.'

'Oh, I don't think she'll be able to tell you anything.'

'I think you should let us be the judge of that,' countered Bassey.

'Could you not speak to her at home? It's very disruptive, the police coming in like this.'

'No, we'd like to speak to her now please,' Atkinson said.

'I suppose so, then,' sighed the Head. 'I'll just check where she is.' Clarke walked over to the large timetable pinned to his study wall and made a big show of examining it. *As if you don't know exactly where all your staff are at all times.* 'She's teaching Year 9 girl's PE at the moment. She has got a student teacher with her who could take over the lesson, I suppose. Are you sure it can't wait?'

'The quicker we speak to her, the quicker you get her back.'

*

It was four o'clock in the afternoon, Atkinson and Bassey were sitting in the canteen at Copy Lane, drinking coffee. They were looking over what they had so far, which basically amounted to not a lot. Ruth Anderson was a teaching assistant in a unit for badly behaved pupils. She was not romantically linked with the teacher in charge, but there was a suspected sugar daddy in the background. She hadn't been seen by anyone since the end of July, and the only thing that pointed to something sinister having happened was the blood on the knife. But whose blood was it? Ruth's? The killer's, if there is one? Someone else's? Atkinson broke the general sense of despair. 'Maybe we should go and have a word with Ruth's landlord – the butcher. What's his name?'

'Cooksey, Mike Cooksey,' supplied Bassey.

Mike Cooksey's butchers' shop was just a few doors down from Ruth Anderson's flat on St John's Road. St John's was becoming a booming little shopping street. It had a large selection of small independent shops mixed in with a good selection of cafes and small restaurants. There was everything from a health food shop to a Goth rock shop, from a greasy spoon to a very good Sri Lankan restaurant. Atkinson had to admit to Bassey that, although he lived locally, he'd eaten a full English more often in the greasy spoon than an aromatic curry in the Sri Lankan. Parking was always a nightmare; the whole road was filled with parked cars and delivery vans. Atkinson eventually found a parking spot, at the bottom end of the road by the level crossing.

As the two detectives climbed out of the car, Bassey started to say something, but it was drowned out by the noise of the Southport to Liverpool train rattling noisily across the level crossing. She tried again. 'So, you live round here then Ron?'

'Yeah. I live in College Avenue, just behind my old school, Merchant Taylors. How about you? Are you around here anywhere?'

Bassey nodded 'I'm not far from here myself, and I live next to a school as well, but not the one I used to go to. York Road, next to that special school that used to be a primary, opposite Merchant's girls' school. Come on, let's get a hustle on, it looks like it's going to rain.'

They walked quickly away from the level crossing and up towards the top of the road, where the main thoroughfare from Crosby to Liverpool ran. Neither of them had said another word by the time they arrived at the butcher's shop. They both stared into the window for a couple of seconds, looking at the joints of beef, lamb and pork. The chops, the cutlets, the mince and the faggots. Atkinson rubbed his shoes on the backs of his legs and pushed the door open.

Bassey found her warrant card in her handbag, 'PC Bassey and this is DC Atkinson,' she said to the man behind the counter, who she recognised as the man who had let her into Ruth's flat, Mike Cooksey.

Atkinson carried on 'Can we ask you a couple of questions about Ruth Anderson, Mr Cooksey, or can I call you Mike?'

'Mike will do. Come through to the back. Oi! Arthur! Get in here and look after the shop!' A boy of about fifteen slowly appeared out of the backroom. He had long greasy black hair and glasses, he kept his eyes firmly on the floor, neither looking at the two police officers or the butcher. Slowly he took up position behind the counter. 'And make sure you get it right and watch the change!'

'I only did it the once dad,' the boy said in a cowed voice as he straightened lamb chops into an orderly pattern on a tray.

Cooksey was a large man with a ruddy complexion and a short stubbly haircut. The back room of the shop contained a deep freeze, a large well used chopping board and a small table with two chairs. Cooksey indicated the two chairs and took up position leaning on the chopping board. The two police officers declined the offer and Bassey started the questioning.

'How well do you know Ruth Anderson?'

'Not that well, really. She's a good tenant and pays her rent on time every month. Which is the important thing. She also had good references from where she'd been living in Oxford. Apart from that, I know very little about her.'

'Is the rent still being paid?' Atkinson asked.

'Standing order. I suppose that'll stop soon if she doesn't come back.' he said grumpily.

'Did you know that she worked at St Michaels School, in the Learning Support Centre?' asked Bassey returning to her original line of questioning.

'She told me she'd be working at the school, when she took on the flat. But she never said which department.'

'Who had the flat before Ruth?'

'No-one. I own that whole building, but I'd never done anything with the flat upstairs. It was a bit of a tip, to be honest. But, just before Christmas I decided to try and rent it out. So, I spent a bit of money on it, not too much, just enough to make it comfortable and put an ad in the local paper. Ruth was the first person to come and look at it. She agreed to take it right away. It was then that she told me that she was new to the area and was about to start a job as a teaching assistant at the school. I had no idea she'd be working in the Unit. I only found that out through the lad,' he nodded towards the front of the shop. 'He attends St Michaels. He said, that she seemed very nice, always smiling and chatting to people, things like that.'

'Was he in the Centre then, Mike?' Atkinson asked.

'No, never, but he did come close once. He's not thick but he can be stupid at times, a right pain in the arse. He had a run in with the Headmaster, Mr Clarke. It was during assembly and he passed a comment of some kind to the boy sitting next to him. Seems Mr Clarke saw him and went ballistic in front of the whole school. Clarke hadn't been at the school long so I suppose he was still trying to set down his markers. So, he threatened our Arthur with a few weeks in the Unit, right there in front of the whole school. I had to go up and speak to him about it, and we eventually managed to smooth it over. In my day I'd have been caned and it all forgotten about. But now, you can't do that. It seems that punishment these days has to be stretched over weeks, rather than being instantaneous. I'd have just smacked him round the back of the head. He was a lucky lad, don't want anything like that on your record. He's hated the Head ever since; says he doesn't like the way he was spoken to in front of everyone and the Head's still nasty to him if their paths ever cross. If I'd been the Head there wouldn't have been any speaking, know what I mean?' The butcher made a sweeping action with his right hand as if slapping someone.

'Is there a flat above this shop?' asked Atkinson, changing the subject.

'Yes. Me and the wife used to live in it, until she got pregnant with our Jenny. It's empty now though. Tends to be used as storage and an office for this place. I have been thinking of sorting it out and renting it.'

'So, the boy's not your only one then?'

'No, he's got two older sisters, they're both nurses. Jenny works at Alderhay, the children's hospital, and Maria works with the Blood Transfusion Service. Arthur's eleven years younger than Maria, but the two of them are as thick as thieves, you'd think they were joined at the hip the way they behave. Finishing each other's sentences, looking out for each other and things like that.'

Atkinson thanked Cooksey for his help and the two police officers left the shop. As they were walking back to the car they quite literally bumped into Charles Clarke. The Head was hurrying along with his eyes on the pavement, when he cannoned into Bassey, almost knocking her over.

'Hello, Headmaster,' Atkinson said. 'You seem to be in a hurry, what are you doing round here?' The look of shock on Clarke's face was quite palpable.

'I'm just getting a bit of shopping on my way home. I have to be quick; I can't leave her for too long,' he stammered. 'I need to go to the butchers and pick up some mince and sausages.'

'Do you live quite close to here then?' asked Bassey.

'No, no, I live in Blundellsands, down by the Leisure Centre.'

'Bit out of your way this then,' continued Bassey. 'There are butchers in Crosby village, just up from the school. And the parking's better. Wouldn't they be more convenient?'

'Yes, yes, they would. But my wife likes the sausages from the butchers here on St John's Road. And it's the least I can do, considering everything.' They looked questioningly at Clarke, but he didn't explain any further. He just nodded and hurried off.

'Considering everything?' Atkinson mused as they continued down the street to the car. 'Let's go back to the school tomorrow, and see if there's anything useful in Ruth's locker.'

Again, they were shown straight to the Head's study. It seemed that reception didn't want anyone to see two police officers hanging around. Whereas the Head seemed to have no problems announcing their presence to all and sundry.

'Of course, you can look in Miss Anderson's locker.' Clarke said. 'But, I don't think you'll find anything in there. It will only be school stuff, I'm sure. I'll go and get the master key from the office.'

In the staff room Atkinson and Bassey watched as Clarke struggled to open Ruth's locker.

'The office assured me that this was the master key.'

'Try one of the others,' Atkinson suggested.

'No, no I'm sure this is the correct one.'

'Here let me try,' Bassey took the small bunch of keys off Clarke. She tried three before she found the one that worked. The locker door came open and all three stared at its contents.

'Bloody hell! That's tidy. Mines a tip, I just cram things in.'

The inside of the locker was indeed extremely tidy. On one side was a small pile of text books, next to which was an empty plastic container with a half-eaten packet of mints balanced on top.

'I'll leave you to get on with it then,' the Head said. As Clarke walked away Atkinson thought he saw a slight look of relief cross his face, but he couldn't be sure. Perhaps he was just happy that there had been nothing in the locker that could have been embarrassing. Bassey had started to look through the pile of books.

'I wish I'd had this one when I was at school,' she said waving a copy of "GCSE Maths for Dummies". As she flicked through the pages a photograph of a new born baby fell out and landed on the floor. 'Look at this Ron,' she bent down to pick it up. Written on the back in shaky hand writing was "Alice Louise 11th November 2006". 'A niece, do you reckon?'

'Could be. We'll hang on to it, it may prove useful. You never know.'

IX

The Head ushered the two detectives out of his office and set off at a brisk pace towards what Atkinson suspected was the gym. But about halfway along the corridor Clarke stopped and opened a door which led to a playground at the rear of the school. He stepped outside, and waited for Atkinson and Bassey to follow.

'The weather is still mild,' he explained. 'So, Miss Carter likes to do a lot of her lessons outside.' Clarke conducted them to the far side of the asphalted playground where there was a group of sixteen girls playing netball, watched by two track suited figures. Atkinson recognised Jan Carter by the blonde ponytail. The other figure must be the student teacher. Both detectives were interested in how Clarke was going to handle this, given his previous record.

'Miss Carter!' he called as they drew near. 'These two police officers need to talk to you. Miss Pruden can look after the girls.' With this he turned on his heels and returned indoors. No change there then.

Atkinson watched as the sixteen girls immediately came to a stop, closely looking at him and Bassey and then quickly switching their gaze to Miss Carter. Jan Carter had a few words with her student and walked over to the two detectives. Behind her the girls half-heartedly went back to their game. They were all obviously listening hard to see if they could collect a piece of juicy gossip about one of the staff. As if a teacher being called away to speak to the police in the middle of a lesson wasn't juicy enough!

Atkinson walked over to the far side of the asphalt, well away from prying ears. 'Sorry to disturb you at school, I'm DI Atkinson and this is DS Bassey,' he began, as he rubbed his shoes on his trouser legs.

'I remember you from when you came into school last time. I covered for Ben when you needed to talk to him about Ruth Anderson.'

'You have a good memory Jan. I can call you Jan? Sorry to disturb your lesson, but we thought it would be easier to catch you here rather than at home. We'd just like to have few words with you about Ben Smart. We understand that you've kept in contact with him since he left the school. Have you seen him lately?'

'I haven't seen him for about two months, why? Has something happened? Is he in some kind of trouble?'

'I'm sorry to tell you, but he went missing, probably about a week ago. So, have you had any contact with him at all recently? Phone calls? Texts? What's App? That sort of thing.'

'He texted me about two weeks ago and said that he wanted to meet. We'd arranged to meet this weekend, he won't be coming now though, will he? Can you come round to my house after school today? About five? There's something that I think you should know, but I don't want to tell you here.'

'OK, five o'clock it is. It's OK we know where you live.' She nodded and began to walk back to her lesson.

'What do you think that's all about?' Bassey asked.

'No idea, I suppose we'll find out tonight.'

*

'Have you managed to get in touch with Ruth's parents yet?' Atkinson asked, as they walked into Copy Lane 'I think we should talk to them as soon as possible.'

'I've left a message on their answering machine every time I've phoned. I've left voice mails on the mobile numbers that we've got. Heard nothing, so I suppose the answer to your question is no.'

'Hey! You two!' called the Desk Sergeant. Jim Brodie had been in the force since he was 22, and was now heading towards what he saw as a well-deserved retirement. Brodie was the 'go to' man in the station. If Brodie didn't know, it probably hadn't happened yet. He was a mine of information. 'Someone phoned earlier, for you Bassey. A Mrs Anderson, said could you ring her back? I'm sure I detected a slight Brummie accent. She the mother of your missing girl?'

'Thanks for that Sarge,' Bassey said. 'And yes, she's the mother.'

Atkinson and Bassey hurried upstairs to the office they'd been allocated for the duration of the case. Atkinson suspected that they been given the room so that they were out of the way of everybody else.

'Home or mobile?' Bassey asked.

'Mobile, and put it on speaker phone.'

She looked up the number in her notebook and dialled it into the phone on the desk. The two officers settled down into chairs while they listened to the phone ringing.

'Hello?' said a female voice with, as Brodie had intimated, a slight Birmingham accent.

'Hello Mrs Anderson, this PC Bassey from Merseyside Police, I've been trying to contact you for a couple of days.'

'Yes. I'm sorry about that, but we've been away and there hasn't been any signal for the mobiles. In fact, we didn't even look at them until we got in yesterday lunchtime. It was then we found out that you've been trying to contact us.'

Bassey looked at Atkinson. They were both thinking the same thing –the police obviously want to talk to you, quite urgently, and you don't think to ring until the day after you get the message?

'OK, Mrs Anderson,' Bassey continued. 'I'm afraid I've got some disturbing news for you. I don't like to do this over the phone, but your daughter Ruth, has disappeared. We only found out about this recently, but no-one has really seen her since the end of July. We wondered whether you or your husband had heard from her or seen her recently?'

'Oh, so that's where she is then, Liverpool?'

'Did you not know she was up here then, Mrs Anderson?'

'No, we've had no contact with Ruth for nearly four years.'

Bassey and Atkinson looked at each other again.

'This is DC Atkinson, Mrs Anderson, would be OK if we drove down to see you tomorrow?'

'Certainly. Come if you want to, but I'm sure we won't be able to help you.' The phone went dead.

'Ever been to Brum, Shirl? No? Neither have I.'

X

As Atkinson and Bassey entered the CID suite a phone started to ring. Bassey easily located it as the one on her desk and she picked it up. Before she could say anything, a nervous voice spoke into her ear. 'Er ... hello? Is that Sergeant Bassey?'

'Yes,' replied Bassey, 'who's this?'

'Oh, hello, yes. This is Artie Miller, Fred .... Fred Lowe said you wanted to speak to me. So, I er .... thought I'd give you a ring.'

'Ah, Artie, thanks for calling, we just wanted to ask you a couple of general questions. Can you pop in and see us at Copy Lane, or should we come out and see you?'

'Er .... can't we do it on phone?'

'I suppose so, we may still need to see you face to face sometime though. But the phone will do for now. So, when did you last see Ben Smart, Artie?'

'It must have been the day before Fred went on holiday,' Artie answered, sounding much more confident now. 'He came into the shop to finalise the arrangements for taking Fred and Ellen to the airport.'

'And you didn't see him again after that?'

'No. Not that I can recall.'

'The last time you saw him, did he seem worried, or different or anything? Something not, quite right?'

'He seemed fine to me. But I only saw him for a couple of seconds, as he and Fred went into the back room and I was serving a customer. I don't think I said more than hello to him.'

'OK, that's great thanks Artie. We'll be in touch if there's anything else. Thanks again,' Bassey put the phone down and relayed the gist of the conversation to Atkinson. They were still no further on with their investigation. Maybe Jan Carter would give them something to go on, when they went to see her later.

Kenmere Road was a quiet residential street off Smithdown Road, near to the junction of Ullet Road and Allerton Road. It was around half past five when Atkinson and Bassey knocked on the door of number 70. Jan Carter quickly answered the door, catching Atkinson rubbing his shoes on the backs of his legs.

'Do all copper's have the same knock? Do they teach it to you at Hendon or wherever it is you go to train?' she said with a smile on her face. 'Come in, would you like some tea, or coffee?' Both officers said that they would love some tea. 'Make yourselves comfortable in there,' she said pointing to a door on the left of the hallway. 'I'll only be a couple of minutes.'

The room behind the door was tastefully decorated and subtly lit. It contained both a two seat and a three-seat sofa, as well as a reclining armchair. All in matching red leather. In one corner was the home entertainment centre, a TV, a Sky box and a Bose Wave music system. The walls were covered with shelves containing books and CDs, Atkinson felt at home immediately. The detectives sat down on the larger of the two sofas and waited in silence. Carter came in and put a tray, with three mugs and a sugar bowl, on a small table between the two sofas. She watched quietly, as Atkinson ladled three spoons of sugar into his tea.

'This looks to be a very nice house,' Atkinson began 'been here long?'

'About six years. I originally bought it with the idea of putting students in and making some extra money. You know, five students, £100 a week each for thirty odd weeks a year, that's about fifteen grand. Plenty to pay the mortgage, with a tidy amount left over. This being a popular student area, and with over 50,000 students in Liverpool all looking for somewhere to live, it sounded easy money. But things have changed since I was a student. The first student house that I was in was actually in this street, number 77. We thought it was exciting and fun, but looking back the place was a death trap. There were five of us, three upstairs and two down. My room upstairs was so small I had to have my wardrobe on the landing! Then there was the electricity. The upstairs electricity all ran from a 13amp plug in the downstairs hallway. If we had too many things turned on, either the fuse would blow or the plug would start to smoulder and smoke. As I said, a death trap. Now you have to have fire doors and safety certificates for everything. So, I decided to live here myself.'

'Over 50,000 students?' queried Bassey.

'Yes, if you think about it, we've got three universities. There's the original red brick university up by the Metropolitan Cathedral. There's John Moore's, which used to be the polytechnic and there's Hope out in Childwall.'

'Hope? I'm not familiar with that one,' Bassey said.

'It's the old teacher training colleges, Christ's College, St Kath's and I.M. Marsh combined together. I actually got my degree from I.M. Marsh. It was an all-female college for girls who wanted to be PE teachers. But when you add up all the students there are about 50 to 60,000 of them.' Carter took a sip of her tea and settled back on the two-seater sofa. 'But I didn't ask you here to reminisce about my life as a student.' She paused for a couple of seconds. 'Ben Smart and I were great friends as well as colleagues, and before you ask, no there was nothing going on between us. He's not my type. When Ruth went missing, he became very paranoid, he thought that you had him down as the prime suspect. It affected him so much that he had to have time off school. Now, while he was off sick, the Head turned the Learning Support Centre back into a Unit. I'm sure Ben must have explained to you what the difference is?'

'Yes,' Bassey said. 'A Learning Support Centre is therapeutic and tries to change behaviours. While a Unit is an isolation and punishment block.'

Jan nodded and continued. 'A lot of staff had complained that Ben was too soft with the kids in there. They thought that these kids needed punishing more than molly coddling, as they thought Ben was doing. So, within two days of Ben being off, the Centre was turned back into a Unit. The work cubicles were reinstated, the kid's work was taken down from the walls, and along with the family shields, thrown into the stock room. And I mean thrown! When Ben came back to school, after about four months, he was in a state of shock about what had been done to his room. And when he looked in the stock room... everything just thrown in there. No attempt made to sort or file it, I thought he was going to burst into tears when he was speaking to me in the staff room. He immediately went to see Clarke and handed in his resignation. Which it seems, Clarke accepted without any argument at all,' she stopped speaking for a moment as if visualising what had happened.

'Ben decided that he was going to leave teaching all together. He had some savings, and said that he was going to open a shop somewhere, which, as you know, he eventually did. Took him a while to find the perfect one. Well perfect for him anyway.

'He was still plagued though by the disappearance of Ruth, and spent most of his spare time trying to find out what had happened to her. He was convinced that she'd been killed, and that it wasn't a random act of violence. He thought she'd been murdered by someone she knew. Someone she knew quite well. So, he spent his time searching for clues, writing everything he learned down in an old exercise book. Then a couple of weeks ago he texted to tell me he'd had what he called a breakthrough, and he was going to come over and tell me all about it.'

'We went through his flat and shop with a fine-tooth comb and we didn't find any exercise books,' Atkinson said.

'You wouldn't,' continued Carter. 'Remember he was not only obsessed, but also paranoid about this whole thing. About three months ago he told me he thought he might be onto something and was worried about anything happening to his note book. So, he gave it to me for safe keeping.' She stood up, went over to one of the bookshelves and pulled out a blue school exercise book and returned to her seat clutching it to her chest. 'Before I give it to you, I want to know, is he dead?'

'I honestly can't answer that,' Atkinson said. 'I can tell you we've found no trace of a body, so there's still hope.'

'There was no trace of poor Ruth's body either,' countered Carter. 'But Ben was convinced that she was dead.'

There was a noise from the hallway as the front door opened. A blonde-haired woman in her mid-forties came into the room. 'I heard voices, sorry to disturb you.'

'You didn't disturb us Josie,' Carter said. 'Detective Inspector Atkinson, Detective Sergeant Bassey, I'd like you to meet my partner Josie. They're here to talk to me about Ben. He's gone missing.'

'Oh, I am sorry, that must be a shock for you. I'm sure he'll turn up though. I'll leave you to it, you don't need me in the way. You've got tea? Good.'

Back out on the pavement about fifteen minutes later Atkinson looked at Bassey, waved the blue exercise book and grinned. 'Looks like teacher has given us some homework. Do you want to read it first, or shall I?' In the end they decided to go to the Brooke House, the big pub much loved by students, just around the corner on Smithdown Road, and read it together.

*

Bassey found the journey down to Birmingham quite enjoyable. Even the interminable road works on the M6, the drivers who don't indicate and the middle lane hoggers didn't spoil things. She wasn't driving, which made her feel more relaxed, they were travelling in Atkinson's car. It was a very comfortable and surprisingly clean and tidy nearly new Land Rover Discovery. All their previous car journeys together had been in a battered Ford Focus pool car. Now though, they were on Atkinson's home turf, and he had access to his "made for the car" CDs. This was what she found so enjoyable, he had such a varied musical taste, not so dissimilar to her own in fact, although a lot of the songs were new to her. Each disc was a mix mp3 CD that could hold up to 70 different tracks. Atkinson must have spent hours putting them together. There was no theme, just random juxtapositions of different genres of music. "How D'Ya Like Your Eggs in The Morning?" by Dean Martin & Helen O'Connell, followed by "Vincent Black Lightning 1952" by Richard Thompson, followed by "Free Falling" by Tom Petty, followed by "I'm A Believer" by The Monkees, followed by "Your

Dad Did" by John Hiatt and on and on…. Bassey really enjoyed it as they sang along together with the tracks, they both knew.

'You sing well Shirl. Do you play an instrument as well?'

'Only air guitar I'm afraid. I was in the choir at school though. Do you play anything?'

'I play real guitar. In fact, I used to be in a band, we were called Instant Karma. Only played locally though, never went too far.'

'Any good?'

'To tell the truth we sounded shite, but we thought we were great. Should've changed our name to Hard of Hearing!'

Bassey smiled as Atkinson went on to recount his adventures as a (failed) rock 'n' roll star. The two and a half hours it took to get to Birmingham went very quickly. It seemed though to take just as long to find the Anderson's address in Solihull.

Solihull. Looking through the window, Bassey could see tree lined streets with a nice mix of detached and semi-detached houses. There seemed to be very little social housing, so she supposed you could call it a "posh" area. The sort of place well to do middle class families moved into to get little Sebastian and darling Hermione into a good school. Thereby pushing up the house prices and denying the benefits of the good school to children from less well to do families. Children who, may very well be brighter and more intelligent than Sebastian and Hermione, but will now have to attend the underfunded, dilapidated, rundown local comprehensive. Not unlike the one she'd attended in Toxteth, she supposed. The comprehensive where the staff battle against the odds and do their utmost to give their pupils the best possible education they can. Knowing all the while that being an alumnus of "Dilapidated Comp" will never carry the same weight in later life as being an alumnus of "Good School". As proved by Atkinson and the school he'd attended. Fucking hell an Archbishop of Canterbury had been to Merchants!

'We're here,' Atkinson said pulling the car up opposite what looked like a small well-kept church. The sign outside said "Highgrove Kingdom Hall". 'Not the church,' he continued seeing the puzzled look on Bassey's face. 'The house next door, on the corner.'

43 Highgrove, the home of Ruth's parents, was a detached three-bedroom house, built of the same materials as the church. It was on the corner of the street and had well-tended front gardens. The two police officers got out of the car and walked up the path to the front door. Bassey pressed the bell while Atkinson busied himself rubbing his shoes on the backs of his trousers. The bell was one of those that played a short tune rather than going "ding –

dong". *Neither of them recognised the tune, but Bassey had it in the back of her mind that it was a hymn. After a few seconds the door was answered by a short rotund lady in her late forties or early fifties. She was wearing a pale green two-piece suit and carrying a large brown handbag.*

'Are you the two police officers?' she asked, and then without waiting for an answer. 'Go in and sit down while I just go next door and get Daddy.' She then squeezed past Atkinson and Bassey and marched off down the path.

Atkinson looked at Bassey, puzzled and amazed, 'Daddy?'

XI

Ben Smart had obviously done a lot of research and been very thorough in his investigation of what he thought had happened to Ruth Anderson. The first few pages of the blue exercise book were filled with notes, diagrams and flow charts. After that there was a list of protagonists, as Smart called them. Every person that had had any connection with Ruth had their own double page spread. He had been very thorough, and obviously thought that Ruth was dead. He had even devoted a double page spread to himself, listing all the reasons the police might think he was the killer. Atkinson had thought all along that Ruth hadn't just disappeared and that Smart had killed her, and could only agree with the points that Smart had made. Only now, with Smart himself missing in what looked like similar circumstances, and the unexpected appearance of the exercise book, was Atkinson starting to think that Smart was not the killer. What Atkinson was beginning to think though, was that the identity of the killer was somewhere in the blue book. Jan Carter had told them that, before he disappeared, Smart had thought that he'd made a break through. To Atkinson's mind that meant that one of Smart's protagonists had found out about the new information and had killed Smart to protect him or herself. Atkinson wanted to know what Bassey thought.

'Well, it looks to me that he spent far longer working on this than we did,' Bassey admitted. 'And I think Ben Smart's dead, as is Ruth Anderson. I also think that the same person killed both of them. Plus, the name of the killer is somewhere in here,' she prodded the blue exercise book which was on the pub table in front of them. 'The killer obviously found out that Ben had turned up something that pointed the finger in their direction. So, he or she, had to do something about it to prevent being exposed. And as they had successfully avoided detection for Ruth's murder, why not follow the exact same MO and kill Ben? What I think we have to do now is go through this book, page by page, line by line, until we find Ben's breakthrough.'

'I agree, but what did he find that we missed? I vote that one of us takes the book home tonight, and shares what they found in the morning. We'll toss for it. Winner takes the book and the loser gets the next round in.'

'I'll go to the bar then. I know you, you want first dibs. If you lose the toss you'll say "best of three". So, another pint?' Atkinson nodded his head and smiled; she knew him too well. As Bassey made her way to the bar to get a Guinness for him and a red wine for herself, he picked up the exercise book and flicked through the pages. You're in here somewhere, you bastard, and I'm going to find you.

It was bright and early the next morning, Atkinson and Bassey were sitting in the canteen at Copy Lane.

'Well?' she asked as Atkinson was spooning sugar into his coffee.

'I was up until three this morning reading that bloody book, and I still can't work anything out. There's a shit load of information there, but nothing leaps off the page, nothing grabs you and screams "Look at me, I did it!". Maybe you'll have better luck than me.'

'It could be that what got Ben excited was a new piece of information, something that he didn't write in his book. Remember he'd given it to Jan Carter for safe keeping before he told her about the breakthrough,' Bassey stopped speaking and just gazed into the distance for a couple of seconds. 'Of course, if he didn't write it down, you have to ask yourself, how did the murderer find out? Did Ben approach him, or her, with what he knew? Has the killer read the contents of Ben's book? Was Ben open with everyone about keeping the book? Did he show it to people?'

'That's a shit load of questions Shirl,' Atkinson observed. 'I think we can answer some of them, if we go back and speak to Fred Lowe, the butcher. He appears to have been a good friend, Ben may have spoken to him about the book, or even showed it to him. Jan Carter knew of the book's existence, but is that a new thing, did he only tell her recently, or has she known for a while? She's known Ben a long time, she knew about his obsession.'

'Let's go and talk to Fred Lowe then,' getting up from the table. 'See what he has to say.' Atkinson nodded his agreement, took one last slurp of coffee and stood up himself. The two detectives hurried out of the canteen and headed for the car park to pick up a pool car.

While Atkinson was settling himself behind the wheel, adjusting the seat and mirror, Bassey was sweeping empty polystyrene cups, McDonalds boxes and other detritus from the passenger seat and into the footwell.

'I wish people would take their shit with them,' she said in an exasperated voice. 'It doesn't take two minutes to pick it all up and drop it in a bin. Look at the state of it. The back seat's just as bad!'

'Finished? Good. Let's get on then, shall we?' He turned the key and the engine laboriously came to life. He sighed, and fought with the gear stick and clutch, trying to engage first gear. The car began to move off, and much to Atkinson's surprise, the gearbox and clutch began to combine together like the finely-honed pieces of cutting-edge mechanical equipment they were supposed to be. He turned left out of the station and then right at the lights onto Dunning's Bridge Road. This was the main artery from the M57 to Liverpool and Seaforth docks, and as always it was very busy with lorries and trucks going to and from the docks. Atkinson knew though that he would only have to deal with the traffic for a short while as he planned to turn left at the lights by Bootle Municipal Golf Course and onto Southport Road. The golf course was known as Royal Bootle by the locals and the golfers who played there. These were the golfers who couldn't or wouldn't pay the fees for courses like Royal Birkdale in Southport and West Lanc's in Crosby. Atkinson had never connected with golf. He'd had a few lessons at a club in St Helens, but never continued after that. He never tired of telling people it was because of what the professional had said to him. "Martin, your main problem is, that you're standing too close to the ball. Usually after you've hit it!".

After turning left Atkinson followed the much quieter Southport Road until turning left into Bedford Road and pulling up outside the butcher's shop. There was no sign of the big Yamaha motorcycle, perhaps Artie had the day off? They climbed out of the car, with much muttering about rubbish, hygiene and thoughtless coppers from Bassey. Fred Lowe was alone in the shop. He had his back to the counter and was boning some meat with what looked like a very sharp knife. He turned with a start when the bell on the shop door tinkled, nearly taking a slice out of his finger.

'Jesus! You gave me a fright there Inspector,' recognising his visitors. 'I was in a world of my own. Now, what can I do for you today? I take it you're not here to maybe pick up a few chops?'

'Perhaps another time Fred. We just want to ask you a couple more questions. Did Ben ever show you, or talk to you about a blue school exercise book?' Atkinson asked.

'That thing,' replied Lowe rolling his eyes. 'He was always dragging it out and poring over it. Everybody knew about it. He was convinced that the young girl he used to work with, in the school, had been murdered. He had all his suspects and theories in that book. He even had himself in there as a suspect! As if he wouldn't remember killing someone and disposing of the body.' Lowe shook his head slowly from side to side. 'I never actually read anything that was in it personally, but I know all about it. Artie, he's the one you should talk to. A great reader of murder mysteries is our Artie. He was nearly as bad as Ben about that book. Quite often I'd meet them in the pub and they'd be having some sort of discussion about what happened to that poor girl. I think Artie looked upon it as an intellectual exercise, you know, as if it was a murder novel and you had to work out the clues. But to Ben, it was real life. I don't think he'd ever be happy until he'd proved that she'd been murdered, and he could tell you lot who'd done it.'

'Did Ben say anything to you about making a breakthrough recently?' Bassey asked.

'No, he said nothing to me. He might've spoken to Artie, but I couldn't say for sure. Did he finally crack it then? Is that where he's gone? After the murderer, by himself, the daft bugger?'

'We're not sure, Fred,' Atkinson said. 'We think that he did make some sort of progress, but we don't think he's gone off looking for the murderer. We think possibly the murderer came looking for him. So, if we can find out what Ben found out, we may be able to identify the killer. The killer of Ruth and also, probably, Ben.'

'So, you think that Ben's dead then?'

'I'm afraid so, Fred,' Atkinson answered. 'Everything we've learned so far points that way.'

'Well, let's hope you're wrong, eh?'

'Let's hope so.'

'Is Artie around Fred?'

'No, I'm afraid he's not. He's gone away for a few days with one of his sisters. Somewhere in Ireland, near Killarney I think.'

'OK, thanks Fred, we'll catch up with him when he comes back,' Atkinson said as they turned to leave the shop.

XII

Atkinson and Bassey walked along the hall and into the kitchen. Inside the house was just as you would expect it to be, judging by the front garden. Everything was clean and tidy. Nothing appeared to be out of place. Everything obviously had a place and, was actually in that place. Bassey compared her present surroundings with the state of her own house. She quickly realised that her house fell well short of the standards set by the Anderson's, and she'd only seen the kitchen so far. She decided that she lived in a tip, and made a mental note to start the big tidy up as soon as she got home. While Bassey was admiring the kitchen, Atkinson took the opportunity to have a quick look in the other downstairs rooms.

'Plenty of photos about the place,' he said on returning to the kitchen, 'but Ruth doesn't appear to be in any of them. Well, not that I can see anyway.' Just then, they heard the sound of the front door opening, followed by the sound of two voices in the hallway.

'Ah, there you are,' Mrs Anderson said as she and her husband came into the kitchen. Mr Anderson was only a couple of inches taller than his wife. He was dressed in a black suit with a crisp white shirt and a maroon tie sporting a full Windsor knot. 'This is my husband, Jerome. Daddy, these are the two police officers from Liverpool.' She looked at Atkinson and Bassey and frowned, 'I'm sorry, but I forget your names.'

'I'm PC Bassey and this is DC Atkinson,' Bassey said, showing the couple her warrant card. 'We spoke on the phone Mrs Anderson.' Mrs Anderson nodded and began to busy herself putting the kettle on and making tea.

'How can we help you?' Mr Anderson asked, looking directly at Atkinson. Atkinson held his gaze for a few moments before he answered.

'We've come to speak to you about the disappearance of your daughter, Ruth. Can you tell me, how long has it been since you last saw or spoke to her?'

'We last saw Ruth in November 2006. She has phoned a couple of times since then, but we have just put the phone down and refused to speak to her. I'm afraid I can't give you exact dates for the phone calls. But we haven't had one for about two years now.'

'What happened for you to stop all contact with Ruth?' Bassey asked. 'Do you mind telling us what happened?' Jerome Anderson looked across at his wife, and some imperceptible signal passed between them as she handed steaming mugs of tea to everyone. Atkinson helped himself to the sugar.

'Well,' began Mrs Anderson. 'Ruth had always been the type of child who got into a lot of scrapes, she was never in trouble with the police mind, but she did get in trouble with the Elders.'

Anderson took over. 'Ruth didn't agree with or, I suppose, really approve of our lifestyle. You see, Mummy and I are members of The Watchtower Society. You'd know us better as Jehovah's Witnesses. I'm one of the Elders of our congregation, so you can see that it was very difficult for me when Ruth got into one of her scrapes, very embarrassing in fact. It came as a sort of relief, I suppose you could say, when Ruth went off to university.'

'When was this, and where did she go?' Bassey asked.

'2005, Magdalen College, Oxford, to study Politics and Philosophy. She may have been a handful and irreverent towards our religion but she was a very bright girl. We naively thought, that living away might make her realise what she had here at home, and encourage her to change her ways. How wrong we were. Mummy and I expected her to come home at the end of her first term. She told us though, that she was staying in Oxford with friends to celebrate Christmas.' Anderson's whole demeanour changed. 'As I'm sure you're aware, Christmas is not something that we, as a faith, celebrate.'

'I've often wondered why is that?'

'Our faith tells us that Jesus was created by God, as was the Holy Ghost. There is no Trinity, they are not God's equals,' Anderson explained. 'Therefore, we do not celebrate either his birth or his sacrifice at Easter. Ruth staying in Oxford to celebrate Christmas was a big blow for Mummy and I. As you can imagine, we spoke to her on the phone at great length about this. How she was damning her eternal soul, how she was going against all that she'd been taught and how much she was embarrassing her mother and myself. All our pleas fell on deaf ears. We hoped that it was just something that she'd do once, get it out of her system and then return to the fold.'

'Daddy and I prayed for her salvation - every night,' interjected Mrs Anderson.

'Yes, we did, Mummy. Nothing appeared to change though, but God has a plan. He doesn't always tell us, his disciples, what that plan is. We have to have faith. Faith in Him and his plan.'

'When was the next time you saw Ruth?' Atkinson asked quickly, cutting off what he feared was going to become a sermon.

'She came home at the end of the Spring term, for about a week or so, wasn't it Mummy? And then she returned to Oxford. Those few days didn't go very well, didn't go very well at *all. She seemed to have something on her mind, but she hardly ever spoke to us. She spent most of the time out of the house, visiting friends and such like. It was a very unhappy time.'*

Anderson nodded to his wife and she took up the story. *'We didn't see her again until the end of November, she hadn't come home at all over the summer.'*

'Did you not go to visit her?' Bassey asked.

'We tried, but she had moved out of her lodgings and left no forwarding address. And I must admit, her landlord wasn't very helpful, not helpful at all.'

'Did you ask at the university?'

'Yes, but they said that they couldn't pass on her address as she'd asked them not to.'

'Strange,' Atkinson said.

'Then she just turned up on the doorstep one day, as I said, at the end of November,' Mrs Anderson continued. *'She hadn't phoned to say that she was coming, and she didn't come alone. I remember it like it was yesterday, it was a very wet and windy day, Daddy had gone out around town knocking on doors, talking to nonbelievers. The doorbell rang about two o'clock in the afternoon. When I opened the door, Ruth was standing there. She was wet and bedraggled, and she was holding something wrapped up in her arms. "Hello, mum," she said, "I've brought someone to see you." It was only then I realised she was holding a new born baby. I got them both inside out of the rain, got her out of her wet coat and sat her down here, in the kitchen. I didn't need to ask; I knew the baby was Ruth's. I made us both some tea. We didn't say anything for a while, just sat and looked at each other and the baby. We'd finished the tea before Ruth spoke. "Mum, I'd like you to meet your granddaughter, Alice Louise, born on the 11th of November." and she passed me the baby, before I could say or do anything. She was such a sweet little thing, lying there in my arms smiling at me. Ruth told me that she'd waited until Daddy had gone out before ringing the bell. I asked how long she'd been standing in the rain with the little mite. She assured me that it hadn't been more than ten minutes or so, but I didn't believe her. We sat and chatted for about twenty minutes while I nursed baby Alice. I'd been avoiding asking the question I really wanted to ask, I thought that she'd tell me when she was ready.'*

Mrs Anderson paused and then looked towards her husband before continuing. *'When Daddy came back, we were still sitting in the kitchen, drinking tea and chatting.'* Anderson stood up at this point and left the room, Mrs Anderson watched him go with a sadness in her eyes. *'Ruth had fed baby Alice a bottle, and she was fast asleep in my arms. I must admit Daddy had such a look of shock on his face when he saw us, that I thought he was about to have some sort of seizure. He collapsed onto that chair, where you're sitting Detective*

Atkinson, and just stared for a long time. When he eventually spoke, he immediately asked the question I'd been avoiding. "I assume it's yours, who's the father?". Ruth said that she wasn't going to say who the father was, as that wasn't important. She said the important thing was that baby Alice was with us and it was a miracle we should all celebrate. I told Ruth that we celebrated the arrival of all babies into this world, even those born out of wedlock. She said that it wasn't Alice's birth that we should celebrate, but the fact that she survived at all. She then went on to explain that it had been a terribly traumatic birth. Alice had unexpectedly turned and presented in the breach position. It was as she was being delivered that they discovered that the unexpected turn had caused the umbilical cord to wrap around her neck, affecting the blood supply to her brain. This meant that the doctors had to perform an emergency caesarean section. Alice came out fine and well, and there appeared to be no lasting problems. But Ruth had lost a lot of blood and very nearly died on the birthing table.'

'I can guess what happened next,' Bassey said. 'Ruth's life was saved with blood transfusions.'

'Yes,' Mrs Anderson continued. 'As I'm sure you're aware, our faith forbids us to have blood transfusions, even in life or death situations. It says in Acts 15:20 that it is forbidden to take in blood to sustain the body, and we as a church abide by that doctrine. My husband, as an Elder of the Church, decided that this was altogether too much. Not only had Ruth had a "bastard", as he called Alice, but she had also broken one of the teachings of the Church. He told Ruth that she was no longer welcome here and that he never wanted to see or speak to her again. The argument that ensued went on long into the night, and only ended when Ruth stormed out of the house.'

'We've found no evidence of a baby, or toddler now, being present in Ruth's life. What happened to Alice?' Bassey asked.

'You'll be able to meet her soon. She's round at a little friend's house, she should be home in the next ten minutes or so,' Mrs Anderson said looking at the kitchen clock.

'She lives here, with you?'

'Oh yes. The only thing that was agreed that night, was that Alice should live here with us. She is the innocent in all of this, even Daddy agrees with that. And it's given Daddy and I the chance to start again with a new daughter. Maybe we'll get it right this time. Ruth knew she was in no position to look after Alice, so we said that we would raise her as our own, but she must promise to stay out of Alice's life.'

'Did Ruth tell you who was the father of the child?'

'No, she never told us, and we knew she never would.'

Atkinson and Bassey decided not stay and wait for young Alice's arrival. They said their goodbyes and left before either Alice or Mr Anderson returned.

'What d'you think?' Atkinson asked as they sat in the car outside.

'I think religion can do strange things to people. How can you shun your own daughter because she had a lifesaving blood transfusion? Those two would sooner have had her dead!'

'Well, they may well have their wish. But I feel that the whole thing was down to him rather than her. It seemed to me that he's in total control there, and she just acquiesces to everything that he says. Did you see how she looked to him for the OK to talk about what had happened? I think this line of enquiry has come to a dead end. I don't think that we'll get very much more out of these two.'

'We did get the answer to a couple of questions though.'

'And, they are?'

'We now know who the baby in the photo is,' Atkinson nodded his agreement as Bassey continued. 'And we know why they call each other Mummy and Daddy!'

Atkinson grimaced a little, started the Land Rover and then said 'OK, let's hit the road.'

'I do think though, that Mrs Anderson has had some contact with Ruth since she was disowned,' Bassey opined.

'What makes you think that?'

'She never asked what Ruth was doing in Liverpool, also, I think that Mr Anderson knows about it, but hasn't let on to her. Maybe he feels that he overstepped the mark, but can't do anything about it now.'

Back inside the neat little house Mrs Anderson turned as her husband returned to the kitchen. 'What have we done?' she sobbed. Mr Anderson held her by the shoulders for a few seconds, staring into her eyes, before he answered.

'The right thing in the eyes of God and the Church. We all have our crosses to bear.'

There was no singing in the car on the journey back to Liverpool.

XIII

It was early the next morning. Bassey was sitting in the canteen staring at the blue exercise book, willing it to tell her something, anything. Atkinson slid into the seat opposite her and started doling sugar into his coffee. They sat there saying nothing for a couple of minutes. It was Bassey who broke the contemplative silence.

'This book doesn't have any information in it that we don't have or haven't deduced. Agreed?' Atkinson nodded. 'Therefore, Ben must have taken an extra step somewhere. He must have seen something here that set him off in such a way that it's frightened Ruth's killer enough for him, or her, to feel threatened so that they had to get rid of Ben as well.'

'Agreed. But what was it that he discovered?'

'I don't know, but I think we have to assume that the killer is in here,' waving the exercise book in the air.

'OK, so all we have to do is get a blood sample from everyone mentioned in the book. One of them should match the blood found at the scenes and… bingo! Case closed. Unfortunately, we can't just ask the people in that book for a blood sample. We'd be up to our necks in lawyers!'

'I know we can't do that. We have to go through everyone mentioned in this book with a fine-tooth comb. The killer is in here somewhere. Ben came close to finding out who it is, we just have to do the same.'

'So, what do you suggest we do?'

'I think we take a page at a time. Question the people in this book, not just about the circumstances around Ruth's disappearance or murder, but also about Ben's disappearance. We should dig deep into everything.'

'We're probably going to piss a lot of people off, but, hey-ho, I can't think of anything better. Who do you think we should start with?'

*

The case didn't appear to be going anywhere. Every line of enquiry so far seemed to come to a dead end. Atkinson wrote down on a piece of paper what they knew:

1. *Ruth Anderson had disappeared sometime between the end of July when school finished and the beginning of September, when school started again.*

2. *Ruth worked as a teaching assistant with Ben Smart in the Learning Support Centre.*

3. *Blood of an unknown origin had been found on a kitchen knife in her flat.*

4. *The flat was forensically clean, apart from the knife.*

5. *Ruth had given birth to a daughter, Alice Louise, on 11th November 2006.*

6. *Ruth's Jehovah's Witness parents have disowned her, not for having Alice but for having a blood transfusion that saved her life.*

7. *No-one except Ruth, of course, knew the name of Alice's father.*

Then on the other side of the paper Atkinson wrote a list of their suspicions.

1. *Ruth Anderson is dead. Killed by person or persons unknown.*

2. *Mrs Anderson had still been in contact with Ruth since her father had thrown her out.*

No matter how you looked at it, there wasn't a lot. He passed the piece of paper to Bassey, who studied it for a short while.

'*Well, I think you've just about covered everything there Ron. We don't know a lot, do we?*'

'*So, where do you think we should go from here?*'

XIV

Atkinson pulled the car to halt and the two detectives just sat and stared for a couple of minutes, nothing appeared to have changed since their last visit eight years ago. Alice would be nearly twelve now, both detectives couldn't help but wonder how she had fared over the last few years. Did she know anything about her real mother? Did she think Mrs Anderson was her mother? Only one way to find out.

'Oh, hello,' said the young girl who answered the door.

'You must be Alice, I'm Detective Sergeant Bassey and this is Detective Inspector Atkinson,' Bassey said as she fished around in her hand bag for her warrant card and Atkinson rubbed his shoes on his trouser legs. She finally found the elusive warrant card in the pocket of her jacket and showed it to the girl.

'How do you know my name's Alice?' Before either detective could answer, she continued to speak. 'There's no one in at the moment, I'm by myself. I suppose I'm safe sharing that information with you, as you're both with the police?'

'That information is perfectly safe with us, and I'm sure you're too smart a girl to go telling strangers that sort of thing,' answered Bassey. 'It's your parents we'd like to speak to, will they be long?'

'They're out, talking to the non-believers. I usually go with them, but I've got a lot of schoolwork to do. They shouldn't be too long though. Do you want to come in and wait? I could make some tea.'

'That would be lovely, thank you,' Bassey said. They followed Alice down the hall and into the kitchen. As Alice made tea she chatted happily with Bassey about French, Maths, boy bands and all the other non-connected things that fire up a near teenage brain. Atkinson let his thoughts wander to his experiences with Jehovah's Witnesses calling at the door. As he remembered they were nearly always accompanied by a child. Was that so that there was less chance of confrontation and stopped the disturbed home owner from just telling them to fuck off? Atkinson recalled, with a smile, how his father had dealt with these often unwelcome callers.

Atkinson's father had been a strong church goer, and one day when Witnesses knocked at the door, instead of leaving them on the doorstep he invited them in. For the next three, or possibly four hours Atkinson senior drank tea and argued theology with his bemused guests. Every point they made, he countered with one of his own. Every passage from the Bible they showed him, he showed them a conflicting passage from his own Bible. He knew that Jehovah's Witnesses used their own version of the Bible, which was obviously edited in such a way that it supported their beliefs. When the poor Witnesses finally managed to escape, Atkinson senior invited them to come back anytime. There were no return callers for many years. Atkinson senior said that this was because he'd been blacklisted after their previous visit. Then, one day there was a knock on the door and there stood two young Jehovah's Witnesses.

"You're not supposed to be here, I'm blacklisted," said Atkinson senior.

"Blacklisted?"

"Yes, come in and I'll tell you all about it." More sheep to the slaughter.

'So, Alice, why aren't you in school today?' Bassey's question pulled Atkinson out of his daydreams. A good question, why hadn't he thought to ask it?

'I don't go to school. Mummy teaches me herself, here at home.'

'And how do you find that, has your Mum got any teaching qualifications or experience?'

'Oh yes, she used to teach science at the big Grammar School in Birmingham before she met Daddy.' The big Grammar School, even Atkinson had heard of King Edward VI school in Birmingham. 'I suppose,' continued Alice. 'That I do miss not having people of my own age to talk to, but, as Daddy says, I can always talk to God. If you don't mind, I've got to get on and finish my work before Daddy gets home. Will you be alright by yourselves? They shouldn't be long.'

'We'll be fine, thanks,' Bassey replied. 'You go and finish your schoolwork.' Alice smiled at both detectives and then left the kitchen, shut the door behind herself, and pounded up the stairs.

'Well, what do you make of that?' Atkinson asked.

'I get the impression that Mrs Anderson had quite a successful teaching career. You have to be good to get a job at a Grammar School, even more so to get a job at that one in Birmingham. It regularly comes near the top of best school lists in the Sunday Times. Then, she met Mr Anderson, fell under his spell and gave it all up for either him or God. Or possibly both. Do you remember when we spoke to them originally, how she told us that they now had a chance to try again with Alice. To get it right?' Atkinson nodded and Bassey continued. 'Well, I presume that Ruth attended school in the usual way, and her parents think that the exposure to "normal kids",' Bassey made quote marks in the air with her fingers. 'Somehow caused her to start to reject what they believed in. So, to stop that happening again, poor Alice is schooled at home and completely misses out on all the social side of school. She seems to be an intelligent young lady, look at her conversation at the door. That was basically a "stranger danger" situation, and she analysed it and talked us both through it in a couple of sentences.'

Atkinson nodded. 'Do you think that home tuition was something that the Andersons discussed? Or do you think it was all his idea?'

'I'd go for it being Anderson's idea and his wife doing as she's told. I get the impression that that's how it goes around here. Did you notice that Alice said she had to finish her work before "Daddy" got home? I thought that was strange as it's her mother who teaches her.'

'I didn't take much notice of it, but I agree with your theory that Anderson controls everything. Could he possibly have found out that his wife was still in contact with Ruth and killed her himself?'

'It's a possibility I suppose. Let's see what happens when we have a chat.'

The Anderson's returned about thirty minutes later. Atkinson and Bassey heard the front door open and then the sound of two voices in the hallway. The couple were still talking to each other when Mr Anderson pushed the kitchen door open.

'Oh my God!' shouted Anderson in alarm as he saw the two detectives sitting in the kitchen. 'Who are you? What are you doing in my house?' He then turned to his wife, 'Alice! Is Alice alright? Go and check! Quickly!' Mrs Anderson immediately turned and ran up the stairs shouting 'Alice! Alice!'

'Mr Anderson, calm yourself,' soothed Bassey, as she and Atkinson stood up. 'You obviously don't remember us, we're police officers. We're sorry if we gave you a shock, we didn't mean to. Alice let us in, and made us a cup of tea, before she went back upstairs to continue with her school work.'

'It's alright Daddy, Alice is safe. She says they're police officers,' they heard Mrs Anderson call as she came puffing back down the stairs. 'I've no idea what they want though.' She walked into the kitchen and stared at Bassey and Atkinson, waiting for them to explain their presence.

Neither Mr or Mrs Anderson had changed very much over the years. Atkinson thought that the Andersons still looked like a bank manager and his wife. Anderson was wearing a dark suit with a white shirt and blue tie, and Mrs Anderson wore a grey two piece.

Bassey pulled out her warrant card as she made the introductions. 'I'm Detective Sergeant Bassey and this is Detective Inspector Atkinson. Again, I'm sorry if we gave you a fright, it honestly wasn't our intention to do so.'

'I remember you now,' Anderson said, thoughtfully, 'you came to see us when Ruth disappeared. Have you found her? Has she turned up?'

'No, I'm afraid not.' Atkinson answered. 'There has though, been another disappearance in similar circumstances to Ruth's.'

'You can't believe that has any connection to us surely?' interjected Mrs Anderson.

'No, no, it's nothing like that.' continued Atkinson, 'The second disappearance is someone that Ruth was working with when she disappeared. A newsagent, he disappeared about two weeks ago, in very similar circumstances to Ruth's disappearance.'

'What possible connection could Ruth have with a newsagent?'

'The newsagents name is Ben Smart, he used to be a teacher, and he worked with Ruth at the time she went missing,' Atkinson answered.

'Smart? Isn't that the name of the man who came to see us a couple of years ago Mummy?' Mrs Anderson nodded. 'He called round out of blue, said he used to work with Ruth and was trying to find out what happened to her. He asked us some questions which we answered the best we could. More out of politeness than anything else. Then he left and we never saw or heard from him again. You say he's now a newsagent and he's disappeared as well? That's very strange, very strange indeed.'

'Can you remember what he said to you?' Atkinson asked.

'I remember he told us that he thought Ruth was dead,' Mrs Anderson said. 'We honestly didn't know what to think at the time. And you coming back, it's just going to churn everything up again. And poor Alice.'

'Does Alice know that Ruth's her real mother? In fact, does she know anything about Ruth at all?' Bassey asked.

At that moment the kitchen door opened and Alice walked in. 'Who's Ruth?' she asked in a very quiet voice, 'And what's she got to do with me?' She looked at each of the Andersons in turn.

'We'll talk about it later darling, when the police officers have gone,' Anderson answered looking pointedly at Atkinson and Bassey.

'No. I want to talk about it now,' Alice said in a much firmer voice. 'You and Mummy must think I'm stupid. I know that you're not my real parents, your much too old to start with. I've been waiting for you to tell me that I'm adopted for ages. It'll make no difference, you know, I'll still love you.'

Mrs Anderson began to sob, rushed across the kitchen and crushed the girl in a strong embrace. 'Oh darling, we're sorry for keeping things from you, but we thought it was for the best. You know we'd never do anything to hurt you, don't you?'

'I know that Mummy, but who is Ruth?'

'It's a difficult story,' began Anderson. 'Are you sure you want to hear it now? Why not wait a bit and hear it later?'

'No, I want to know now please. Please tell me who she is. Is she my real mother?'

'Come on, let's go and sit in comfort in the living room,' Mrs Anderson suggested, walking towards the kitchen door holding Alice's hand. Everyone followed, Atkinson was very interested in how the Andersons were going to explain this. Once they were all settled, Mrs Anderson began the story.

'Well, darling, you're right, Ruth was your real mother.' there was a long pause before she continued. 'Ruth was our daughter, which makes you our granddaughter.'

'What happened .... Grandma?'

'Ruth was just like you, a clever, pretty and lively girl with definite ideas of her own. She did very well at school and went to Oxford University to study Politics and Philosophy. She came to see us one day in November 2006, bringing you with her. You were so small. She wouldn't tell us the name of your father, no matter how often we asked. Obviously, Daddy and I were not exactly delighted about the situation,' Mrs Anderson glanced threateningly at the two detectives before carrying on. 'We all agreed that it would be best for you to live here with Daddy and me so that your Mum could complete her studies, and you could go and live with her when she was settled.'

'But,' interrupted Anderson before Bassey or Atkinson could speak, 'she disappeared when you were three, so we have continued to look after you.' He nodded towards Atkinson and Bassey, 'That's why these police officers are here. They've come to update us on the situation concerning your mother.' Alice looked at Atkinson. He could see the mixture of hope and fear in her eyes, could he sugar coat things as well as the Andersons had?

'Your grandfather's right. We're the police officers investigating your mother's disappearance. We came here today to give them an update and to ask a couple of questions about someone your mum used to work with. Because he's been looking for her as well, and now he's disappeared'

'Do you think he's found her and they've run off together? Is he my father? If he can find her, surely you can?' The questions just tumbled out.

'No Alice, I'm afraid he's not your father, he's someone she used to work with in Liverpool. And you're right, if he found her, we can as well. And we're going to continue to do our best to find your mother, and her friend.'

'This must be a shock for you, love,' Mrs Anderson said taking Alice's hand. 'Come upstairs and I'll try to answer any questions you might have. We'll leave Daddy down here to talk with the police officers.'

Once they were alone in the room, Anderson looked at the two police officers. 'Thank you for not saying anything. We'd decided a long time ago what we'd say if this moment ever arose. We must have known it would happen someday, and today's the day. Thank you again.'

'I must admit, I thought it was a very smooth performance,' Bassey said. 'Just enough truth for it to be believable, and all the unsavoury bits left on the cutting room floor. Clever, very clever. But isn't it going to cause more problems and heartache if the real truth comes out?'

'Well, I think that's probably up to you. At this point in time, I'm sure you'll agree, Alice doesn't need to know that Ruth's probably dead. And if by any chance you actually find out what happened to Ruth and her friend Mr Smart, I don't think that revealing the details of our family estrangement will be of any practical use to anyone.'

Atkinson and Bassey nodded their agreement. Why turn the young girl's life into more of a maelstrom if they didn't really need to? 'We'll do what we can Mr Anderson,' Atkinson said. 'But, if it all needs to come out, either for us to solve this case or to ensure we get a conviction in court, then I'm afraid all bets are off.'

Anderson nodded his thanks. 'I'm sure you will do everything you possibly can to find out what happened to our daughter and to keep our granddaughter safe.'

'Can I ask Mr Anderson,' Bassey said. 'Were you or Mrs Anderson in contact with your daughter at all after that night in November?'

'I never contacted Ruth, but I found out that my wife had been in quite regular contact. Keeping Ruth informed about Alice's progress and things like that. At first, I wondered if I should stop it, but I decided that it was obviously something my wife needed to do so, I let it continue.'

'So, your wife knew that Ruth was in Liverpool all along?' Atkinson asked, Anderson nodded sheepishly. 'Do you have any idea how often your wife contacted Ruth and when the last time was?' he said changing the subject quickly.

'We have an Elders meeting at church on the third Thursday of every month. I'm pretty certain that that was when she made the phone calls. I presume August would have been the last time they spoke as you came to see us in the September to tell us Ruth had disappeared.'

'Do you mind if we ask your wife about these phone calls? Does she know that you know about them?'

'She knows that I know, but we've never spoken about it. I'll go and get her for you.'

When Anderson left the room Bassey looked at Atkinson and whispered 'More secrets?' Atkinson nodded. Mrs Anderson joined them a couple of minutes later.

'Daddy says that we have been remiss in our roles as hosts. Would you like some tea?' Both detectives nodded and Mrs Anderson turned to go to the kitchen. As she reached the door, she turned and looked directly at Atkinson. 'I knew that he knew about the phone calls to Ruth, but we never spoke about them.'

This is getting like a game of I know that you know that I know that you know.... Why can't people just be open and honest with each other? Especially families?

Mrs Anderson returned five minutes later carrying a tray holding a tea pot, milk jug, sugar bowl, three mugs and a plate of Fondant Fancies. 'Please help yourselves,' she said. As Atkinson piled sugar into his tea and stuffed a whole Fondant Fancy into his mouth, Bassey began the conversation.

'We suspected when we visited all those years ago that you were in contact with Ruth,' Mrs Anderson nodded. 'Did you phone her on Thursdays while your husband was at the Elders meeting?' Mrs Anderson nodded again. 'So, when you phoned in August, the month before we came to see you, did you speak to her then?'

'No, I spoke to Ruth in the July, a couple of days before she broke up from school.'

'So, when we came to see you eight years ago you knew where Ruth was and what she was doing?'

'Yes, I'm sorry about that. I didn't want Daddy to know that I'd been in contact with Ruth. I didn't think he knew about the phone calls then. And no, I didn't speak to Ruth in August at all, her phone just rang out whenever I tried it.'

'So, when we came to see you, you'd had no contact with Ruth since the third Thursday in July?' queried Atkinson.

'That's correct, but I didn't begin to worry about her until you and Sergeant Bassey showed up that day. You must understand that I only ever had a two-hour window to speak to Ruth, as that was how long the Elder's meeting lasted. I'd rung a few times previously and got no answer, so I wasn't worried when she didn't pick up.'

'OK, just one final question,' Atkinson paused a couple of seconds before continuing. 'Did Ruth ever tell you the name of Alice's father?'

'No, never.'

Ten minutes later, Atkinson and Bassey were driving back towards the M6 motorway and Liverpool.

'I think we can scrub Anderson from our list of possible killers.'

'Why's that?' Atkinson asked.

'Well, he knew all about the phone calls, and I get the impression he knew about them from quite early on, and didn't really have a problem with them. Why wait until they'd been going on for years before doing anything about it? He's obviously the boss in that household, all he needed to do was tell Mrs A to stop and desist and she probably would have done. OK, we don't agree with his religion and the way he treated Ruth, but I don't think he killed her. In fact, I think he regretted what they'd done, but just couldn't find a way of putting it right which would square with his religious beliefs.'

'Shirley, I think you're right there. Scratch Mr Jerome Anderson, Elder in the Solihull branch of the Jehovah's Witnesses from our list of starters and riders.'

'Yes boss.'

XV

'At the moment we only really have one suspect. And that's if Ruth was murdered, and hasn't just gone off to the Greek Islands,' Atkinson said.

'Ben Smart,' Bassey agreed. 'Maybe we should go and visit him again, and see if we can get him to change his story.' Atkinson nodded. 'Do we have his home address?' continued Bassey.

'No, but we can give the school a quick ring and get it. In fact, we can kill two birds with one stone and get the Head's home address as well, I think he's worth another chat. And, I think it would be good to talk to both of them away from the school - no distractions, if you know what I mean.'

It took more than a quick call to secure the two addresses. The school secretary refused to give out the addresses of two members of staff over the phone to someone claiming that she was a police officer. If she wanted the addresses she would have to come into school and show some ID.

An hour later Atkinson and Bassey were back, sitting in the canteen, looking at the neatly folded piece of paper which contained the two addresses. It was too early for home visits; school would still be in session. They decided to make their calls in the early evening.

It was about half past six when Atkinson cut the engine to the pool car. He looked at the piece of paper in his hand and then at the front door, the numbers matched. Number 30 Mariners Road looked to be a pleasant, well-kept, four bedroomed detached. It was a short walk away from Crosby Leisure Centre and the beach. People came from all over the country to visit this beach. Not because of its golden sands or sparkling waters, they came to see Antony Gormley's art installation "Another Place". This was art on a massive scale. It consisted of one hundred life-size cast-iron human statues, scattered along three kilometres of beach, all staring out to sea. Each statue a cast of the artists own body. Many of the statues disappearing and reappearing with the tides. It had originally been planned that the Iron Men, as they are known locally, would only stay for a fixed period of time. They were then going to be dug out of the sand and a fresh installation made of them in New York. Their popularity though took everyone by surprise and in 2007 Sefton, the local council, decided to keep them. It cost one and a half million pounds to make Crosby beach their permanent home.

There was a look of complete shock on Charles Clarke's face when he opened his front door and found the two police officers standing on his step. 'What are you doing here?' he demanded, glancing over his shoulder and looking back down the hallway. 'The secretary told me that you only wanted my address for completeness on your forms.'

'We'd just like to have a little chat, Mr Clarke,' Atkinson said, gurning what might be seen as an apology for telling a little white lie, and rubbing his shoes on the backs of his legs.

'Couldn't it have waited until tomorrow? You could have come to see me at school.'

'Who is it Charles?' called a voice from inside one of the rooms before he could say anymore.

'It's no-one for you to get worried about dear. Carry on with your jigsaw,' Clarke called back. 'They're just going.'

'It's the police!' shouted Atkinson, looking straight at Clarke, who became very flustered and looked again down the hallway. One of the dark wooden doors off opened and a woman, about the same age as Clarke, purred out into the hall in an electric wheel chair.

'Oh, how exciting,' she said smiling, 'do come in and have a cup of tea while you're interrogating us. Charles, take these lovely police officers into the front room and I'll put the kettle on. Sugar anyone?'

'Three please.' Atkinson answered. Mrs Clarke looked at him, shook her head in obvious dismay, did an expert three-point turn in the narrow hallway and retreated into the kitchen. Atkinson looked expectantly at Clarke.

Defeated he said, 'You'd better come in then.' He turned and ushered the two police officers into the front room. Clarke didn't speak again until Atkinson and Bassey had settled themselves into two large armchairs. 'You must forgive my wife, her life is a little humdrum and something like this she sees as an opportunity for some, what shall we say, excitement. Yes, excitement, that's the word.' Clarke had stopped looking flustered and seemed to be coming more to terms with the fact that there were police officers sitting in his front room. 'Anne watches a lot of television and her favourites are always the detective programmes. She quite fancies herself as a Miss Marple.'

'We could definitely do with someone like that at the moment,' quipped Bassey as the door was pushed open and Mrs Clarke came into the room with a tray on her lap. The tray had four mugs balanced on it, and Mrs Clarke began to distribute them. When she got to Atkinson, she looked him squarely in face and said 'I've only put two spoons in. Three's far

too many, you need to cut down young man.' Atkinson just nodded, whether in agreement or because he realised it was no use arguing, Bassey couldn't work out.

'I suppose you've come about that poor young girl who disappeared? Charles has told me all about it. It's very sad. A pretty young thing by all accounts,' she glanced at Clarke. Giving him what Bassey thought was quite a funny look. 'Have you found her yet? Do you think she's still alive? Any clues?'

Atkinson took his chance when Mrs Clarke appeared to stop for breath. 'We've actually come to a bit of a dead end. It may be that Ruth has just gone off, decided to start again somewhere else. A fresh start where no one knows her.'

'You don't believe that though do you detective? You think she's dead, and I'm inclined to agree with you,' Atkinson raised his eyebrows and Mrs Clarke continued. 'I'm sure that you've circulated her photo, and if she's as pretty as my husband says,' another glance at Clarke, who seemed a little disconcerted to Bassey's eyes. 'Someone would have spotted her. So, this leaves two possibilities; kidnap or murder. She's not been kidnapped as there has been no contact from the kidnappers, so it has to be murder. But who did it? I think you'll find that it was someone she met in a club or a pub, that's usually the way. Well, I can't stay chatting, you've obviously come to speak to Charles and Midsomer Murders starts in five minutes.' And with that Mrs Clarke executed another perfect three-point turn and left the room.

Clarke started the conversation. 'Do you agree with my wife that Miss Anderson is dead?'

'Without a body, we have to think that there is a chance that she's still alive,' Bassey began. 'But on the whole, we tend to agree with your wife. As to the identity of the killer, we don't know the answer to that yet,' Bassey put her tea cup on the small coffee table and continued. 'Can you tell us anything more about Ruth? We've spoken to her parents in Birmingham, but all they could tell us was that they've not seen her since late 2006.'

'A dead end as my wife would say. Sorry, no pun intended. I honestly know very little about Miss Anderson, she's only been with us for two terms. She seems to be a very capable person, the young people she works with obviously like her. You must understand, I don't want to sound callous in anyway, but I have far more important things to do in school than worry about what my staff get up to in their free time. As long as they are performing well and getting results then I'm happy.'

'So as far as you are aware, there are no great friendships?'

'Not that I would know of.'

'How about Ben Smart?' Bassey asked. 'Do they get along well?'

'As far as I know, yes. Whenever the Unit is brought up in staff meetings Miss Anderson and Mr Smart always appear to have a united front.'

'So, there's nothing you can tell us about Ruth Anderson then.'

'No, I'm afraid not,' said Clarke shaking his head.

'Where did she come from? I mean, where did she work before she joined you?'

'Somewhere down south, as far as I recall. Without her file I'm afraid I couldn't tell you for sure.'

'Did you know that she had a child? A little girl, named Alice, she's nearly four now.'

There was a slight hesitation before Clarke replied 'No, no I didn't. It was not something that came up at the interview, and as I'm sure you know, you can't ask that type of question anymore. Plus, I never heard the child mentioned by herself or other staff members. But if anyone would know, it would be Mr Smart, she had the closest working relationship with him. She could well have spoken to him about it.'

'OK, thanks for your help,' Atkinson said getting out of the chair. 'Come on Shirl, let's leave these good people to enjoy the rest of their evening.'

Outside in the car Atkinson looked at Bassey and said 'He claims to not know a lot about his staff, but from what we've seen at the school I don't think that's true. How about you?'

Bassey nodded. 'He's got benches positioned so he can see what's going on in the classrooms. I think he's almost voyeuristic,' Atkinson looked puzzled so Bassey explained. 'He likes to know what's going on, but doesn't want to be involved or be seen to be involved. I'd bet a big gold clock that there's not a lot he doesn't know about any of his staff. And I'm positive he knew about Alice. Did you notice he didn't ask anything about her? I'd have thought that he would have asked about where the child was, and who was looking after her.'

'Good point. Let's go over to Ben Smarts and see what he has to say,' Atkinson said, starting the car. Neither he nor Bassey noticed Clarke watching them from the window of the darkened front room.

XVI

Once again Atkinson and Bassey were sitting in the canteen at Copy Lane, trying to decide who to visit next. 'How about we go to the school and see the Head, and we can have a word with Jan Carter as well?' ventured Bassey.

'Do we really want to talk to them at school, or would it be better at home?' Atkinson mused. 'They may be more amenable at home, no pressure of work and things like that.'

'Well why not do both? If it's inconvenient or doesn't seem to be going anywhere at school we can always go and visit at home.'

'Great idea Shirl. I knew I kept you around for something,' joked Atkinson finishing his coffee and getting up from his chair. 'Let's go and get a car.'

*

'Did you ever find out about that tie incident that Smart mentioned?' Atkinson asked as they drove towards Ben Smart's address in Thornton.

'I did actually.'

'Well......?'

'I think it's best to hear Smart tell it from his point of view. It sounds very interesting and I don't think there'll be a problem getting him to talk. Do you?' Atkinson smiled in agreement.

There was a light on in the front window of Ben Smart's house in Thornton. It looked a well-kept three bedroomed semi-detached in the estate by Saint William Of York's church. Bassey pushed the bell, shaking her head as she watched Atkinson wiping his shoes on the back of his trousers. Ben Smart opened the door wearing jeans and a white T shirt.

'Oh, hello officers, you're working late, would you like to come in?' Smart turned and walked down the hallway. Bassey and Atkinson followed into a living room piled high with books, CDs, magazines and newspapers. 'Sorry about the mess, but I live here.' grinned Smart as he moved things around to make room for the two police officers to sit down.

Once they were settled and more tea politely refused, Atkinson kicked off.

'We'd like to ask you a few more questions about Ruth Anderson, if that's OK?' Smart nodded. 'How well do you know her? For example, do you know where she'd been working, before she joined the school at the start of the year?'

'Ruth's a lovely girl, great with the kids, who all adore her. She is though very tight lipped about her past. She did let it slip that she'd moved up here from Oxford, but it didn't take a genius to work out that she isn't from there. Her Brummie accent gives it away. She's never said what she'd been doing in Oxford, but I got the feeling that she'd been to university there.'

'Does she have any friends amongst the staff?' asked Bassey.

'No, not in particular. She seems to get along with everyone, but doesn't seem to have any great friends.'

'How about you, would you class her as a friend?' Bassey continued.

'I'd like to think so, but I think she sees us more as colleagues who get on well together, rather than friends. We have each other's backs in school, but we rarely see each other out of school.'

'How do you mean "we have each other's backs"?' interrupted Atkinson.

'I don't know if you've picked up the vibes around school, but a lot of the staff don't like the way we run the Learning Support Centre. They'd prefer to have the old Unit back. Somewhere where they can send kids to get rid of them from their classes. Both Ruth and I believe that what we are doing is the right thing to do to help these emotionally fragile kids. And so, we support each other. Especially in staff meetings, where the subject gets brought up a lot. Also, she's there as a witness in the LSC if anything happens with the kids.'

'A witness?'

'Yes, a witness. I'm sure you both know what one of those is. Let me explain what I mean though. A few years ago, in the late 90's, I was working at a residential school in Formby for kids with emotional and behavioural problems. It was run by the Catholic Social Services - one of my references for the job even had to come from a priest. Anyway, one Monday morning I was called in to see the Head who informed me that one of the pupils, Nathan White, who had gone missing on the previous Friday morning had turned up, back at school. I wondered why the Head was telling me this, I taught the lad but had nothing to do with the residential units. It soon became clear. Nathan said that he'd gone missing because in my lesson, on the Thursday before he disappeared, I'd strangled him with his tie and he'd collapsed unconscious. Of course, I denied this, asking had he said anything about the bucket of water I threw on him to bring him round? Because if I'd been stupid enough to strangle him, I'd have been stupid enough to do that as well. The Head, unimpressed with my sarcasm, said he would write me a good reference if I resigned there and then. Or, he could *suspend me and the police would become involved. I told him to fuck off, if you'll excuse my French. So, he suspended me.*

'I was asked by the police to attend Southport Police Station. I met my solicitor, supplied by my union, outside and asked him what was going to happen? He said that they were just going to ask me a few questions and there was nothing to worry about. When I presented myself at the front desk, the first think they did was arrest me. I wasn't expecting it and looking at the face on my solicitor neither was he. I was taken down to the Custody Suite where I had to empty my pockets, and hand over my belt and my shoelaces.'

'It must have been terrifying for you,' interrupted Bassey.

'It was, it was. My solicitor asked me if I'd actually strangled the boy, because it looked like the police thought they had an open and shut case. I told him there was no way had I done anything so stupid. I was eventually interviewed by two police officers, one female, one male - I don't remember their names. They outlined the charge against me and informed me that they had four eye witnesses to the assault. The initial questioning was very heavy, and I had little opportunity to put my side of the story. My solicitor eventually called a halt and said that he wanted to confer with me privately.

'He said he thought that they were bullying me and I shouldn't answer any more of their questions. I told him that I had a few points that I wanted raise. So, when we returned to the interview, he said that I'd be answering "no comment" to their questions but that I would like to make some points at the end.

'And that's what happened. They asked their questions, produced their witness statements and I kept schtum. Their case was that I had strangled Nathan unconscious in front of four witnesses, and that when he recovered consciousness he had immediately run out of the room and informed the Head of Care. I first asked about the four witnesses, as none of them were in Nathan's class, how had they seen what had happened? They did though live in the same residential unit. I then asked the two officers how much they knew about strangulation and unconsciousness. I had spoken to a friend, a doctor, and he told me there was no way that a strangulation victim who had become unconscious could wake up and immediately run out of a room. I then asked where was the statement from the Head of Care? They admitted that they hadn't even spoken to him! My final question to them, and the killer if I may say so, was - had they spoken to my teaching assistant who would have been present in the room at the time of the alleged offence? Again, they said no. So, they hadn't spoken to any of the adults involved.'

'Doesn't sound like very good police work,' Bassey said.

'The eventual outcome was that the police said the case was unproven, and I found myself another job. So, that's what I mean about teaching assistants being witnesses.'

'Did you ever find out why he accused you?' asked Bassey

'I'd always got on well with Nathan, in fact, he'd given me a handmade birthday card the week before, so I was baffled by it all. It seems though, that the residential unit he was living in were going away for that weekend and he didn't want to go, so, he'd run off and gone home.

'When he returned to school, he needed a good reason for running off, not just that he didn't want to go on holiday. So, he concocted the strangulation story with four of his friends from the unit, who all said they'd be witnesses.

'It could all have gone to shit for me I know. Three members of the care staff at that school were arrested and jailed for sexual offences against children. They all served the major part of their sentences before it was found that all the allegations had been false. Unfortunately, that was the kind of kid we were trying to help.'

'It sounds as if you had a very rough time of it,' Atkinson said. 'Did it not put you off working with that type of child?'

'No, in fact, it made me more determined to try and help them to turn their lives around. Basically, to keep as many as possible out of your clutches!' Smart smiled. 'But you didn't come here to listen to my war stories. How can I help?'

'We're still trying to build up a picture of Ruth, what she was like, what she did in her spare time, things like that,' said Atkinson.

'I'm afraid I can't help you there very much. The only contact I had with Ruth outside school was on staff nights out and things like that. Apart from those I only ever saw her in school.'

'Did she ever tell you she was a mother?' Atkinson asked.

'Good God no! Who's looking after the child? How old is it? Is it a boy or a girl? Did Ruth just leave it or did she take it with her?' Atkinson looked at Bassey, that's the sort of reaction you expect from a friend or colleague.

'It's OK,' Bassey said interrupting the flow of questions. 'It's a little girl, her name is Alice, she's nearly four years old and she lives with her grandparents in Birmingham, as she has done all her life.'

Smart let out a sigh, 'Thank God for that. Ruth never mentioned her at all.'

'OK Mr Smart, I think we've taken up enough of your time, so we'll be going,' Atkinson said, standing up.

Smart escorted the two police officers to the front door, just as he was stepping outside Atkinson turned and asked one final question, à la Columbo. 'When you left the school in Formby, Ben, where did you go?'

'I got a job down south at a Pupil Referral Unit in Woodstock.'

'And you came back......?'

'2006 to take this job.'

'OK, thanks and goodnight.'

Atkinson and Bassey sat in the car discussing all the new information.

'So, Ben Smart worked in Woodstock until 2006, the year Alice was born. Do you know where Woodstock is Shirl?'

'You mean apart from the one in New York State that had the festival?' Atkinson nodded. 'It's Oxford way isn't it?'

'Exactly! Is Ben Smart telling us the truth? Does he know Ruth better than he says he does? Is he Alice's father? Is he Ruth's sugar daddy? Did he kill Ruth? He has possible previous, the strangling charge wasn't dismissed it was "case unproven", he said so himself. I think we need to talk to the people who interviewed Smart back in the 90's.'

XVII

The school receptionist recognised them this time. She took them to a small room off the entrance hall, explaining that the Head was busy. The room was obviously a waiting area. It held a small sofa and a side table with a sprinkling of magazines. The pair sat in silence, thumbing through out of date copies of Hello magazine. After about ten minutes the receptionist appeared at the door and informed them that the Head was ready to see them. They assured her that they could find their own way, and she returned to her position as custodian of the school doors.

The Head was sitting in his usual seat, looking like a shadow. 'Good morning officers, and what can I do for you today?' he asked, making no effort to get up.

'We'd like to ask you a few more questions about Ruth Anderson and Ben Smart,' Atkinson said. 'Did you know that Ben Smart was looking into Ruth's disappearance?'

'No, I didn't, and what difference would it have made if I had?' Clarke snapped.

'We're just trying to get a complete picture, Mr Clarke,' soothed Atkinson. 'Do you think Ben could have been the father of Ruth's daughter? She was at Oxford and he worked in Woodstock around that time.'

It was difficult to see Clarke's face in the shadows, but Bassey was sure she saw an emotion of some kind quickly flit across his face. When the Head spoke again, his voice had lost a little of the arrogance. 'I can see where you're going inspector, but geographical closeness does not mean sexual closeness, does it now?' Clarke looked purposefully first at Atkinson and then at Bassey. 'If it did, would any of us be safe from rumour and gossiping tongues? And why would they pretend not to know each other? It seems a strange way for parents to behave.'

'Yes, I suppose you're right there. Would it be possible to have a quick word with Miss Carter while we're here?' Atkinson asked.

'I suppose so,' grumbled the Head. 'Break starts in a couple of minutes, so if you go down to the staff room you can speak to her there.'

'Just out of interest Headmaster, do you have any children?' Atkinson asked as he turned towards the door.

The Head paused for a moment before replying. 'I don't know what relevance that question has, but no, I don't have any children. Unfortunately, my wife's accident and resulting condition means children are not an option for us.'

'Did you see the way he looked at us? Pervert!' Bassey grumbled as they walked towards the staff room.

'Don't get so worked up about it. Would it really be so bad?' Atkinson smiled.

'Yuck!' barked Bassey. 'I do hope you're joking!'

The staff room door had a new keypad entry system, so they had to wait for a member of staff to let them in. Bassey thought that it had been very petty of Clarke not to give them the code. Even though break had only just started, the staff room was already full of teachers chatting, drinking coffee and marking books. Atkinson looked around for Jan Carter and found her sitting with a hot drink at a table by the staff lockers. She had a pile of exercise books in front of her and was going through them with all the enthusiasm of one of Henry VIII's wives walking to the execution block. Atkinson coughed and she looked up. Jan Carter looked totally knackered. Her eyes were rheumy with large bags under them. Her skin had a ghastly pallor to it and when she smiled in recognition it looked to be more of a grimace.

'I take it you've come to talk to me,' she croaked. 'Far too many people in here, let's walk down to the gym. We can talk there in private.'

'If you don't mind me saying so,' Bassey said as they were walking to the gym. 'But you look awful.'

'I've not been sleeping so well, since I found out about Ben's disappearance. I've not been eating, and I've been drinking too much. I just can't seem to get any of it out of my head. Is he dead? Do you know for sure yet?'

'We still don't have a body, but we're assuming that both Ben and Ruth are dead,' Bassey answered handing Carter a tissue to help mop up the tears starting to flow.

'Thank you,' she sniffed, opening the door to the gym and leading the two police officers to a small office at the end of the girl's changing room.

Once they were settled into chairs Atkinson started the conversation. 'We can't find anything in Ben's exercise book that points to a possible killer. We think though, that Ben was getting close. Have you read it?'

'I read it when he gave it me to look after, but nothing rang any bells.'

'Did he say anything when he gave you the book to look after?' Bassey asked.

'He said that he was worried it would fall into the wrong hands and that I should put it somewhere safe and not speak to anyone about it. He didn't say anything else that I can recall.'

'Did you not think it was odd, that after all this time when Ben had made no secret of the book, he wanted it hidden and not talked about?' Atkinson asked.

'I did think it was a little strange, but I just thought he was going through one of his paranoid episodes. He used to have panic attacks, and I thought it was one of those. I did ask him about it, but he said I was not to worry.'

'OK, thanks Jan. If you think of anything let us know please. You've got our number?'

'Yes, Sergeant, its pinned on the notice board in the kitchen.'

Once they were back in the car Atkinson decided that they should go to Fred Lowe's butchers' shop and see if Artie Miller was back from Ireland.

XVIII

Bassey put the phone down and looked across at Atkinson. 'I've managed to trace one of the officers who interviewed Ben Smart in the 90's. Name of Susan Jeffries, now retired and living over the water in Neston. She's agreed to meet us this afternoon. Says that she has a slight memory of the case, but she'll look through her notes in the spare bedroom to see if there's anything there. Before you ask, she retired as a DCI, and before you ask again, she told me that she hasn't seen her co-interviewer, Bob Wainwright, since she left the job.'

'We really need to find Wainwright as well Shirl. He may remember things that she's forgotten.'

'Well Jeffries said that the last she'd heard was that he'd also retired and was living somewhere in the Southport area. We'll just have to keep looking. Ben's interview took place at Southport nick, I'll ring them again and see if I can find anything else.'

Across the river Mersey from Liverpool was the Wirral, and the two were connected by two tunnels. Queensway, built in the 1930's, and Kingsway, built in the 1960's. It was through the Kingsway tunnel that Atkinson was driving. He was always quite excited about visiting the Wirral, he didn't know exactly why, but he always felt a frisson of excitement as soon as he was enveloped by the tunnel. All scousers thought that people who lived on the Wirral were posh, and people who lived in Neston were amongst the poshest. But Atkinson and Bassey both knew that it didn't matter how posh an area was, there were still people there who lied, cheated, stole and even murdered. So, being posh didn't affect their thought processes at all.

Jeffries lived by the University of Liverpool botanical outpost, Ness Gardens. The house was a large 4 bedroomed property set well back from the road. The gravel drive crunched as Atkinson pulled the car to a halt outside the front door. Closer inspection showed that the house was in need of a little TLC, the paint was peeling from the windows and the rendering was patched and mismatched. Cat Lady, was Atkinsons first thought as he rang the bell and dragged his shoes up and down the back of his trouser legs.

To Atkinson's surprise the door was opened by a slim attractive woman, he guessed in her late fifties, with no cats in sight. Susan Jeffries was in fact 55, she had short brown hair and a welcoming smile.

'Come in, you must be Atkinson and Bassey.'

They, both wiped their feet on the mat and entered the large square hallway. Atkinson was immediately taken with the neatness of what he could see. Maybe the outside belied the inside. They followed Jeffries into a large well-appointed sitting room.

'Coffee?' she asked gesturing towards a pot and cups on the table in front of one of the 3 sofas in the room. 'Help yourselves. I don't drink it myself.'

Atkinson and Bassey sat on the sofa and poured themselves coffee. Atkinson added milk and his usual 3 sugars. Once they were settled Atkinson began the conversation. 'Susan, can I call you Susan?' Jeffries nodded. 'Can you tell us what you remember about your interview with Ben Smart.'

'Well, luckily I've managed to find some of my paper work from the case. It was in June 1997 that Smart came to our attention. He was working at Clarence House in Formby, a school run by the Catholic Social Services. It looked after kids with emotional and behavioural problems from all over the north. A lot of them were completely out of control, especially the ones that boarded. We had umpteen call outs a month from the school and local residents – violence, stealing, abuse. Well, you know what I'm saying.

'One of the pupils accused Smart of strangling him, with his tie, until he became unconscious. We thought it was the usual load of bollocks, the kids were always making accusations against the staff. I was a DS at the time and Bob Wainwright was my DC, and we got the job of going to interview the kid, Nathan White his name was. Well, this kid was adamant that Smart had set upon him in a science lesson, grabbing his tie and pulling it tight causing him to pass out. This seemed to be a little more than the usual he hit me, or he touched my leg accusation, if you know what I mean?'

Atkinson nodded his understanding.

'We interviewed White in the Head's study, in the presence of the Head. White told us that he'd been chatting with the kid sitting next to him as Smart was explaining something about the lesson. He said that Smart started screaming at him, rushed over, grabbed his tie and began pulling it tighter and tighter round his neck. He said that his vision began to swim and he lost consciousness. We asked if there had been any witnesses. We knew there should be in a class of kids. White gave us four names and we asked the Head if we could speak to them. They were brought to us one at a time and all gave similar versions of events. We couldn't speak to Smart at this stage as the Head had suspended him, so we made arrangements to interview him at the station in Southport.'

Bassey had been quietly drinking her coffee while Jeffries had been talking. 'Did the Head tell you what had happened when he suspended Ben Smart?' Jeffries shook her head slowly as Bassey continued. 'It seems that he gave Smart the option to resign and be given a good reference, or be suspended and have police involvement. Doesn't sound like a Head who was over worried about the welfare of a child. But it does sound like one who's worried about the reputation of his school.'

'That never came out to us, and Smart never mentioned it when we questioned him.'

'What happened at the interview?' Atkinson asked.

'Smart arrived with his solicitor and we took them down to the Interview Suite.'

'Hold on a minute,' interrupted Bassey. 'Smart told us that he was arrested as soon as he came into the building, and the custody sergeant removed his belt and shoe laces. This shocked his solicitor so much that he actually asked Smart if he'd done it.'

'Yes, that is what happened. But you must understand that with four witnesses we thought it was nailed on. Maybe in hindsight, we should have arrested him after the interview,' she shrugged. 'But we didn't want him hanging himself in one of the cells with his belt or shoelaces.'

'Surely, there was plenty of time for all that after the interview. At that moment in time, he was either sitting in the waiting room of the interview suite, with his solicitor, or in an interview room with you and Wainwright. How was he going to hang himself in those circumstances?' Atkinson demanded angrily.

'Look, you don't know what it was like then in Southport nick. We'd had two prisoners attempt to hang themselves in the Custody Suite in the space of a month. We couldn't afford another one having a go. We thought he'd done it. So, who could blame us for using a belt and braces approach?'

'OK, what's done is done. What happened in the interview?' Bassey interjected before there was any real bad feeling between Atkinson and Jeffries.

'We'd been questioning Smart for about five minutes or so when his solicitor called a halt and asked to speak to Smart. So, Bob showed them to another room, and about ten minutes later they returned. The solicitor said he thought that we were bullying his client and he had advised him to answer "no comment" to the rest of our questions. The solicitor also said that Smart had some things that he'd like to say when we'd finished with our questions. Well, I'm sure you know how frustrating it is to deal with a no commenter.'

'We do,' Atkinson agreed nodding his head and smiling, trying to repair bridges.

'So, it was at the end of the interview that Smart put forward his points,' Bassey said, looking at her notebook. 'Can we just go through those one at a time? Smart said the four *witnesses were not in the same class as Nathan White and could therefore not have witnessed anything. Did you not think about that?'*

'We naturally assumed that to have witnessed the assault that they would all be in the same class,' shrugged Jeffries.

'Smart pointed out that White and all his witnesses said that when he recovered consciousness he immediately ran from the room. Smart then queried whether a "strangulation victim" could physically do that. He said he'd checked with a medic who said it was very unlikely. Did you check that out?'

'No, no we didn't,' a shake of the head.

'Any reason why not?'

'We assumed that that was what had happened,' said Jeffries quietly, looking a little embarrassed.

'Smart also asked you if you'd spoken to the Head of Care, who White is supposed to have gone to when he ran from the room. You said that you hadn't. Is there a reason for that?'

Jeffries thought for a moment, 'He wasn't available when we went to see him, and he sort of got……. forgotten about.'

'Forgotten, possibly because you thought you had Smart bang to rights?' Jeffries didn't reply. 'This brings us on to Smart's ace in the hole, his teaching assistant. Did you honestly not know anything about her? Did the Head not say anything?'

'We knew nothing about any teaching assistant until Smart mentioned her. The Head never said anything about her, or White, or any of his witnesses. We just didn't know she existed.'

'What did she say when you spoke to her?' Atkinson asked.

Jeffries looked even more embarrassed, 'We didn't speak to her. We thought our case was blown, so we just left it there.'

'Left it there, but it wasn't dismissed was it? It was filed as unproven. So, did you still think that Smart had done it?' asked Bassey.

'There's no smoke without fire. We were certain that he'd done something, and we hoped he'd get cocky and slip up.' Jeffries suddenly became defensive, 'Other things did go on at that school. We nicked three or four Residential Social Workers for abusing kids in their care.'

'Yes, yes you did. But those convictions were eventually overturned,' Atkinson replied. 'OK thanks for your help Susan,' standing up abruptly and heading towards the door, followed by Bassey.

'I know it doesn't look like the finest police work in the world, but we were trying to do the best we could at the time,' Jeffries said quietly to herself as she shut the front door after her visitors.

'Assumptions, forgotten witnesses, how the fuck did she ever make DCI?' questioned Bassey as they pulled off the drive and onto the road.

'You know how it is Shirl, sometimes they promote people to their level of incompetence, just to get them out of the way. I don't think it's worth finding Bob Wainwright now though, after what we've just learned.'

'Agreed. And I think we can probably remove Ben Smart from our list of suspects.'

Atkinson nodded his agreement and steered the car back towards the tunnel.

XIX

They were in luck; the Yamaha was parked outside the butchers. Bassey led the way into the shop, said hello to Fred Lowe and asked if Artie was available.

'He's just in the back – Artie! Those two police officers are here to see you!'

Thirty seconds later, Artie Miller appeared at the doorway from the backroom. He smiled shyly and looked a little confused. They had never seen him without his motorcycle helmet before. His head was completely shaved, in stark contrast to his face with its neatly trimmed hipster beard. Ginger. Atkinson was surprised he hadn't spotted that last time.

'DS Bassey and DI Atkinson,' Bassey reminded him.

'Can we borrow him for half an hour Fred?' Atkinson asked.

'Yeah, no problems, just don't arrest him today,' laughed the butcher. 'We often get busy later on.'

On the corner of Stuart Road and Bedford Road was the Stuart pub, it was here that Atkinson led Bassey and Miller. Atkinson hadn't been inside for years, but what he remembered of the place was not especially good. His memory did not disappoint him. Inside was dingy and the carpet gripped his feet with a suction that he'd only seen with infants and bottles. Looking around, it was obviously a pub dying slowly. They had no problems finding an empty table and Atkinson went to the bar. He returned after a few minutes with a pint of Guinness and two orange juices.

'You two are driving,' he explained with a smile as he saw the look on Bassey's face. 'I'm not. And you have to set a good example to young Artie here. We don't want him falling off his bike on the way home.'

'It's OK Mr Atkinson, I don't drink when I've got the bike,' said Artie as he moved the beermats around the table until he was satisfied with a neat regular arrangement.

'Sensible lad,' continued Atkinson as he pulled a beermat closer to rest his pint on. 'Now, Artie, we want to talk to you about the blue exercise book that Ben Smart had.'

'The one with the info on the missing girl, Ruth Anderson?' answered Artie as he rearranged the beermats again to take into account the new position of Atkinson's.

'Yes, that's the one. Now Fred tells us that you and Ben used to look at it together, trying to find out what had happened to Ruth,' Artie nodded slowly. 'Now what exactly did you talk about at these sessions?'

'Well, Ben always thought that Ruth had been murdered, that she wasn't just missing. The book contained all his notes about what he called "the case". Every possible person who was involved, no matter how slightly, was in that book.'

'Yes, we know,' said Bassey.

'Oh, you've seen it then?'

'Yes, we've seen it,' continued Atkinson, 'and what we'd like to know is, did Ben make a discovery? Did he come up with a possible answer to the puzzle? And do you know what it was?'

'No, he didn't tell me about any new information. But I haven't seen it for a couple of months now. We just kept going over and over the same stuff. How did you get hold of it? The book I mean, was it in his flat?'

'No, he'd given it to someone for safe keeping,' answered Atkinson.

Artie's eyes narrowed and he looked as if he'd made a decision of some sort. 'So, do you think he'd found something new?'

'Can't be sure, but yes, I think he did. Well, we both think that he did,' Atkinson looked at Bassey, who nodded. 'We also think that Ben was murdered by someone, possibly named in the book, who realised that whatever the new information was, it pointed towards them.'

'Well, he never mentioned it to me,' said Artie as he quickly downed his orange juice. 'I'd better get back to the shop, Fred's right, it does get busy. That's if you've finished with me?'

'We've finished Artie. You go back and thanks for your help.'

As Artie stood to leave, Bassey asked 'Oh, Artie how was your holiday? Ireland wasn't it, with your sister?'

'Yeah, it was great, thanks.'

'Do anything interesting?'

'Just the usual, she made the messes and I tidied them away,' he said cryptically.

The two officers watched as Miller left the pub. Atkinson started stroking his chin in thought, then shook his head as if clearing it of what he'd been thinking about. 'Strange way to describe a holiday,' he said, more to himself than Bassey. 'C'mon let's go back to the station.'

XX

'We need to go somewhere quiet and think about what we know,' said Atkinson as they exited from the tunnel 'and I know the perfect place.' He pointed the car north and headed towards Bootle and Crosby. He turned left at the traffic lights at the top of Crosby village and negotiated the two mini roundabouts. At the next roundabout he took the second exit onto Cooks Road and then turned left into Victoria Road.

'The Crow's Nest?'

'Too right,' Atkinson replied. 'It's a lovely little pub, sells good beer and should be quiet at this time of day.'

Atkinson parked the car on the small carpark and they entered the pub by the side door. While Atkinson got the drinks Bassey went to powder her nose. The bar maid, Brenda, told him to sit down and she would bring them over. One of the great things about the Crow's was that you could still get table service, when it wasn't too busy. Bassey returned from the toilet and looked around the room searching for Atkinson. She found him in a corner half hidden by the coat rack, went over and sat down. Atkinson was having a large gulp of his pint of Guinness, Bassey looked at the drink waiting for her on the table.

'Red wine? Don't I get a pint?'

'Sorry, do you want something else? I just thought that you looked like a red wine sort of girl.'

'A red wine sort of girl,' Bassey repeated, emphasising every word.

'I'm sorry, I'll get you something else,' stammered Atkinson, standing up to go to the bar.

'No, it's OK,' Bassey said. 'I quite like red wine, but I'd rather have a Guinness. Just ask next time OK?'

Atkinson nodded and sat back down. They both sat in silence for a short while, enjoying their drinks and the peacefulness of the pub.

'Well, we'd better get started,' Bassey began 'what do we know?'

Atkinson expertly split a beer mat to make a list of what they knew. 'We know that Ruth Anderson worked at St Michael's school. She was Ben Smart's teaching assistant. She was reported missing on the 10th September and no-one has really seen her since the end of the summer term. We know that she's got a daughter, Alice, who's cared for by her grandparents in Birmingham. I need another pint; would you like another?'

'Please, I'll have a Guinness,' Bassey replied with a smile.

Atkinson ordered the fresh drinks, and Brenda again said that she'd bring them over.

'OK, what don't we know?' Bassey asked on Atkinson's return.

'We don't know who Alice's father is. We don't know whether Ruth is dead or alive. We don't know of anyone with a motive to kill her. That's if she is dead. We don't know who she went to meet when she left the end of term party. If she left to meet anyone. We've got the knife with the blood on it from the flat, but we don't know who's blood it is. We haven't got means, motive or opportunity. We're stumbling around in the dark looking for something, anything. But we don't know what that something is.'

'Do we need to know who Alice's father is?'

'I'm not sure, but it's part of the puzzle and it would mean we'd at least have one concrete fact. Has the father killed Ruth because she took the baby away from him? Or has he reappeared in her life and they've run away together?'

'I don't see the running away together bit. No-one knows that Ruth has a daughter, well up here in Liverpool anyway, so why would there be a need to run away with the father? Ruth could have just introduced him as her new boyfriend.'

'Is he the one she left the party to meet? We seem to be running around in circles. Let's have another drink. And before you start, we can leave the car here and walk. You're not too far away and I'm not much farther.'

Bassey nodded her silent agreement. And that was it, one drink led to another and they staggered out of the pub just before it closed. As they hung onto each other for support they agreed that they had got no farther with the case, but that they had both needed the opportunity to relax and let their hair down.

Atkinson walked Bassey to her door, wished her a good night, turned and staggered off back up towards the main road. Bassey watched him until he went out of sight, smiled to herself and turned to begin the struggle to get the key in the lock.

XXI

Back at Copy Lane Atkinson rubbed his shoes up and down the back legs of his trousers as he stood outside DCI Mitchell's office, waiting for the traffic light to switch from amber to green. He was going to inform his boss about how the case was progressing. The light turned green and he pushed open the door. Atkinson's first surprise was that Mitchell was not alone. Sitting rather untidily on a chair in the corner was Superintendent Tom 'The Todger' Rogers. The surprise must have shown on Atkinson's face.

'Don't worry Martin, it's not a court of enquiry into the Ben Smart Case. The Super's got something he wants to ask you, off the record.' Surprise number two, the Super never did anything off the record.

Rogers looked at Atkinson for a short while, coughed to clear his throat and then began.

'DCI Mitchell has been keeping me up to date with your investigation Inspector. And I'm sure you'll agree that not a lot of progress has really been made in finding out what has happened to Mr Smart. I think I have to agree with you that his disappearance is linked to that of Miss Anderson. I also agree with you that both these people have probably been murdered. But, as I understand it, there is no suspect, no bodies and no motive?'

Atkinson nodded. This is it – case closed.

'Now to my unusual request,' continued Rogers clearing his throat again, 'I want you to pursue this case, vigorously, we need to know what happened to these two people,' Atkinson looked a little shocked. 'I assume that you thought I was going to close the case?' Atkinson nodded. 'Well in normal circumstances I probably would, as it does seem to be going around in circles a little. But I have to confess to a personal interest.'

*

Atkinson groaned again as he took another loud slurp from his coffee. He looked at Bassey, sitting across from him. How could she look so bright and up for the day after last night? How much had they had to drink? He couldn't remember a lot of what had happened, especially after the pub. He didn't think he'd made a fool of himself, well not too much of one anyway. He remembered walking Bassey back to her house, and then waking up on the sofa in his flat. Fully clothed with a mouth like a gorilla's armpit. What happened in between? Had she invited him in for "coffee". How had he responded to that?

He stole another glance at her over the top of his cup. She was just sitting there. Eating some toast, drinking coffee and looking at her phone. Not a care in the world. She was very attractive. You definitely didn't need beer goggles to see that. But what had happened? How should he proceed?

Bassey caught Atkinson looking at her and decided to ignore him. Let him suffer. He obviously had very little recollection of last night. He looked very hungover, and also confused. She also had a hangover, but was hiding it better. Looking at him she could tell what was going through his mind. As if! He wasn't too bad looking, but definitely not her type. Plus, you don't get involved with work colleagues, causes far too many headaches and problems. How long she was going to leave him in this state she had no idea. But it would be fun while it lasted.

XXII

'You could have knocked me over with a feather, Shirl,' concluded Atkinson.

'OK,' mused Bassey. 'Run it by me again, only less garbled this time.'

'Well, when I went in, The Todger was sitting there in the corner. He said that in normal circumstances he'd be asking us to wind the case up, as we were making little progress. But he said he had an interest in the case, a personal interest mark you, and wanted it brought to a successful conclusion.'

'Go on.'

'He said that many years ago, when he was a young copper in the West Mids. force, he met a girl called Mary Vickers. She was a young teacher at a Birmingham Grammar school. It seems he courted her diligently, my words not his, for a year or so. Then one day she told him that it was all over, she'd met someone else. Not only had she met someone else, but she was becoming a Jehovah's Witness as well. It seems that Mary Vickers is none other than Mary Anderson. Ruth Anderson's mother and Alice's grandmother.'

'So, she split up with The Todger to take up with Mr Anderson! And the Todger wants us to find out what happened to Ben Smart and therefore by extension what happened to Ruth Anderson?'

'That's about it,' agreed Atkinson.

'So, do you think The Todger is Ruth's father? I know the way your mind works.'

'It's a possibility I suppose,' Atkinson agreed. 'He didn't give me any specific dates, but they won't be difficult to dig up. Not for someone as accomplished at digging around as you.' Atkinson quickly ducked to avoid the block of post-it notes that Bassey threw at his head. 'C'mon, you're much better at it than I am.'

'OK, I'll do it. But it'll cost you a drink tonight.'

'I've a dental appointment later this afternoon, so I'll see you in the Crow's about seven?'

'Sounds good to me. I'll bring whatever I've been able to dig up.'

*

'OK, where do we go from here?' asked Bassey.

'I've literally no idea. We've not got a lot to work on. No motive, no opportunity and no means.'

'What about the blood on the knife?'

'We don't know who's it is. It might be Ruth's, it might not. It could be the blood of someone who came over and helped chop a few carrots for all we know.'

'It might be Ben Smart's,' Bassey mused.

'It may well be. But we've ruled Ben out, and we can't ask him for a few drops to see if it matches. Not without probable cause.'

'It's all dead ends. It doesn't matter how many times we go over it - all we've really got is a missing person. It doesn't matter whether we think Ruth's dead or not, there's no evidence,' Bassey paused before continuing. 'There's a couple of things though. Why was the flat so tidy? Everywhere was clean, scrubbed clean. Why did she leave all her clothes? There were some really expensive ones there, cost more than I can afford. Where was her phone? I don't remember seeing one anywhere, do you? Plus, the smell of bleach in the hallway. Had there been a big industrialised size clean up and the bleach was the lingering smell?'

Atkinson sat quietly for a few seconds before he answered Bassey. 'OK, what do you think of this? A person or persons unknown gain access to the flat. There's no damage to the door, so, Ruth must have let them in.'

'Or they had a key.'

'Or, they had a key. Please don't interrupt again Shirl, I'm going to lose my train of thought,' she nodded as Atkinson began again. 'A person or persons unknown gain access to the flat. There's no damage to the door so, Ruth let them in. So, she probably knows them, let's say it's just one person. Some sort of argument ensues and the visitor grabs a knife from the knife block and stabs Ruth to death. Our killer decides to clean up the mess to make it look like Ruth has just done a moonlight flit. That would account for the cleanliness of the place and the smell of bleach. The blood on the knife is some of Ruth's that he missed.'

'Or he nicked himself while cleaning the knife and didn't quite remove all of the blood?'

'Possible. I don't think we'd have found the blood on the knife if I hadn't knocked the block over.'

'Forget about the blood for now. Your theory fits with what we know and what we suspect. But who was the visitor? It had to be someone she knew. Because if you think about it, Ruth had to let them through two locked doors – the one on the street and the flat door itself,' Bassey paused. 'Or, she was bundled into the building by someone off the street as she was entering or exiting the street level door.'

'If that was the case, why bother with the tidy up? You've just pushed someone through a door and upstairs into her flat, where you violently murder her. The last thing you do is tidy everything up. You get out quickly. You don't know her routines, or whether she was expecting a friend. And surely someone would have seen her being pushed through the door. Someone in the café?'

'OK, it's somebody she knows,' agreed Bassey. *'But in your scenario, why leave the clothes and what happened to the body?'*

XXIII

It was almost 8 o'clock when Bassey pushed her way into a busy Crow's Nest. She looked around the room and spotted Atkinson sitting at the corner table under the golf trophies, to the left of the door leading to the toilets. When he looked up from his phone, she signalled to him, he nodded and she turned to the bar and ordered two pints of Guinness when her turn came.

'I'll bring them over,' said Mike, the barman.

As she made her way to the table, she noticed two older men with grey hair sitting in the mirror seat to Atkinson, on the right of the toilet doorway. They looked at her, looked towards Atkinson and sighed audibly. Sitting in your seats are we boys? Tough!

Atkinson waited for Mike to bring the beer and for Bassey take a gulp before he tried to say anything. 'Where've you been? What kept you?' a note of irritation in his voice.

'I've been digging up information about The Todger, like you asked me to. It took me longer than I thought it would.'

'OK. Sorry. But, what did you get? Anything?'

'Well, from 1983 to 1988 he was a police constable with the West Midlands police force,' she held up her hand as he started to interrupt. 'He made sergeant in '88 and inspector in '94, and was made chief inspector in 2002. He moved to Merseyside and was assigned his present lofty state in 2014.'

'So, he didn't join us until well after the Ruth Anderson case?'

'Looks that way, or we would have had pressure from him then.'

The pair sat quietly for a while drinking their beer.

'So, The Todger was in Birmingham around the right time to be Ruth's father,' Bassey said breaking the silence.

'He was also there at the right time to be Alice's father.' added Atkinson.

'Christ!' muttered Bassey.

Atkinson's phone rang, he pulled it from his pocket and began to walk towards the door, calling over his shoulder. 'Reception's crap in here. I'll go out to the car park.'

Bassey settled down with her drink and thought about what they'd just been saying. The Todger was in the right place at the right times to be either Ruth or Alice's father. She couldn't see it herself, but it was perhaps something they should look at. She was pulled from her reverie by Atkinson shouting to her across the room that they had to go. As she was leaving the pub, she looked behind her and saw two happy looking grey-haired men sliding into the seats that she and Atkinson had vacated.

Bassey looked expectantly at Atkinson as she climbed into his car.

'I've just had a phone call from Jan Carter. She's just got home and found her partner, Josie, dead in the kitchen. And there's lots of blood. I told her to phone 999 and tell them what's happened. We should be there before the locals if we hurry.' He put the car into gear and headed towards the southside of Liverpool and Kenmere Road.

*

Bassey sat at a desk in the CID suite, feeling a little out of place. She may have been in plain clothes but she didn't fit in, she wasn't part of CID. She looked over at the door that Atkinson had walked through 10 minutes before. It led to the office of Detective Inspector Owen Reynolds, and Atkinson was in there being quizzed about their progress. As she was looking at it the door opened and Atkinson stuck his head out

'Shirl, the boss wants a word.'

Bassey stood up, took a deep breath and paused on the threshold of the open door. This, she realised, was an important moment in her career. If she made a dick of herself now, she could kiss goodbye to ever being in CID. 'I can do this,' she muttered to herself and walked, she hoped, with confidence into the office.

DI Reynolds was sitting behind a large untidy desk. He was about 35 years old, with a mop of ginger hair and a short neatly trimmed beard. Directly in front of the desk were 2 hardback chairs, Atkinson occupied one.

'Sit down Bassey,' Reynolds said, pointing towards the empty chair. 'Now I've listened to what Martin has had to say, and I wondered what your thoughts were?'

Martin? She only ever thought of him as Big Ron, Atkinson or possibly wanker. She'd almost forgotten his name was Martin. Before she could say anything, Reynolds continued to speak.

'He says that he thinks it's not just a missing person case, it's a murder case. Do you agree?'

'Yes sir, I do, for a couple of reasons,' Bassey began quietly. 'The flat is just too clean and tidy. I'm a woman who lives alone, and I consider myself reasonably tidy. But that flat? It's as if an obsessive-compulsive lives there, and we've had nothing from anyone to say that Ruth Anderson is that sort of person,' Reynolds nodded encouragingly, and Bassey continued

with more confidence. 'There doesn't appear to be any of Ruth's clothes missing. She has some very expensive stuff and if it were mine, and I was going to disappear, I'd be taking it with me. Both Ron, I mean DC Atkinson, and myself wondered if she had a sugar daddy. She wouldn't be earning a great deal as a teaching assistant, not enough to afford some of the things in her wardrobe any way. Once she'd paid rent, bills etc there wouldn't be a lot left over. Her parents have had no contact with her, so they aren't sending her any money. So, sugar daddy seems the obvious answer. Who is he? We thought probably the father of her child,' both Reynolds and Atkinson nodded their agreement, giving Bassey even more confidence. She felt a shiver of excitement go through her body. She was actually a valued member of an investigation. Not just a body in a blue uniform whose opinion was never asked for. She took a heavily disguised deep breath and continued. 'The knife we found with the blood on it is a puzzler though sir. If Ruth was murdered in her flat, and the killer cleaned everything up, how did he miss the blood on the knife? If the blood's not Ruth's, we can guess that it's the killers. But why did he not clean it? Is he one of those people who thinks that they are so safe from being discovered that they can afford to leave a clue to their identity just to wind us up?

'At the moment we have no motive, it could possibly be the father of the child. Upset with Ruth for some reason - lack of access or recognition maybe? It could be some random, but I doubt it, I think Ruth knew her killer. Why would a random clean everything up as thoroughly? Finally, we don't have a body, which leads me to believe the killer took it with him. He was obviously trying to make it look like Ruth had done a midnight flit, so he couldn't leave the body behind. How he moved it and where he took it, we don't know. Did he have an accomplice?' Bassey paused and looked at Reynolds. 'And that's about it sir.'

'Excellent summing up of the available evidence, Bassey. So, we have no body, no motive and no suspects but, we do have a possible murder weapon,' Reynolds sat quietly scratching his beard, looking at Atkinson and Bassey in turn. 'OK, what I'm going to do is this. I want you two, to continue with this investigation. I agree with you that Ruth's probably been murdered. Proving it looks like it's going to be difficult though. Find me some suspects, just one would do if they have a good motive. It'd help if they also had the opportunity. Finding the body would also be a bonus. I think we're in agreement about the method and the weapon, so find out who that blood belongs to. Is it some smart arse, or is it just a visitor to the flat who had nothing to do with the murder? Now get out both of you and keep me informed!'

Atkinson and Bassey quickly exited the office before Reynolds could change his mind.

'How much longer do you think he'll give us to come up with something?' Bassey asked.

'I'd say a week, two at the max. So, we'd better pull our fingers out Shirl. I really want to crack this.'

'So do I Ron, so do I. Let's have that blood on the knife run through the system again, see if it belongs to anyone on there. We only had it matched for Ruth's blood group, so it may belong to someone in the data base somewhere.'

'I don't really think anything will come back though, do you?'

'Don't be so negative. We can have it DNA tested as well. We may get a hit.'

'OK, let's make some phone calls and get things rolling.'

This was the best that they had both felt about the case for a while. Having the backing of DI Reynolds gave them both a great confidence boost. Bassey just hoped that her performance in Reynolds' office been good enough to help in her efforts to get into CID.

XXIV

It took just 30 hair raising minutes to get to Kenmere Road. Unfortunately, the locals were quicker off the mark than Atkinson had anticipated. A young constable stopped them at the cordon that had been set up on the pavement outside number 70.

'DS Bassey and DI Atkinson,' Bassey said as she flashed her warrant card.

'You'd better get suited and booted before you go in there,' the young bobby said with a grim smile. 'It's a bloody mess. And I mean bloody in all senses of the word.'

Bassey and Atkinson quickly dressed themselves in white plastic Tyvek suits, nitryl gloves and blue plastic overshoes. They ducked under the cordon and climbed the three steps to the front door. Inside Atkinson saw someone he knew standing in the hallway.

'Hello Russ, what's going on then?'

DI Russ Muir turned to look at Atkinson with an ashen face. 'Fucking hell Martin, what are you doing here?'

'Woman who lives here is helping us with one of our cases.'

'Not the dead one I hope?'

'No, her partner, Jan Carter.'

'She's outside in the squad car. She found the body; in a terrible state she is. Hardly surprising really,' Muir started shaking his head. 'Now we've all seen some terrible things, but this? A first as far as I'm concerned'

'Mind if we have a look?' Atkinson asked.

'Be my guest, but I'm taking no responsibility if you're traumatised for the rest of your lives, and please don't contaminate the crime scene by throwing up. She's in the kitchen.'

Atkinson and Bassey squeezed past Muir in the narrow hallway and headed towards the kitchen. Atkinson put his hand on the handle of the closed door and turned to look at Bassey, who was standing behind him. She took a deep breath and nodded. Atkinson slowly opened the door, but made no effort to go into the room. The colour drained from his face as he quickly shut the door and turned to Bassey.

'You can stay out here if you want to.'

She had caught just a glimpse of the kitchen over Atkinson's shoulder. A glimpse had been enough. She could feel the colour draining from her own face. The two police officers were both as white as proverbial sheets. 'No, it's OK. Let's go in and have a proper look, it's what we came for,' she whispered.

*

'OK, that'd be great. Can you get the results to us a quickly as possible? Thanks, greatly appreciated.' Bassey put the phone down and looked across at Atkinson. 'They'll have the blood results with us as soon as possible. No later than tomorrow afternoon.'

'Good, now let's have another think about at what we've got. We all think that Ruth's been murdered, and that it was by someone she knew. So far, we've concentrated on Ben Smart, but it doesn't look like it was him. Let's spread our net a little wider. Let's start by talking to any of the staff at school who knew her, or worked with her.'

Bassey nodded her head in agreement. 'How do you want to do it?'

'Let's go to the school and start talking to everybody. Anyone who had even the slightest contact with Ruth. We'll ask the head for a room and pull 'em in one by one.'

'He's not going to like that,' and how right was Bassey?

XXV

The kitchen looked as though someone had raided a blood bank and sprayed the proceeds everywhere. There didn't seem to be a single surface that didn't have blood on it - congealed blood now. There was blood up the walls, on the counter tops and the floor as well as the sink and draining board. It also looked as if blood had dripped from the light fittings. But it wasn't the blood that caused the two police officers to gag. There, on the kitchen island, was Josie's body, hands tied to the tap on the sink and feet tied to the handles of cupboard doors. She had been split open from throat to crutch and all her internal organs were neatly stacked around her. It was no longer a kitchen it was a slaughter house. Who could have done something like this? And why?

Atkinson and Bassey couldn't take their eyes off the carnage in front of them as they edged backwards through the kitchen door. Once back into the hallway, Atkinson gently closed the door and they looked at each other dumbfounded. What the fuck had happened in there?

'It looks like scene from a Jack the Ripper movie,' Atkinson said once he was able to speak.

'One difference though,' whispered Bassey. 'This is for real. Some mad bastard has done that. Actually, stood there and removed what looks like every organ in her body cavity. I hope to God that she was dead when he started. Because if she wasn't …. I just can't imagine it.' She turned from Atkinson and rubbed at her eyes to remove the tears. Atkinson took the opportunity to do the same while her back was turned.

The pair eased their way past Muir again, with all three officers giving each other little nods of not understanding.

'We're going to go and have a word with Jan Carter, if that's OK with you Russ?'

'Be my guest, Martin lad. I doubt if she'll have much to say, she's in a hell of a state, almost catatonic when I saw her ten minutes ago. From what we can gather, Miss Carter was late home from school because of a parents evening. She came into a quiet and dark house and went into the kitchen, turned the light on and found poor Miss Rutherford, just as you've just seen her.' Rutherford. So that was Josie's surname. Neither of them had known, or in all honesty had cared before now. 'We thought that she'd phoned us immediately, but she obviously found time to phone you as well.'

'She…. they had my card. I told her to phone if she thought of anything or if anything happened. But I didn't expect this.'

'Do you think this has anything to do with your case?' Muir asked.

'I'm not sure, it could just be a coincidence. And I'm not a big one for coincidences. But I'm struggling to see a link anywhere. Our killer is far tidier than this. In fact, we can't really say with 100% certainty that we've actually got a killer. We've got two missing people, eight years apart with scrupulously clean crime scenes. The only thing we really have is smears of the same blood group on kitchen knives, and they'd been put back in the knife block!'

'Sounds complicated, I'm glad it's yours and not mine. At least with this one we know we've got a killer. We'll let you know whatever we find, just in case it is the same killer.'

'Thanks Russ,' Atkinson said as he nodded to Bassey and the pair went outside to Jan Carter in the waiting squad car.

On the pavement away from Muir, Bassey turned to Atkinson and asked 'Do you think our man did it?'

'I'm not sure Shirl. Jan Carter's got a connection with our case and Josie Rutherford has a connection with Jan. So, it could be. Let's keep an open mind and not jump to any conclusions.'

After removing their protective clothing, they walked over to the squad car and asked the female constable who was sitting with Jan to give them five minutes. Once the constable had got out of the car, Bassey sat next to Jan in the back and Atkinson sat in the front passenger seat. He turned and examined Jan quietly. Her blonde hair was a mess, tears had smeared her make up all over her face. But she wasn't crying now. Jan Carter sat stock still in the back of the squad car, just staring forwards into the distance, almost catatonic as Muir had said. It took a while before she finally focused on Atkinson.

*

'You want to do what?' asked the Head. 'Am I getting this right? You want me to give you a room where you can interview all of my staff?' Atkinson nodded. 'Do you know how much disruption that would cause to the school day? I'm sorry, but it's not going to happen.'

'Well headmaster, we could do this in a more formal way, if you'd like,' Atkinson said. 'We could arrange to interview your staff over at Copy Lane. We could give each one an allotted time, starting at 9 and going through to 4.30.'

'Doing it that way though,' interjected Bassey. 'May take two or three days - possibly four.'

Clarke looked at the two police officers and could tell by the looks on their faces that this was not just an idle threat. 'Alright, alright. You can use my office. But please try to get it all done today.'

'We'll try Headmaster. Now, do you think we could have a staff list please? We'll need teachers, teaching assistants as well as ancillary staff. Thanks,' smiled Atkinson.

With a look of exasperation, Clarke turned on his heel and headed for the door, where he stopped and turned to look at the two police officers. 'Please be as quick as possible,' he pleaded as he opened the door and stepped out into the corridor.

Two minutes later the Head's secretary delivered the staff list.

'Thank you miss...?' began Atkinson.

'No problem. And it's Mrs, Mrs Palmer.'

'Well I wonder Mrs Palmer, is it OK if we kicked off the proceedings with you? We have to start somewhere,' Atkinson shrugged apologetically, pointing to a chair.

'Not at all,' Mrs Palmer answered taking a seat.

Bassey found Mrs Palmers' name on the staff list and put a pencil line through it as Atkinson started the interview.

'How well do you know Ruth Anderson?'

'Not that well at all. My only real contact with her is at staff meetings. Oh, and the times that I've seen her come to see Mr Clarke.'

'To see the Head?'

'Yes, my office is across the corridor and I always leave my door open. I suppose it's my way of keeping an eye on who goes in and out of Mr Clarke's office. And Miss Anderson was quite a frequent visitor. But, that's not unusual for new members of staff who are still in their probationary period. Mr Clarke likes to make sure that they're settling in OK and that they're having no problems with the children. Things like that.'

'So, you have no contact with Ruth outside school?'

'No, none at all,' replied Mrs Palmer shaking her head. 'I'm afraid we move in different circles. The academic staff don't really mix with the clerical, either in school or out. It's a little bit us and them, with clear lines of demarcation.'

'OK, thanks for your time Mrs Palmer.'

'I hope we get something a little more enlightening than that,' Atkinson said after Mrs Palmer had left the room. 'We didn't exactly learn a lot there.'

'What about Ruth's visits to see the Head?'

'Normal procedure by the looks of it. If you're on probation you have regular meetings with the Head.'

'But, wouldn't you have these meetings with your line manager? The boss teaching assistant, or someone like that?'

'Look Shirl, we know what sort of head Clarke is. He likes to be in control, know everything. I can't see him waiting for a line manager to report. He'd want any information first hand, from the horse's mouth.'

'Yeah, I suppose your right. Who shall we see next?'

'Let's just start at the top of the list and work our way down. In that way we've less chance of missing anybody.'

By lunch time Atkinson and Bassey were nearly three quarters of the way down the staff list. All the interviews had been similar to that of Mrs Palmer. Clerical staff hardly new Ruth at all and academic staff only new her a little better. The reason given for this was that the Learning Support Centre had different break and lunch times to the rest of the school in an effort to keep the pupils in LSC segregated. It also seemed to work for the staff.

'Are we actually getting anywhere?' Bassey asked.

'No, but we'll see it through. You never know.'

XXVI

All three sat in silence for a short while.

'Find the bastard who did this inspector!' Jan Carter suddenly shouted. Her voice sounding all the louder in the confines of the car. She looked at Atkinson and then Bassey. 'Please,' she whispered. 'Please,' her shoulders began to shake and tears began to fall down her cheeks.

'Jan? I know it's a difficult time, but we need to ask you some questions,' Bassey said in a quiet voice. Carter nodded imperceptibly so Bassey continued. 'What time did you get home tonight?'

'About quarter past eight,' sniffed Carter wiping her eyes. 'I'd been at a parent - teacher evening at school.' Atkinson nodded. That was about the time that he'd received the phone call.

'Did you expect Josie to be in when you got home?' Bassey continued gently.

'Yes. But when I got here, the house was in darkness,' Carter murmured. 'I didn't think she was in. She usually has all the lights on when she's in. I'm forever telling her to turn lights off. I suppose I won't have to do that now though will I?' bursting once more into floods of tears.

'OK Jan,' Atkinson said in a quiet voice 'we've got no more questions for you at the moment. Inspector Muir will want you to make a statement, but I'm sure there'll be no rush for that. For what it's worth, we're both very sorry.'

Atkinson and Bassey climbed out of the car and beckoned to the female constable to get back in. They walked quietly back to Atkinson's car and leaned against it, keeping their own thoughts for a couple of minutes.

'I could use a drink!' Bassey said cutting through the silence.

'There's a pub just at the top of the road,' answered Atkinson and he started to walk.

Bassey had to break into the occasional trot to keep up. He pushed open the door to Kelly's Dispensary, looked around, pointed to an empty table and went to the bar for drinks. Bassey sat where she had been directed and was lost in her mainly unpleasant thoughts when Atkinson arrived with the drinks. He put two pints of Guinness and two large Irish whiskeys on the table. They raised the whiskey, clinked glasses and threw the warming liquid back in one go. Atkinson stood up and returned to the bar. He came back with two more large whiskeys. Again, they clinked glasses and threw them back. As he started to get up again,

Bassey put her hand out and pushed him back into his seat. She stood up and went to the bar, returning with four large whiskeys. There were another two rounds of clinking glasses and throwing back. This time neither of the pair attempted to get more. Their appetites were satiated and their feelings just about numbed enough for them to talk about what they'd seen.

'It's just beyond comprehension,' Bassey said. 'I mean, it's just …. barbaric! What sort of person could do that to another human being? It …it's disgusting! They've got to be caught. We've got to catch them and get them locked up! How can they sleep at night? What would their mother think?'

Atkinson let Bassey get it all out of her system before he spoke. 'Look Shirl, there are some sick bastards out there and I'm sorry you had to see that. But what we've got to do, me and you, is decide if this is anything to do with us.'

'Of course, it's got something to do with us! We're police officers, it's our job to get scum like that off the street!' Bassey whispered urgently.

'No, you got me wrong. What I meant was, is it anything to do with our case? And yes of course, it is our job to get shitheads like that locked up. But if it's not connected to our case it's got sod all to do with us. Russ Muir's a good copper, he'll catch the scrote who did it.'

'Yeah, I'm sorry,' Bassey apologised. 'But it's just got me so worked up.'

'I understand. Right, we going to talk about this now or wait 'til the morning?'

'I think the morning would be best. We'll be sober and hopefully more objective.'

'Agreed,' he looked at the two empty pint glasses on the table and then at Bassey. 'If we're going to get pissed, we might as well do it properly.'

Bassey stood up and wandered over to the bar for refills. 'We'll have to leave your car here, you know, and get a taxi,' she said when she got back to the table, no whiskey this time, just pints of Guinness.

'Suppose so,' Atkinson agreed. 'We'll have to get a taxi. Let's toss to see who pays.'

'No, it's OK, I'll pay. You'll only want to borrow the money off me any way.'

With their journey home settled the two detectives settled down to attempt to wipe from their minds what they had just seen. Both of them knew though, deep down, that the alcohol would not do it. It would dull the horror for a short while, but they would recall that kitchen island and its contents for the rest of their lives. It would always be there at the back of their minds. That's not to say that they didn't give it a good go. In fact, neither of them remembered that the bar staff had helped them into a taxi and that Bassey had just given her purse to the driver and told him to help himself to the fare. Luckily, the driver was a relatively honest man and only took £20 for his tip. It was his last job of the night and he was sure that that's how much his passengers would have given him, and there was still plenty of money left.

*

At 4.30, as the door closed for the – he didn't know how many times, Atkinson stretched and looked at Bassey.

'That was the last one?'

'The only ones we haven't spoken to are the Head and Ben Smart,' Bassey answered. 'We going to bother with them, or what?'

'No. I don't think we need to talk to them again at the moment,' Atkinson paused for a couple of seconds. 'Did we actually learn anything? From anyone?'

'Well, we know that no-one really knew Ruth very well. Everyone said she was pleasant enough and chatty when they met her around the building. But she spent most of her time in the Unit. Did you notice how they all called it the Unit?' Atkinson nodded his head and Bassey continued. 'Must be only Ben Smart who calls it the Learning Support Centre. Anyhow, no-one had anything to do with Ruth outside school. She attended all the get togethers, at the end of term and such like, but she never stayed too long. Just long enough so that people didn't think that she didn't want anything to do with them, I suppose.'

'I wonder where she went after those get togethers? Did she go straight back to the flat, or did she meet someone the other staff knew nothing about? Was she meeting her killer?' Atkinson mused.

The opening of the door interrupted their ruminations.

'I hope you found today beneficial for your enquiry,' the Head said as he entered the room. 'I personally, think that it has been an utter waste of time. Both yours, my staff's and mine,' Clarke looked at the two police officers and carried on. 'Did you find anything useful?'

'I'm afraid we're not allowed to discuss an ongoing investigation with members of the public, Headmaster,' Bassey answered.

'Huh! I'll take that as a no then. And when, do you think, I can have my office back?'

'Just as soon as we've got our things together, Mr Clarke. We'll be out of your hair in a couple of minutes,' Bassey said smiling. 'Thank you for your cooperation today.'

There was nothing spoken between Atkinson and Bassey, but they took as long as possible to get their few bits and pieces together.

'About time!' the Head said as they stepped out into the corridor. 'I hope that you won't be taking over my office and disrupting my school again after today?'

'We hope not,' Bassey replied with a smile. 'Anyone we want to talk to again we'll do it at the station.'

Once they were out of the school Bassey turned to Atkinson. 'Did you see the look on his face, when I said any further interviews would be at the station?'

'I did yes. There's something he's not telling us. I don't know what it is, but I intend to find out. Come on. Let's get back to the station and review the notes. Let's see if we did get anything today, or was it really a waste of time.'

XXVII

'Oi!' shouted DI Muir from an upstairs window, 'I suppose you've come back for that heap of junk you left here last night.'

Atkinson nodded his head, looking sheepish. Bassey just grinned like a Cheshire cat at his discomfort. They were standing outside number 70, where parked half on the pavement and half on the road, at an angle of more than 45 degrees was Atkinson's car. He still had the Land Rover, and it was blocking a lot of the pavement as well as quite a bit of the narrow street.

'I was going to get Traffic to come and impound it, I thought you'd forgotten all about it.'

'Can you not be so loud? I've got a banging headache,' Atkinson called back, regretting it immediately.

'Are you sure you're fit to drive? I can get one of my lads to chauffer you if you want?'

'Don't start. I've had that all the way here,' Atkinson cast a sideways look at Bassey, who continued to grin. 'It's not funny!' he hissed.

'Oh, but it is, it is.'

Atkinson jumped into the Land Rover and straightened it out so that it was no longer blocking either the pavement or the road. 'Come on,' he said to Bassey, 'let's go in and see what's happening.'

As the two detectives ducked under the tape barrier and climbed the steps to the front door They stopped on the top step, each taking a deep breath before entering the house. Inside everything had changed from the night before. The hallway was a blaze of arc lamps. Every nook and cranny lit up like Blackpool. A large yellow plastic curtain now hung in front of the kitchen door, both preventing any sight of the interior and providing a barrier to access. Only SOC would be allowed in there now. The pathologist would have long been by now and removed the body and its internal organs for examination. Atkinson knew from experience that nothing would have happened here last night until McKenzie, the pathologist, had declared the body dead. Not a difficult call to make.

'Up here!' shouted Muir. The detectives dragged their eyes and their thoughts away from the yellow curtain and climbed the stairs. They found Muir in the front bedroom, whose window he had shouted from. 'What do you think?' he continued.

Atkinson and Bassey looked carefully around the room, it was obviously the master bedroom. There was a king-size bed with its head board pushed up against the party wall.

There were bed side cabinets and what could best be described as a low chest or foot locker at the end of the bed. Closer inspection showed that the chest had six draws in three banks of two. Leading Bassey to think that it may have been on legs originally. The wall facing the bed was filled with fitted wardrobes and in the bay window a dressing table with a long bench. So that two people could apply make-up at the same time?

Every flat surface in the room was piled with what was obviously the contents of all the drawers and cupboards. Someone had searched the room methodically and with great care.

'Every room's the same,' Muir said. 'Not a drawer that's not been turned out and not a cupboard emptied. Our intruder was obviously looking for something. Did they find it though?'

'All this took a lot of time,' Bassey put in. 'They killed and eviscerated poor Josie, and then carefully searched the house. This must have taken them hours. Must have been sure that they wouldn't be disturbed. Do we know what time Josie got home last night?'

'According to Miss Carter, Josie was usually home by four,' Muir answered.

'And Jan Carter didn't get home until eight. So, to do all this they must have been waiting for her, either in the house or outside. If they was already in the house, Josie could have disturbed them. With both Josie and Jan being out at work they could have got in at any time. Were there any signs of forced entry?' Bassey asked.

'None that we've found.'

'So, they either had keys, was adept at gaining entry without leaving marks or Josie let them in,' picked up Atkinson.

'What's the lock on the front door like?' Bassey asked.

'Just a Yale I think.'

'They're not too difficult to get past,' Bassey mused. 'Does that trick with a credit card actually work? You know, the one they use on the telly all the time.'

'I've never tried it,' Atkinson answered. 'But I suppose it might.'

'It doesn't really matter how they got in though, does it? They got in and were methodically searching the house when Josie arrived home. She may have been earlier than expected. They heard her enter the house and go into the kitchen. Crept downstairs and did,' Bassey paused, shaking her head. 'What they did. Then they either left or finished their search.'

'Go on,' Muir encouraged.

'Now, cutting Josie up like that, obviously sent blood everywhere, look at the state of the kitchen. So, chummy would also be covered in blood. Therefore, if any of Josie's blood is found in any of the rooms, we can say that they were disturbed in their search and went back to it. Or Josie let them in, they killed her and then searched the house.'

'Very good,' complimented Muir. 'But it doesn't really matter if they were here already or she let them in. They were searching for something, and we need to know what.'

Atkinson and Bassey looked at each other and nodded their agreement.

'Where's Jan Carter?' Atkinson asked changing the subject. 'Is she coming to grips with all this?'

'She's doing as well as you would expect,' Muir answered. 'She's staying with friends in Formby. Still think this is involved with your case?' Atkinson shrugged. 'I'll text you the address if you want to talk to her.'

'That'd be great Russ. Thanks. We'll get from under your feet and let you get on.' As they headed for the stairs Muir caught hold of Atkinson's sleeve, causing him to turn.

'She's bright, that Sergeant of yours. Is she OK with all this?'

'Well, what do you think?'

'No, I suppose not,' Muir said shaking his head. Atkinson turned and went to catch up with Bassey, but Muir spoke again, stopping him. 'Something your Sergeant hasn't thought of though. She touched on it but didn't follow it through. It doesn't matter if our killer was disturbed or was let in; there was a hell of a lot of blood. They would be covered with it, but we've found none anywhere else in the house yet. How did they manage that? How did they get out without leaving a mess?'

'Did any of the neighbours see or hear anything?'

'Not the ones we've spoken to. Most of the properties round here are full of students. They would have had music blaring and been half pissed by four o'clock.'

'Cynical, Russ, cynical.'

'I'll see you back at Copy Lane,' Atkinson said to Bassey as he left the house and climbed into his Land Rover.

'OK,' Bassey replied as she opened the door to the pool car, they'd both arrived in.

*

Atkinson and Bassey were sitting in the canteen and reviewing their notes from the day's interviews.

'It doesn't get us any further,' Bassey said. 'We know a little more about Ruth, but none of it is relevant or pushes the case forward.'

'Complete waste of time,' agreed Atkinson. 'The only positive thing out of the whole day is that we ruffled Clarke's feathers. I'd really like to bring him in and lean on him 'til he tells us what he's not telling us. There's something, I don't know what, but, there's something.'

'Unfortunately, we can't pull him in without a good reason.'

'I know, I know, we'll just have to come up with one.'

XXVIII

After parking up the pool car, Bassey went into the station to look for Atkinson. She found him in the canteen, sitting hunched at a corner table with two steaming mugs of coffee in front of him.

'I thought I'd have to drink them both. What kept you?' he asked as she approached the table.

'Speed limits. I tend to stick to them; unlike some people I know.'

'Perk of the job Shirl, perk of the job.'

Bassey sat down and took a long drink from her coffee. Placing the cup back on the table, she looked at Atkinson. Despite the very obvious hangover his eyes still sparkled with what might be intelligence, but more probably mischief.

'That was some good theorising you did back there Shirl, really impressed Muir. But, as he said it doesn't matter how the killer got into the house, it's obvious that they were looking for something. If we can find what that something is, we 'll have a better idea where to look.'

'So, do you think Josie's murder has something to do with our case? And why kill Josie?'

'Collateral damage?' queried Atkinson. 'What if they were looking for Ben's book? We both thought that up in the bedroom. Was Josie just in the wrong place at the wrong time? It's all questions again Shirl. Would it be wrong of us to assume that it was the book they were looking for? Or is it just a coincidence?'

'We don't believe in coincidences though, do we Ron?'

Atkinson tapped his fingers on the table, and came to a decision. 'I'm going to phone Muir and ask him for the address in Formby where Jan Carter's staying. He said he'd text it but we can't wait for that. And then, we're going to go and see her, see if we can tie this in or not.'

They both got up from the table. Atkinson strode off as purposefully as he could, in his delicate state, towards his office to make the call. Bassey waited for him to disappear out of sight and went to the canteen counter.

'Can I have a packet of paracetamol please?' although she hadn't shown any outward signs, Bassey had a hangover of equal proportions to Atkinson's. She was buggered though if she was going to let him know. Grabbing a cup of water from the dispenser, she swallowed three of the capsules, shook her head, instantly regretted it and set off in pursuit of Atkinson.

*

In the end Atkinson and Bassey didn't have to find a reason to get Charles Clarke to the station to answer their questions. He came of his own accord. Bassey answered the phone on its third ring.

'Hello, Bassey speaking.'

'Oh, hi Shirley, it's Jim Brodie,' did everyone in the whole fucking station call her Shirley? She'd have to have words with Atkinson. 'There's someone down here at the front desk who wants to speak to you or Martin. Names Clarke, Charles Clarke.'

'Is there an interview room available? ..... number two is? OK, put him in there. I'll just find Ron and be right down,' making a point of using "Ron" in an effort to get her nick name for Atkinson around the station.

Bassey found Atkinson in DI Reynolds' office. 'Sorry to interrupt sir but can I drag Ron away?'

'Ron? Oh, you mean Martin. Of course, you can Shirley. A break on the case?'

'Hope so sir. Too early to say yet,' Reynolds as well! Fucking hell!

Outside in the corridor Atkinson looked at Bassey and said 'This had better be good Shirl! Dragging me out of the boss's office like that.'

'Guess who's just presented themselves at the front desk?'

'No idea. Bob Dylan? Bruce Springsteen?'

'Not even close, Charles Clarke!'

'Charles Clarke! Fucking hell! What does he want?'

'No idea, let's go and find out. I've had Jim Brodie put him in Interview Room 2. Maybe we'll find out that thing that he's not telling us. Maybe he's come to confess to it all.'

With grins like Cheshire cats the two officers headed for the Interview Suite, where in Room 2 Charles Clarke paced nervously up and down the room.

XXIX

Jan Carter was staying with friends in Friars Walk, on the Redgate estate in Formby. Atkinson and Bassey had been sitting in the car outside for twenty minutes. No one had answered when they knocked so it was a no-brainer to sit outside and wait.

Bassey knew the area and there were a few shops and a café at the other end of a walkway that went along the side of the house. On her walk to get coffee Bassey was able to take a look at the back of the house. From what she could see it looked like a normal family home with a well-tended garden.

They had just finished their coffees when a car pulled into the driveway. A woman in her early forties, with short copper coloured hair got out and opened the front door of the property. The two detectives waited for five minutes before knocking on the door. As they waited for the door to be answered Bassey searched in her bag for her warrant card and Atkinson rubbed his shoes on the backs of his trouser legs. Before the door opened Atkinson and Bassey heard a chain being put on. The woman with the copper hair looked out of the gap at the two detectives.

'Hello,' Bassey said holding up her warrant card while Atkinson busied himself with his shoes. 'I'm Detective Sergeant Bassey and this is Detective Inspector Atkinson, can we come in please?'

'Bassey and Atkinson,' said the woman taking the chain off the door and standing back. 'Jan said you'd probably turn up at some time. I'm Chris, Chris Williams, a friend of Jan and Josie's. We're in the kitchen, go through, would you like hot drink?'

The door opened up onto a hallway with an oak effect laminated floor. There were two doors to the left and the stairs to the right. At the end of the hallway was an open door, the kitchen, and there sitting at the table was Jan Carter, looking a little better than last night, but not much. The two detectives looked quizzically at each other and at Chris Williams.

'I told Jan not to answer the door to anyone while I was away. And also, not to curtain twitch to see who it was. I'm sorry, but I thought it was for the best.'

'Excellent advice,' offered Bassey, 'you can never be too careful.'

'So, tea or coffee?'

*

Atkinson and Bassey entered the interview room together. Clarke, stopped pacing and sat at the table. The two officers sat down opposite him and just looked at his face, waiting for him speak. It was nearly two minutes before Clarke broke the uncomfortable silence.

'I've not been entirely honest with you,' he began. Atkinson looked at Bassey, there was a gleam in his eye. A gleam that translated as "I told you so".

XXX

Only when everyone had a cup of coffee in front of them did anyone say anything.

'Do you have any ideas about who killed Josie?' Jan Carter asked in an almost whisper.

'No, I'm afraid we don't,' Atkinson answered, speaking nearly as quietly as Carter. 'DI Muir is running the case, unless we can find a link with the disappearance of Ruth Anderson and Ben Smart.'

'Do you think there is a link?' Carter asked without looking up from her cup on the table.

'That's why we've come to see you Jan. I know it must still be very raw and painful for you, but I'm afraid we have to ask you some questions. DI Muir said that if it is a separate case then he'll come and see you in a couple of days. At this stage he wouldn't ask you any different questions to what we're going to ask, so he'll just accept our report of the interview.'

'I'm glad about that, he seems to be a nice man but, at the moment, I feel more comfortable talking to people I know.'

Atkinson took a sip of his coffee and began with his first question. 'Can you tell us about what you can remember about last night? Everything you remember, no matter how small and insignificant you think it might be. What's a small detail now could prove to be very important later.'

Carter stood up from the table and slowly circled around the kitchen. As she walked, she began to speak. Quietly at first and then with more volume. 'Josie usually got home from work about four o'clock. She only works .... worked part time in a small café on Allerton Road. She worked the lunch period and finished about half past three. So, by the time she'd walked home it'd usually be about four. She loved to cook, so she'd always prepare something for our tea. I was at a parents evening at school. It started around four, the same time Josie would have got home,' Carter stopped walking and speaking for a short while, and stood looking out of the window at the back garden. She wasn't seeing anything though, just staring into the distance. 'Sorry,' she continued. 'It just hit me that while I was talking to parents some animal was doing that to Josie.'

'It's hard, I know. But please carry on. You're doing well,' encouraged Bassey.

'The parents evening was tailing off about seven. I'd spoken to everyone I really needed to, so I tidied up and left about quarter past. Some of the staff were going for a drink, but I passed on that. I was driving and I knew that Josie would have a meal ready. I pulled up at the house about eight o'clock. The first thing I noticed was that there were no lights on in any of the rooms. Usually the house looks like Las Vegas, Jodie can, sorry - could turn a light on but had problems turning it off. So, in the dark from outside it's possible to see which rooms she's been in. I thought it was a bit strange, and it was very quiet when I went inside. Josie usually has the telly or music on.'

'Can I ask,' interrupted Bassey. 'Was the front door open or did you have to use a key?'

'A key, I used a key.'

'I noticed that you only have a Yale on the front door and no mortice lock.'

'Yes, we've been meaning to fit one, but have never got around to it for some reason. Why are you asking about the lock?'

'We're trying to work out how the killer got into the property. Did he by-pass the lock or did Jodie let him in?'

Carter nodded her understanding and continued. 'Anyway, I called Josie's name and got no answer, so I assumed that she was out, maybe at Tesco's on Smithdown. I dropped all my school gear in the hall by the front door and phoned Josie's mobile as I walked down the hall to the kitchen to put the kettle on. Before I got to the kitchen, I heard Josie's phone ringing. It was in the kitchen. I was a little confused, she always has her phone with her. So, I went into the kitchen and turned the light on ......' at this point Carter let out a huge sob and tears began to run down her cheeks. Williams immediately shot up and put her arms around the sobbing figure, casting accusatory glances at Atkinson and Bassey before escorting Carter from the kitchen.

'I'm sorry,' Atkinson said when the two women returned ten minutes later. 'But we have to ask these questions. We have to know Jan's movements up to when she discovered the body.'

'You think she might have done it!' hissed Williams.

'I'm sorry,' Atkinson said again. 'But we have to be able to rule her out.'

No one spoke for the next ten minutes. The only sound in the kitchen was the ticking of the wall clock. When she had recomposed herself, Carter began again.

'It was horrible, I've never imagined anything like it, let alone seen it with my own eyes.'

'You don't have to go into detail here Jan,' Bassey said kindly. 'Both DI Atkinson and I have both seen inside the kitchen. Can I ask though, did you touch anything in there?'

'Nothing apart from the light switch. Once I'd seen Josie, I ran to the downstairs loo and threw up. Oh yes .... I might have touched the fridge because I went back in to get the Inspectors card so I could call him.'

'That was very brave of you to go back in. But why didn't you just phone 999?'

'It just came to me as I was puking in the loo. There's a police Inspectors phone number on the fridge door – I should call him. I suppose in the back of my mind I was thinking that maybe things would happen quicker if I phoned the Inspector than if I phoned 999.'

'OK,' Bassey said quietly. 'Now do you know anyone who could have done this? Someone who had a grudge against Josie maybe?'

'Like someone she'd short changed in the café?' snorted Williams. 'Josie was loved by everyone who knew her. I don't think she had an enemy anywhere in the world.'

'I have to agree with Chris,' Carter said. 'Josie didn't have any enemies. Well, none I'm aware of anyway. I suppose she might have some in her past, before I knew her.' Carter shrugged.

'How long have you known Josie?' Bassey asked.

'We met about seven years ago when she moved down here from Newcastle. We started going out together and she moved in with me about eighteen months later. We were talking about getting married next year,' sighed Carter, more tears forming in her eyes.

'You're doing great Jan, just a couple more questions,' Atkinson said. 'Did you know that your house had been thoroughly searched?'

'No. A nice policewoman threw a few things in a bag for me so that I didn't have to go back inside. And I never noticed anything downstairs, I stayed in the loo while I waited for the police. I didn't turn a light on when I dumped my school stuff, and I was too surprised to hear Josie's phone ring in the kitchen to go in any of the other rooms. And of course, the kitchen...well, I only saw one thing in there.'

'Any ideas why someone would want to search your house? Or what they might be looking for?'

'No. No, we've got no expensive jewellery and we don't keep cash in the house.'

'Did Josie know Ben or Ruth?' asked Bassey.

'She'd met Ben, but I wouldn't say she really knew him. She arrived in Liverpool after Ruth had disappeared, so no, she didn't know Ruth. Do you think this is anything to do with their disappearance?'

'Not sure yet,' Atkinson replied. 'But I don't believe in coincidences. Thanks for your time Jan, and thanks for the coffee Chris. Sorry we had to ask you all those questions, but...'

'It's OK Inspector, I know you're only doing your job. And I want you to catch this bastard. A few upsetting questions is nothing compared to what Josie went through.'

'Well, if you think of anything give us a ring. Me or DI Muir.'

'I will Inspector,' said Carter slowly turning away and starting to sob again. Atkinson and Bassey said their goodbyes, but no one heard them, and headed out towards the car.

Outside Bassey looked at Atkinson. 'Do you think it's anything to do with Ben and Ruth?'

'As I said, I don't believe in coincidences. Josie has links to people in our case, and the killer could have been looking for Ben's book, so I'm going to see the boss when we get back and put forward a strong argument to have this case tied in with Ben and Ruth.'

XXXI

Clarke became quiet again, looking at the expectation in the faces of Atkinson and Bassey.

'You've come here voluntarily Mr Clarke. So, you must have something you want to tell us, or you need to tell us. You're not under arrest, and you can leave at any time. But I urge you, that if you know anything that can help us find out what happened to Ruth Anderson, please tell us,' Atkinson said.

'Well, I wanted to tell you …. I did know that Miss Anderson had a child. I didn't find out until the end of the Summer term, a few days before we broke up. I had occasion to go down to the Unit, and when I went in Miss Anderson was in there alone. She was sitting with her back to me and didn't hear me approach her. She was concentrating on something she was holding. I'm afraid to say that curiosity got the better of me and I peeked over her shoulder, to see what she was looking at. I was surprised to see a photograph of a young child. Miss Anderson suddenly realised I was there and turned to look at me. There were tears in her eyes. I asked who the child was and she told me it was her daughter who lived with her parents in Birmingham. At this point, she burst into full floods of tears and laid her head upon my shoulder. It was quite embarrassing, what if a pupil had come into the room? She made me promise not to tell anyone about the child. I think she was embarrassed that she was unable to look after her. She didn't want other members of staff tittle tattling about it. I gave her my word not to tell a soul, which is why I didn't mention it at our previous meetings. But since Miss Andersons disappearance, it has weighed heavily on my mind. So, I thought I should come and tell you.'

'Thank you for coming in and telling us, Mr Clarke,' Bassey said. 'It's a pity that you didn't tell us originally,' Clarke looked somewhat abashed. He rose slowly from his chair and looked directly at Bassey.

'I am sorry I didn't tell you before, I truly am. Please find Miss Anderson.'

After Clarke had gone Atkinson and Bassey sat quietly in the interview room for almost five minutes. Both officers trying to work out in their minds if this new piece of information progressed their investigation or not. It was Bassey who broke the silence.

'In all honesty does it really help? So, he knew Ruth had a daughter. It doesn't change anything about the case. Does it?'

'No, I don't think it does. But he felt the need to come and tell us. Why?'

'You were right though, there was something he wasn't telling us.'

'I don't think that that's what it is though. I wonder if we'll ever find out what he's really not telling us? Did the DNA test come back yet?' quickly changing tack.

'It hit the desk just before this none event with Clarke kicked off.'

'Well?' There was just a glimmer of hope on his face. This could be their last roll of the dice.

'Sorry Ron, no matches. We still don't know whose blood is on the knife.'

'Well, that's it Shirl, we're fucked. We've no witnesses, no motive and no fucking body. We've got nothing but dead ends. I suppose I'd better go and tell Reynolds and you'd better get your uniform out of the wardrobe.'

'So, case unsolved then?'

'For now, Shirl, for now. I'll get to the bottom of it one day. I don't know when, but I will.'

'Give it six months and she'll turn up after being in the Greek Islands or somewhere like that,' they both knew she didn't mean it. They both knew that Ruth Anderson was dead, and they couldn't prove it. Atkinson stood up and kicked his chair across the room, looked at Bassey with a grim expression, turned and left the room.

Bassey sat quietly for a couple of minutes. Her time being seconded to CID had come to an end. They hadn't got a result, but she thought she'd performed quite well. Well enough for a permanent transfer? Only the powers that be could answer that question. She hoped so any way.

PC 637 Irene Bassey slowly got up from her chair, returned Atkinson's chair to its correct spot and quietly left the room, walking back to her life in uniform.

*

Atkinson had been in DCI Mitchell's office for over half an hour. Bassey was comforted by the fact that she had heard no raised voices. Would Mitchell agree to them taking on Josie's murder as part of the Smart and Anderson case? She had noticed that there had been a lot of shoe polishing on trouser legs before Atkinson had even initiated the traffic light sequence. It gave her the impression that Atkinson wasn't 100% sure of his ground. Bassey felt deep down in her waters that the three cases were linked. How, she didn't know. But crack one and she knew they would crack all three. In her opinion the Josie Rutherford murder was the one. If they could find Josie's killer, they would find out what had happened to Ben and Ruth.

When Atkinson finally came out of Mitchell's office, he had a big grin on his face.

'The boss says we can have it Shirl. We can fucking have it!'

'Great!'

'He's phoned Russ Muir and Russ is sending us everything that he's got.'

Bassey was feeling happy that they'd picked up the case, but was wondering where they were going to start.

'Right,' Atkinson said sitting on the edge of Bassey's desk. 'If Josie's murder is connected, then I think that she was collateral damage. It's to do with Jan Carter not Josie.'

'So, the killer was looking for something in the house, something that Jan had, not Josie. Josie came home and disturbed him and he killed her. It's got to be Ben Smart's exercise book.'

'You're right, it's got to be the book. If it's the same killer in all three cases and they knew about the book they'd want to get it back. They were looking for the book. They didn't find it though because we've got it.'

'So, who knew about the existence of Ben Smart's book?'

Their deliberations were interrupted by the phone in Atkinson's office ringing. He quickly got up and went to answer it. Bassey didn't hear what he said but there was a lot of head nodding.

'That was Russ Muir, he says that McKenzie, the pathologist, is doing Josie's autopsy in an hour if we want to go. As its now our case.'

Bassey nodded her agreement, she didn't really like autopsies. Who did apart from pathologists? Pathologists – the only doctors who did actually know everything - usually about two days too late! They gathered up their bits and pieces and walked slowly to the car park. They both knew how important autopsy findings could be for a case. But they also knew that most of the autopsy had already been carried out by the killer in the kitchen. They were in no real hurry to get to the morgue.

XXXII

The problem with going to the Royal Liverpool Hospital, as with all hospitals, is the parking. There are no little side streets to park in, the only option is to use the multi storey over the road from the hospital.

They were running a little late so Atkinson decided to take a chance and park in an ambulance bay, right by the main hospital entrance, much to Bassey's disapproval. He scribbled a note which said "Police Business" and gave his rank and mobile number and left it on the dashboard in full view. He hoped that this would cover it.

Bassey hated coming to RLH, or any of the local hospitals come to that. Not because she had a thing about hospitals or anything. But they were all supposed to be no smoking sites, and to reach the entrance of any of them you had to pass through little gaggles of smokers - both visitors and patients. Usually standing under signs that said "No Smoking". Patients! Not just visitors. She had once asked a doctor she knew why they couldn't confine the patients to their wards. In that way it would stop them damaging their health any further and also stop people having to walk through all the smoke as they entered the hospital. He'd told her that to keep patients on the ward was infringing their human rights. So, if a patient was mobile, they could leave the ward, go to the shop, the in-house Costa or, although not really permitted, to have a cigarette. Bassey didn't agree with this and thought that this movement of patients could also account for the spread of MRSA around a hospital. The doctor could only agree with her.

Once they had negotiated the ranks of smokers and entered the hospital, they quickly made their way to the morgue, which like all morgues, was in the basement. The basement of the RLH though, unlike in the films, was well lit and sign posted.

'Ah, you've made it Inspector, just in time as always,' quipped the pathologist. 'DI Muir told me you might be dropping in.' Atkinson and Bassey were well acquainted with Dr Alexander McKenzie. It was he who did all the police autopsies and, like many of his colleagues, he had a very dark sense of humour. Bassey supposed it was his way of not getting too upset about some of the things he had to see and do. She often wondered if pathologists developed the black humour because of the job, or were they spotted at medical school with a black sense of humour and funnelled into pathology. To Bassey it was a chicken and egg situation.

'Sorry if we kept you Doc,' Atkinson replied rubbing his shoes on his trousers, 'but we're here now. So, you may begin.'

'Thank you, Inspector, but we've finished.' McKenzie gestured towards his assistant, Kevin, who was replacing a green sheet to cover Josie Rutherford's body. 'As you will no doubt be aware,' McKenzie continued. 'The victim underwent what we'll call severe and drastic surgery. All of the removed organs were present in the kitchen - saved me the job I suppose. Kevin has weighed them and there appears to be no abnormalities. Now the question I'm sure you'd like an answer to is was the poor girl dead before her body organs were taken out?'

Both Atkinson and Bassey nodded. They needed to know the answer and they both hoped, no prayed, that Josie had been dead before the mutilation started.

'Well Inspector, I examined the kitchen closely, probably much closer than you did when you had your look,' he smiled knowingly. 'You will though have noticed that the walls and flat surfaces were covered with the victim's blood. Now no blood had actually been smeared onto any of the surfaces, which leads me to only one conclusion I'm afraid. The blood on the walls and surfaces was caused by arterial spray, which means the heart was beating and the poor girl was alive when her organs were removed. Well, when some of them were cut out. She would have died of exsanguination and shock well before our killer finished his grisly task. There is a small flicker of light at the end of this dark tunnel, though. There is a large bruise that had started to form on the left side of her face. It looks like she was struck with a heavy object before the frenzied attack took place. Hopefully she was unconscious, but we'll never know for sure.'

All the colour drained from Bassey's face as she imagined what Jodie had gone through. But why would anyone do that? Killing and mutilating was bad enough, but mutilation before death? That was just horrific. She looked at Atkinson, he still appeared to have some colour to his face. His eyes though had taken on a steely, hard look.

'We've got to get this bastard,' he said through gritted teeth, nodded at McKenzie and turned and walked out of the room. Bassey quickly recovered herself, thanked McKenzie and followed Atkinson. There was no sign of him in the corridor so she hurried towards the hospital entrance. She finally caught up with Atkinson at the spot where they'd parked the car – the ambulance bay was empty.

'Fuck,' Atkinson exclaimed. 'They've towed the fucking car.'

'Was that your car sir?' enquired an officious voice from behind him. Atkinson turned and pulled out his warrant card, shoving it right into the face of a hospital security guard.

'Yes! It fucking was!'

'Now, now sir, there's no need for profanities. We recognised it as a police car, it's all the rubbish inside you see, gives it away immediately.'

'Well, if you knew it was a cop car why didn't you ring me? The number was there on the note on the dashboard.' Atkinson demanded.

'We tried to sir, but your phone just went to voice mail. We needed to free up the space for an ambulance, because that's what it is sir,' he said pointing to the lettering on the floor. 'An ambulance bay.' Atkinson felt like hitting the supercilious shit, but refrained himself.

'I was in the morgue; I didn't hear my phone ring.' He looked at Bassey who nodded in agreement. No phone had been heard.

'Ah, the morgue,' said the security guard, nodding sagely.

'Yes, that's what I said,' Atkinson answered, just about keeping a lid on it.

'You see sir, the morgue's in the basement,'

'Yes, I fucking know that,' Atkinson countered, getting even more worked up.

'That'd be why you didn't answer then sir. There's no mobile signal in the basement.' More nodding sagely on the part of the security guard.

Bassey could almost see the steam coming out of Atkinson's ears.

'Well, as I said sir, we knew it was a real police car, because of the mess inside. They'd be less easy for villains to spot if you tidied them up a bit, you know? So, what we've done is we've just towed it up to the second floor of the staff car park. You'll need this to get out.' He handed Atkinson a credit card sized piece of card with a bar code on it. 'Please be careful where you park in future sir,' he tapped his cap, turned and walked away.

'Bastard! Who does he think he is talking to me like that?'

'Calm down Ron,' soothed Bassey. 'You know he's right in what he says. Lucky for us they only towed it to a car park. Funny though isn't it? He knew it was police car because of the shit in it, not because of your note.'

XXXIII

'Have you calmed down now?' Bassey asked as they drove back to Copy Lane.

'Yeah, I suppose so. The bastard could have given us more information than just the second floor though. We wasted, what? Fifteen minutes, looking for the car?'

'Stop moaning. It was more like three or four minutes and it could have been worse. The car could have been towed to the pound. And where would you be then? Having to explain parking in an ambulance bay at the busiest hospital in the city to the DCI.'

'That wouldn't have been a problem,' Atkinson cut in before Bassey built up a head of steam. 'I'd have told him you were driving!'

'Piss off!' Bassey said as she hit him.

Thirty minutes later the two detectives were sitting in the canteen at Copy Lane, Bassey with a diet coke and Atkinson with a heavily sweetened cup of coffee.

'So, we think that Ben's blue exercise book is the key to Josies murder then?' Bassey asked.

Atkinson nodded as he took a noisy slurp of his coffee. 'Hot,' he explained.

'Whoever knew about the book has to be a suspect then,' Bassey continued, looking at Atkinson with a slight expression of disgust.

'Every bugger knew about it,' he replied, shaking his head. 'He showed the bloody thing to anybody who'd pay attention.'

'So, there's going to be people who've seen it that we don't know about. That means we have to concentrate on the people who we do,' Bassey paused for a moment before continuing. 'OK, we know Fred Lowe's seen it and so has Artie Miller. Then there's Jan Carter, she obviously knew all about it as he asked her to look after it. Jerome and Mary Anderson, they knew, because Ben had been talking to them about it. Did Charles Clarke know about it?'

'I don't recall him mentioning it at all. But then again if he was our killer you wouldn't expect him to volunteer that information. We'll have to ask him.'

'So, that's five possibly six, anymore?'

'Well, there's Josie Rutherford, she probably knew.'

'She's dead Ron. I don't think she mutilated herself, do you? It's taking alibis a little too far.'

'I know she's dead,' spluttered Atkinson slightly embarrassed. 'I'm just saying she probably knew about the book as well, that's all.'

'Did she know that the book had been passed to us? Did she tell the killer as he cut her up? Because, if she did, we could be next on his list,' Bassey said these last seven words in as menacing a voice as she could. Atkinson just laughed at the possibility. But he had to agree, it was a possibility.

'What time is it Shirl?' Atkinson asked suddenly.

'Six o'clock. Why?' Bassey answered with a puzzled look on her face.

'Because we're going to see Clarke, and at this time he should be at home,' Atkinson explained getting to his feet.

Thirty minutes later, one of the detectives was rubbing his shoes on the backs of his trouser legs and the other was knocking on the door of Clarke's house in Mariners Road. She was about to knock a second time when the door swung open. Anne Clarke looked up at the two detectives from her wheel chair with a look on her face that said: I know you from somewhere but I can't just place you.

Bassey pulled out her warrant card and put Mrs Clarke out of her misery. 'Hello Mrs Clarke, I'm DS Bassey and this is DI Atkinson. We have met before, about eight years ago.'

'Yes, yes, I remember now. You called about the disappearance of that young girl from Charles' school. Ruth…. Ruth Anderson that was her name wasn't it?' she looked at Bassey who nodded. 'Please come in. I take it that you've come to see Charles? He's upstairs I'll give him a shout.' With this she executed a neat turn in the hall way and shouted up the stairs. 'Charles! Charles! Visitors!'

'I'll be down in about 5 minutes dear, just finishing off,' they heard Clarke reply as they were shown into the sitting room.

'He's working on a report for the governors, he's got a meeting next week. Can I get you a drink while you're waiting? Coffee? Tea?' Both detectives settled on tea. 'Now I'm afraid we only have rice milk. We haven't used cow's milk for about three years, will that be OK?'

Bassey saw Atkinson's grimace; luckily Mrs Clarke didn't notice it. 'No, it's OK Mrs Clarke, we'll just have black coffees, thanks,' she said quickly.

Mrs Clarke was back with the drinks before her husband had come down stairs. Both Bassey and Atkinson looked a little perturbed: for black coffee it looked very light.

'I'm afraid I put some rice milk in – sorry, my mind was on other things,' explained a thoughtful looking Mrs Clarke.

Atkinson and Bassey exchanged puzzled looks and Bassey said, 'It's fine Mrs Clarke, don't worry about it.'

'I'll get back to my ironing if you don't mind. Charles shouldn't be long,' Mrs Clarke said as she pulled off another tight turn and left the room.

Atkinson took a sip of his coffee. 'Jesus!' he whispered. 'This is shite, have you tasted yours?' Bassey nodded in answer to his question and in agreement with his description of the coffee. 'It's only instant Shirl, why didn't she just pour it away and start again when she realised?'

'Good question,' Bassey answered. 'You going to ask her?'

Before Atkinson could speak again Clarke entered the room. He was obviously taken aback at the identity of his visitors.

'Detectives, what can I do for you now? I thought we had finished our ...er... relationship.'

'I don't know whether you are aware of the fact that Miss Carter's partner, Josie Rutherford, has been murdered,' began Atkinson.

'No, no, I didn't know,' Clarke said sitting down. 'Miss Carter had someone contact the school office to tell us that she wouldn't be in for a while, for personal reasons. But I had no idea that her partner was dead. Josie Rutherford you say. That's terrible. Absolutely terrible. Thank you for coming to tell me personally.'

'We're sorry to be the bearers of such bad news, but we think the killing is associated with the Ruth Anderson and Ben Smart cases,' Bassey explained.

'In what way?'

'We're not one hundred percent sure yet,' Bassey said. 'We have got a working theory though. As we've told you, Ben was obsessed with Ruth's disappearance. He desperately wanted to know what had happened to her. He kept his thoughts in order by writing them down in a blue exercise book. Before he disappeared, Ben gave this exercise book to Jan Carter to look after. We think that he'd discovered something significant and thought that he was in danger, so he gave the book to Jan for safe keeping.

'Obviously, Ben was right to be worried. Jan contacted us about the exercise book, and we took possession of it. It's full of information about everyone who Ben thought was in any way connected to Ruth. We think that the killer found out that Jan had the exercise book, thought there was something incriminating in it, and went looking for it. He killed Josie when she disturbed his search, or she died while he was attempting to get information from her. Now we've read the book and we can't find anything in it that points a finger at anyone,'

Bassey concluded, realising that this was the first time that she or Atkinson had put the whole thing into words.

'And where do I fit in?' an obviously puzzled Clarke asked.

'Well, Mr Clarke,' Atkinson said. 'You're mentioned in the book, and we wondered if you knew anything about its existence?'

'Me! In the book! What on earth for?' Clarke exclaimed; obviously agitated in some way.

'You're there because you knew Ruth, you were her boss,' Bassey cut in. 'As we said, everyone connected with her was in there. There was a page for everyone. Ben even had a page for himself. By your reaction I take it that you didn't know of the existence of the book?'

'No, I knew nothing about it at all. You can't think that I killed poor Miss Carter's friend while looking for the book surely?'

'No, Mr Clarke,' Bassey continued in her best soothing voice. He was still agitated. 'If you had no knowledge of the book there was no reason for you to go looking for it, was there?'

'Well?' Atkinson said when they were sitting in the car ten minutes later.

'I believe him. Did you see his face? He knew nothing about the book, he's not Josie's killer.'

'Anything else?'

'Yes, his wife makes terrible coffee! Rice milk! Her mind was on other things! What an excuse.'

'You finished? Good, let's go for a proper drink and wash that fucking coffee away.'

XXXIV

Atkinson was sitting in his office with his feet on the desk. Bassey looked at his shoes, they had a slight shine to them. He must have rubbed them on his legs recently. She wondered if she had any little habits or tics that he'd noticed. She didn't think so and even if she did, he never mentioned them. She was brought out of her thoughts by the sound of Atkinson's voice.

'Eh?'

'I said Shirl, that that theory you gave Clarke last night is probably what happened. We don't have all the details yet, but I think that's what happened.'

'Yeah, it fits the overall picture. We just need to fill in the details.'

'Talking of filling in the details, I suppose I'd better boogie on down and update Mitchell on our progress,' Atkinson thought for a moment before continuing. 'I can call it progress, can't I? I don't want him or The Todger getting too excited. Well, not just yet.'

After Atkinson had left, Bassey collected a cup of coffee from the CID coffee machine. Having put the requisite thirty pence in the tin she returned to her own desk. She sat quietly for a few moments before getting out the list, Atkinson had made, of people who were known to have had knowledge of Ben Smart's book. She stared at it as she drank her coffee, letting her mind run little movies of each person. In her mind she watched each person in turn mutilate and kill Josie Rutherford. Thankfully her mind movies were always in black and white. Did anyone look right doing the deed? There were two people on the list that she decided would have been comfortable with the amount of blood and removing the organs. They would also have the knife skills - the butchers Fred Lowe and Artie Miller.

There was only one problem, as far as she knew, neither Fred nor Artie had ever had anything to do with Ruth Anderson. Their only link to Ruth had been Ben Smart. And Artie had probably still been at school when Ruth disappeared. Bassey shook her head trying to clear her mind of all thoughts, trying to get a mentally clean slate.

Fred and Artie? Was there a connection between one of them and Ruth that they didn't know about? Would it be worth asking them? Of course, it would be worth asking them! It would be piss poor police work if they didn't. Their job was to go down every blind alley until they found one with a gate at the end. And this would probably be a very blind alley, but it was one they had to explore, never the less. Again, she was woken from her reverie by Atkinson's voice.

'Well, that went better than I thought it would Shirl. Mitchell understands the difficulties we have. That in itself surprises me, must be something to do with The Todgers input.' Atkinson sat on the corner of Bassey's desk and looked at her. 'You've spilled coffee down yourself. So, you must have been deep in thought not to notice. Nice shirt by the way.'

Bassey immediately started rubbing at her blouse. 'Shit, shit, shit. I hope it doesn't stain, I paid a fortune for this and it's the first time I've worn it for work.'

Atkinson shook his head and smiled. 'You'll have to use some of that Vanish stuff when you wash it. Do you want to share your deep thoughts?'

'Actually, I was thinking about who, out of the people we know who knew about Ben's book, would be capable of killing Josie. The only ones who I think would be able to do it are Fred Lowe and Artie Miller.'

'But Fred and Artie have no connection to Ruth Anderson that we know of.'

'Agreed,' Bassey said nodding. 'I think we should ask them though, don't you?'

'Most certainly, get your coat – you've pulled!' Atkinson shouted jumping to his feet. The two detectives booked out a pool car and Bassey drove them to Bedford Road and Fred Lowe's butchers' shop. It was only en route that Bassey realised that they didn't have home addresses for either of the two men. They'd have to correct that oversight she determined. The car she was driving was a three-year-old Ford Focus and it looked to have three years of worth of rubbish rattling around in it. Maybe there was something to the hospital security man's theory.

Atkinson was out of the car as soon as it came to a stop opposite the shop. He's got some sort of bit between his teeth – thought Bassey. 'Come on Shirl, get a move on.'

It was when she saw the bulky figure of Fred Lowe on the step of the shop locking the door, she understood Atkinson's hurry; it was closing time. There was no sign of the Yamaha so Artie must have gone home already. Even more reason to get his home address.

'Fred! Fred!' Atkinson shouted as he managed to avoid an oncoming cyclist and then a car travelling in the opposite direction, as he crossed the road. Lowe turned around to see who was shouting his name. His face turned from questioning to recognition as he saw Atkinson stepping onto the pavement.

'Glad we caught you,' Atkinson gasped as he approached Lowe. 'Can we ask you a couple of questions?'

'I'll open up again and we can talk inside, be more private,' Lowe replied turning the key in the lock and pushing the door open. Bassey followed them through the door and pulled it shut.

'Well, what can I do you for you two then? I take it you've not come for some of Artie's faggots. He makes them all now y'know, thanks to Miss Round.'

'No, it's not faggots we want Fred,' Atkinson said. 'It occurred to us that you and Artie had both seen Ben's book and talked to him about it,' Lowe nodded and Atkinson continued. 'And then we got to thinking, did either of you know Ruth Anderson?'

Lowe sniffed before he replied. 'I'd certainly never met the girl. I only knew of her and about her through Ben and his book. I'm pretty sure Artie didn't know her either. But you'd be better off asking him yourself.'

'That's what we're going to do,' Bassey said. 'Unfortunately, we don't have his address. I'm sure you'll be able to let us have it though.'

'Of course. He lives with his sister in a flat, Ford cemetery way. The exact address is ……. Flat 31 Daleacre Drive I think, off the top of my head. Yes, that's it, Flat 31 …. no Flat 13, that's it, I'm sure, Flat 13. I always get the digits the wrong way around for some reason.'

'It's OK Fred, we can always try both,' Atkinson smiled. 'We'll leave you to lock up then. Thanks for your help.'

'Do you know where Daleacre Drive is Shirl?' Atkinson asked as Bassey got behind the wheel of the Ford and started the engine.

'Yes, I had to go there once when I was back in uniform. There's a Pupil Referral Unit there, I think that's what they're called. It's a school where they send kids mainstream schools can't cope with. The staff thought some young lads were selling drugs to the pupils from a flat opposite the school. I went over there with another officer and had a look around. From the look of the kids we met they were probably selling drugs to the guys in the flat. Jesus! I'd have locked them up! I wouldn't have put them into a nice building like they had there. It reminded me of Colditz.'

'Colditz? You said it was a nice building.'

'It was a nice building. But if you remember, Colditz was where the Nazis put all the prisoners of war who kept trying to escape. Probably working on the theory that if you had all your bad eggs in one basket, they'd be easier to keep an eye on. Plus, they couldn't infect other prisoners with their ideas.'

'Ah, so this school is where the kids who didn't cut it in places like Ben Smart's Learning Support Centre might have ended up? The real hard nuts.'

'Probably,' Bassey agreed.

It took less than fifteen minutes to get from Bedford Road to Daleacre Drive. It then took a further five minutes to find Flat 13. It was not on the road itself, but off on a side walkway. Bassey prepared her warrant card and knocked on the door, Atkinson rubbed his shoes on the back of his legs. The door was opened by an attractive timid looking woman in her early thirties. She had curly black shoulder length hair and she was wearing a baggy FC Barcelona tracksuit.

'Sorry, to disturb you,' Bassey began waving her warrant card. 'I'm DS Bassey and this is DI Atkinson, we're looking for Artie Miller. Does he live here?'

'Yes, I'm his sister. He's not in at the moment, he shouldn't be too long though. He's not in any trouble, is he? What do you want to see him about? Can I get him to contact you?' The voice was almost a whisper.

'He's not in any trouble Miss Miller, we just want to have a quick word with him,' assured Bassey.

'Is it something to do with the disappearance of his friend, Ben?' Artie's sister asked so quietly that Atkinson had to strain to hear her.

'Yes, yes, it is,' Atkinson answered nodding.

'Have you found him?' quiet again.

'No, I'm afraid not,' Atkinson replied. 'Sorry that we disturbed you but can you tell Artie that we'd just like to have word with him about Ruth Anderson.'

'Ruth Anderson,' pondered Miss Miller. 'Isn't that the name of the girl that went missing about ten years ago?' she continued hesitantly. Atkinson gave Artie's sister a questioning look.

'Oh, I know all about Ben's obsession and that he kept a note book, Inspector,' she explained in her soft, quiet voice. 'My brother's spoken about it many a time. I've never seen it myself though, but he did tell me that before he disappeared Ben gave it to a friend to look after. He never said who. My brother thought Ben might have made a breakthrough in his search for what happened to that poor girl. I don't suppose anyone knows where it is, so we'll never know.'

'We know where it is, Miss Miller,' Atkinson said. 'We've got it.'

It was Artie's sisters turn to look quizzical.

'Ben's friend gave the book to us when he disappeared,' Atkinson explained with a smile. He thought that she looked like she was going to start clapping and jiggling with excitement. 'Tell Artie we'll catch up with him at the shop tomorrow, and that there's nothing for him to worry about. Again, sorry for disturbing you.'

As the two officers walked back to the car, Atkinson proposed that they call it a day and meet in the pub later for a drink. Bassey quickly agreed, if they were going to spend time talking about the case why do it at the station when they knew a perfectly good pub. Look out Crow's Nest here we come! In the end they decided not to go home and meet later, but to go straight to the pub.

XXXV

Bassey dropped Atkinson at the door while she parked the car. She was delighted to see that Atkinson had already got a round in when she entered the pub. He was sitting at a table which gave a good view of the door and of most of the pub, a good spot for people watching. And the first thing she saw as she sat down were the two grey haired guys sitting at their usual table. Happy tonight then boys.

'Cheers,' Atkinson said lifting his pint of Guinness.

'Cheers,' Bassey replied taking a mouthful from her own pint of the black stuff. They both just sat, drank and watched the ebb and flow of the pub for five minutes or so, comfortable in each other's company. It was Bassey who broke the silence.

'So, what did you think of Artie's sister then Ron?'

'Pretty,' he began, but noticing the look on Bassey's face quickly changed tack. 'Pretty .... Quiet, I thought she was probably a quiet girl. You know, someone who stays in the background and never pushes themselves forward.'

'Well recovered,' Bassey's round of sarcastic applause got other drinkers looking in their direction. She smirked back at them. 'I think I agree with you,' she went on. 'She didn't strike me as being a confident person at all. Probably why she's sharing a flat with her brother rather than having one of her own. But, as you were about to say, she's a very attractive woman. You'd have thought that she'd be sharing a flat with a partner not a brother.'

'Maybe she's had a bad experience with a man.' Then seeing he may have upset Bassey again quickly added, 'or a woman.' He took a drink before continuing. 'Could have made her withdraw into herself, lose confidence and all that sort of thing. I suppose we can add her to our list of people who knew about Ben's book. I think she falls straight into the Jan Carter - Josie Rutherford territory though.'

'Somewhere between dead and alive?' Bassey smiled grimly. 'You make her sound like Schrodinger's cat.'

Atkinson looked blank.

'Come on, you must know about Schrodinger's cat?'

He shook his head slowly. 'Never heard of it, but, I'm sure you're going to tell me.'

'Schrodinger's cat,' Bassey began in her best school teacher voice, 'is one of the greatest thought experiments in quantum physics. . . .'

Atkinson's face crumpled and his eyes rolled at the mention of thought experiments and quantum physics.

'Schrodinger said what if there's a cat in a sealed box? In the box with the cat is a flask of poisonous gas, a hammer, a Geiger counter and small amount of radioactive material. The amount of radioactive material is small enough so that there's only a 50:50 chance of it registering on the Geiger counter. If the Geiger counter goes ping it sets off a train of events which leads to the hammer breaking the flask and the gas being released. But because quantum physics is all about probability, you don't know if the cat's alive or dead until you open the box. So, it's technically both dead and alive.'

He interrupted her in full flow. 'Hang on Shirl, what's all this bollocks got to do with Artie's sister?'

'Fuck-all,' Bassey admitted. 'But you didn't think I'd let you get away with a crack about her being another lesbian, did you? I was trying to make a little joke. And if you'd known about Schrodinger's cat and I hadn't had to explain it, you would've got it and we could've moved quickly on. Sometimes I think I'm wasting my time with you. I'll get another round.' She smiled inwardly, stood up and walked to the bar.

Why did Bassey have to do this sort of thing? Ok she was a clever girl and she was pissed off because he still out ranked her, but this parade of intellectual superiority was getting them nowhere. The Cat in the Hat he could handle, but a cat in a sealed box? Surely it would die of suffocation before the poison gas got it? So, it was always going to be dead – case closed.

When she sat down again saying Mike would bring the beer over, Atkinson decided to stick to things he was confident with. 'So, we'll go and see Artie at the shop in the morning and that will be the end of that.'

'Yeah, I can't see Artie having known anything about Ruth Anderson until Ben Smart started talking to him about her.'

Atkinson nodded and turned the conversation to other more general topics, where it stayed until closing time.

XXXVI

Once outside in the car park, the fresh air hit Atkinson and the Guinness he'd consumed began to take its toll. His head began to spin and he became unsteady on his feet. So unsteady that he had to sit down on a bench at one of the tables that were placed just outside the door, on the edge of the carpark. Bassey, who was feeling only slightly better, plonked herself down next to him.

'I think we'd better get a taxi Ron,' she slurred. 'And leave the car here.'

'Good idea Shirl,' Atkinson slurred back and pulled his phone from his pocket. He stared at it for a while with an uncomprehending look on his face and then started to get up. "I'll ask Mike to ring for one.'

'No, you sit there, I'll do it. I'm more capable.'

Atkinson nodded and slumped back onto the bench and started to minutely examine the table. In his drunken state he found the grain in the wood fascinating. To an observer he was just staring blankly, whereas in his reality he was trying to memorise the intricate patterns of grain and stain. So, it was safe to say, he was staring blankly.

'Mike's on it,' Bassey said interrupting his stare.

'Oh good. Fancy coffee at my place? No ulterior motives.... honest.'

'Yeah, go on. I trust you; I wouldn't trust just any one.... but you? Yes.'

At that moment a taxi pulled into the carpark, the driver stuck his head out of the window and looked at them. 'Holmes and Watson?' Fucking Mike!

'That's us,' Atkinson said struggling to his feet, steadying himself and offering his hand to Bassey. She batted it away and struggled up herself. The taxi driver let out an audible sigh, got out of the car and opened the back door in an attempt to speed things up.

'College Avenue, please driver,' Atkinson said. 'And don't spare the horses.' There was another long sigh from the driver as he put the car into gear and pulled out of the carpark. He was glad that neither of his passengers spoke to him for the duration of the short journey. He hated having to hold conversations with drunks. Too often they became abusive, and then there was always the possibility of violence. The quicker his picture framing business got off the ground the better, and he could give up this taxi driving lark.

'Here'll do driver,' Atkinson called from the back seat. The driver came to a halt and put on his interior light, so he could calculate the fare.

'That'll be £3.40 please, folks.'

Atkinson gave him a fiver and told him to keep the change. In return the driver gave him a business card. Atkinson stared at it, shrugged and fumbled it into his jacket pocket. Now it was time to concentrate on getting out of the car without falling over. He was pleased to see that Bassey had accomplished this difficult feat and was safely on the pavement, so he had great hopes of doing likewise. He pushed the door open and levered himself out. He'd been sitting directly behind the driver and so had a surprise when a small white car flashed past him, just avoiding his toes. 'Kinell. He put his hand on the roof of the car to steady himself and shut the door.

'G'night driver,' he said as he lurched towards the door to his flat. He'd seen a little white car like that recently, but he could just not think where. There were lots of little white cars on the road, probably driven behind one today. He caught up with Bassey and fumbled for his keys. After picking them off the floor twice, he allowed her to open the door.

They bounced off the walls as they climbed the stairs to the first floor. Here, there was a small landing and another door. Again, after repeated failed attempts by Atkinson, Bassey opened it. Behind the door was a hallway, about twelve feet long and six feet wide. There were two doors to the left and one directly in front. Atkinson waved in the general direction of the two doors. 'Bathroom,' he slurred and led Bassey through to the living room.

Bassey looked drunkenly around the room, she'd been in worse "bachelor pads". At least this one was tidy and tastefully furnished with two Chesterfield sofas separated by a small coffee table. In the alcove to the left of the fireplace was a low cupboard supporting a not too large television and DVD or Blue Ray player. In the right alcove was another matching cupboard, which held Atkinson's hi-fi equipment - turntable, CD player, tuner and amplifier.

It was only after taking in the furnishings that Bassey started examining the walls. He hadn't spoiled the effect with "tasteful" nudes, had he? It took her a couple of seconds to get things into focus. There were no nudes on the walls, but there was shelving, must be miles of it! The shelves positively groaned under the weight of CDs, vinyl, books and DVDs.

'Fuckin' hell, Ron!' she exclaimed. 'Is this a library or a branch of HMV?'

'Forgot.... You've never been round before,' replied Atkinson between deep breaths. It was true, in their eight years of working together, Bassey had never been inside his flat. 'D'you like my little collection?'

'Little? There looks to be hundreds of albums and thousands of CDs,' Bassey paused. 'And hundreds of books and God knows how many DVDs.'

Atkinson took another deep breath before speaking. 'I've got them all cata ... cata ... catalogued on the computer. Last count there was ... no idea' he shook his head. 'Coffee?'

'Yes please.' Bassey flopping onto one of the Chesterfields.

'Put some music on first,' Atkinson chose a CD from one of the shelves. Two minutes later the room was filled with sound. Bassey concentrated on listening to the music.

'I like this, who is it?' she called into the kitchen, where Atkinson was struggling with cups and his coffee machine.

'Richard Shindell.'

'Who's he?'

'American. Lives in Argentina.' He came back into the room studiously hanging on to two cups of coffee.

'Oh,' said Bassey her drunken curiosity satisfied.

Atkinson managed to give her one of the cups without spilling too much and sat down on the other Chesterfield. They concentrated hard on listening to the music and drinking their coffee without making any more mess on the carpet or sofas. Both were having trouble with the room, which was starting to spin before their eyes.

'I'll drink this, have a wee and get off home.'

'I'll walk you home,' volunteered Atkinson at his most chivalrous.

'No, you won't, you're pissed. Chances are we'd never make it to my house, and if we did, I wouldn't give much for your chances of finding your way back here. I'll have another taxi ride.'

'Wonder if it'll be the same driver? He'll be pissed off if it is,' Atkinson giggled.

'Right!' fighting her way off the Chesterfield. 'I'm going for a wee.'

'Not in there you're not! That's the kitchen. You need the other door. One hundred and eighty. Yes, that's it. Straight on. Excellent!'

She eventually found her way out of the living room and into the hallway. She squinted at the two doors in front of her and chose one at random. Wrong! She came back out of Atkinson's bedroom and went through the second door and into the bathroom.

XXXVII

Bassey tried to open her eyes and found it quite difficult, but she managed it with effort. She then tried to yawn. This she found impossible, due to the fact her mouth was held shut with some sort of tape. Next, she tried to bring her hands down from above her head to peel off the tape. What an unnatural position to fall asleep in. There was very little movement, but whatever was around her wrists began to dig tighter. Fucking hell, he'd tied her up! He said there'd be no funny business. I'll kill him! I will, I'll kill him! She stopped pulling as the binding was only getting tighter. She looked around the room, as well as she could from her position, and saw that she was on the bed in Atkinson's bedroom. She forced her head around so that she could see up the bed to where her hands were attached by bell wire to a bed post. Her feet were tied to the bottom of the bed with more of the wire. She hadn't known Ron was into bondage ...... She wasn't. I'm definitely going to fucking kill him!

She started to look for a way out of her predicament. It appeared that the wire around her hands hadn't been tied to the bed frame, just looped over the bed post. She tested to see if there was any give in the bonds around her feet. There was, only a small amount, but it might be enough. Wriggling as far as she could up the bed, she started to wave her arms up and down, hoping that her movements would lift the wire off the bed post. It took a while. It seemed like hours, but it worked. The wire flipped off the post and Bassey was able to sit up. Breathing heavily, she steeled herself to rip off the tape. Something made her stop and listen before she did it. She could hear a voice, someone shouting, and it didn't sound like Atkinson.

She peeled off the tape without screaming and untied her feet. Then using her teeth managed to free her hands. She climbed off the bed, stood up and wobbled precariously. Taking a few seconds to master the art of standing upright, she thought about what she was going to do. Mind made up, she edged towards the door and cracked it open just enough to see into the hallway. Squinting through the gap she could see along the hallway and into the living room. Fucking hell!

Atkinson was sitting in a wooden chair facing the open door. His wrists were taped securely to the arms of the chair, his ankles were taped to the legs, and his mouth was taped shut, all with silver duct tape. There was a large bruise starting to make an appearance on his right temple. An unknown figure was dancing around with its back to the door waving a large kitchen knife and shouting - what, she couldn't make out. But it looked like the knife had already been used. There was heavy bleeding from a slash on Atkinson's left cheek. The intruder was wearing a Tyvek suit, like SOC officers wear. The hood was up and the face was covered by a scarf so that only the eyes could be seen. This is serious!

Bassey stepped back from the door and into the bedroom. She needed a weapon. Propped in the corner was an old acoustic guitar. It looked like kids had been scribbling on it with black felt pen. Bassey wobbled over and picked the guitar up by the neck. She tried a couple of practice swings. It wasn't perfect, but it would have to do.

She stole a look out of the bedroom door, the stranger's back was still to her. She inched out and edged along the hallway towards the living room. She made it through the open doorway before she was spotted. Not by Atkinson's tormentor, but by Atkinson himself. She raised the guitar in preparation to strike, but Atkinson, his eyes suddenly wide, started violently shaking his head and mumbling behind his tape. This caused the white suited figure to turn and stare at Bassey standing there with the guitar raised above her head. Smack! The body of the guitar shattered, leaving Bassey holding the neck and the intruder face down on the floor.

Bassey dropped the remaining wood and strings and smiled at Atkinson. There were tears in his eyes. She ripped the tape off his mouth.

'Aaaaaaaagh!' he screamed. 'Fucking hell Shirl, what have you done?'

'Saved your life by the look of it.'

'No, no, not me, the guitar? Look at it!'

Bassey saw a tangle of wires, a neck and some bits of wood on the floor. 'That old thing?'

'Old! Old! That's a Martin D35 acoustic guitar. Well, it was until you came over all Pete fucking Townsend!'

'And your point is?' asked Bassey as she started peeling off the tape that held him to the chair.

'It's the same type of guitar that David Gilmour played when Pink Floyd recorded the title track of the album "Wish You Were Here".'

'It wasn't the actual one though. Was it?' Bassey said belligerently.

'No, no it wasn't. But did you not see the inscription on the body?'

Bassey shook her head.

'It said …. It used to say: To Martin on a Martin. All the best David Gilmour.'

So much for kids' scribble. Bassey stopped releasing Atkinson and stood back. 'I'll just stay over here then, while you calm down, shall I?'

'No, it's alright Shirl,' he sighed. 'You're right, you saved my life. I'm sure I'm worth more than an irreplaceable guitar.'

'Only just, only just.' Ungrateful bastard! Bassey turned back to the duct tape around Atkinson's arms and legs. 'I'm sorry, it was the only thing I saw that might do the job.'

'Don't worry about it,' said Atkinson rubbing his wrists and trying not to look at what was left of his prize possession. 'Let's see who we've got here then.'

Neither of them moved for a few seconds. Both were trying to work out who it could be lying on the floor. Eventually, Atkinson bent down and rolled the unconscious body onto it's back and removed the hood and scarf.

'Fucking hell!' they both exclaimed together.

XXXVIII

It was just after one o'clock in the afternoon when Atkinson arrived at Copy Lane. He'd been checked over for concussion and had the slash on his cheek attended to. He went straight up to his office, from where he collected Bassey, and they went down to the Interview Suite.

'Anything yet?' Atkinson asked a young police constable who was stationed outside Interview Room 3 as he rubbed his shoes on his trouser legs.

'No sir,' she replied. 'Arrived from the hospital at around twelve, and hasn't spoken a word, not to anyone. And going by the shaking of the head, doesn't want a solicitor. So, don't expect much conversation or witty repartee.'

'Thanks, Claire,' Bassey said opening the interview room door. The prisoner was staring unseeing at the table, but looked up when they entered and smiled in recognition. They took the seats opposite the prisoner - the ones which weren't screwed to the floor.

Bassey shook her head slowly and looked into the prisoner's eyes before starting the interview. 'Well, what do we call you? Miss Miller sounds very formal to my ears.' Artie's sister just looked back and smiled. 'Miss Miller it is then, until we have something a little more friendly. Because, believe me, we do want this to be an amicable process,' Bassey said in the most pleasant voice she could manage. Atkinson just touched the dressing on his cheek. 'We don't want to have any unpleasantness, there's been enough of that. So, please talk to us so that we can understand what's been going on.' Artie's sister just tilted her head and smiled.

'Now, I know that you will have been read your rights,' Atkinson said. 'And I know it says somewhere in there that "anything you say may be taken down and used in evidence against you", but not saying anything doesn't really help either.'

Smile.

'Come on Miss Miller, it's going to be a long day if you don't say anything. Please help us to help you. You may not believe it, but at this stage of an investigation we're not just interested in a conviction. We actually want to help. Please allow us to do so.'

Smile.

'OK then, what we'll do is this - the Sergeant and I will go and have a late lunch and let you think about what you want to do. We won't put you back in the cells. It's a little more comfortable here, not much, but better than a cell. Would you like something to eat? A drink perhaps?' He and Bassey got up from the table and headed towards the door. Turning and looking back. 'Please think carefully about this. It is in your own best interests to talk to us. I'll send you a cup of tea and some sandwiches.'

Another smile.

Once out in the corridor the drippingly pleasant tone fell from Atkinson. 'Fucking hell Shirl, I don't think she's going to say anything. Ever!'

Bassey nodded, and they made their way to the canteen. She thought it a good idea not to let Artie's sister know that they knew her Christian name. If she eventually offered up the name Maria, it would signal a crack in her defences.

XXXIX

It was an hour later, Atkinson and Bassey were standing outside DCI Mitchell's office. Atkinson gave his shoes a quick "polish" and pressed the button on the traffic light system. The green light immediately lit up and Atkinson pushed open the door. Mitchell was sitting behind his desk and Superintendent Rogers was sitting just to one side. The DCI waved to the two chairs in front of the desk and they sat down.

'How are you two?' asked Rogers with a note of concern in his voice.

'Fine, thank you sir,' Atkinson answered for both of them, touching the dressing on his cheek.

'Nasty cut you've got there Martin, must make sure it doesn't get infected. Worst thing that could happen that. How are your tetanus jabs? Up to date? Don't know where that knife might have been.'

'He's OK sir,' said Bassey. 'He's just miffed about his guitar.'

'Oh, yes. I hear it was quite valuable .... in its way. Ah well, better to have you here Martin than a guitar. I don't think either I, or DCI Mitchell play?' Rogers looked at Mitchell who shook his head with a slightly doleful look on his face. Frustrated musician. 'So, where do we go from here then? I hear that little Miss Gobshut is living up to her name and still hasn't said a word. The only time she's opened her mouth it seems is to eat or drink tea.'

'I think we need to have a word with her brother, Artie,' Bassey said. 'See if he can throw any light on what's been happening. If nothing else we'll get a bit of background information.'

'I agree. Why do you think she attacked the two of you? How did she know where to find you?'

'Well,' Atkinson began. 'I remember, vaguely, getting out of the taxi last night and a small white car whizzing passed me. Nearly ran me over! I thought I'd seen it somewhere before but I put it out of my mind. Uniform have found a white Nissan Micra parked near my flat. According to the DVLA the registered keeper is one Maria Miller, Flat 13 Daleacre Drive. So, the reason I thought I knew the car was that I'd seen it parked outside her flat. So, best guess is that after we left the flat, she followed us. It was, I suppose, fortuitous for her that we went to the pub and stayed together after that. It made things far easier for her when it came to overpowering us.'

'You mean you were both spark out pissed,' chipped in Mitchell with a grin. 'But, how did she get in?'

'That TV trick with the credit card must actually work,' postulated Bassey.

'More likely you were too pissed to shut the doors properly,' Mitchell countered with another grin.

'OK,' Rogers said. 'Let's get back to our next move. I agree with Shirley.' Fucking hell, him as well! 'We should bring in the brother, see if he's got anything to say that might be helpful. But for now, you two go home, it won't hurt Miss Miller to have a night in the cells. It might even loosen her tongue. We've got plenty we can keep her for. Pick the brother up in the morning. Late in the morning. The pair of you look like you could do with a bit of a lie in.'

They said their goodbyes and went straight home. After last night, they both needed the space and the time.

XXXX

It was after eleven o'clock when the tinkling of the bell caused Fred Lowe to come out of the backroom. A look of disappointment crossed his face as he saw who it was.

'Morning Fred,' Atkinson said. 'Is Artie in at all? I know his bike's not outside, but I thought he might be out on a delivery....'

'Actually, I hoped that you were him. He hasn't turned up this morning and he's not answering his phone. He's not gone missing like Ben, has he?'

'No, we're pretty certain that he's still around .... somewhere,' Atkinson answered. 'We'll go over to the flat, see if he's there.' Halfway to the door Atkinson turned. 'We'll let you know if we find him Fred, so don't go worrying.' But it looked as if Lowe had already started.

Out on the pavement, no communication was needed. The two officers climbed into the car and headed towards Daleacre Drive.

'Do you think he'll be there?' Bassey asked after a few minutes.

'I hope so, because if he's not, I've got no idea where to start looking for him,' admitted Atkinson.

The rest of the journey was spent in silence, trying not to think about what they would do if Artie proved not to be at home. The sigh of relief was almost audible when Artie's Yamaha was parked outside the flat, but was he at home? Bassey knocked on the door and after a few seconds, that felt like hours, a dishevelled and worried looking Artie appeared.

'Ah Artie,' said a relieved Atkinson. 'I'm afraid we've got some bad news for you. Your sister, Maria, we've got her down at Copy Lane,' he touched his cheek. 'She attacked Sergeant Bassey and myself last night.'

'Attacked you! Why?'

'We don't know the answer to that Artie, we hoped that you might be able to give us some ideas,' Bassey answered. 'Do you mind coming down to the station with us?'

'No, no, of course not. Will I be able to see her?'

'I don't think that'll be a problem. We'll wait for you in the car.'

'Looks like he's been up all night,' Atkinson said as they settled themselves into the car. 'Obviously worried about his sister being out all night.'

'Yeah, looks that way. Here he comes now.' She started the engine.

Once Artie was settled in the back seat, Atkinson turned to look at him. 'She hasn't spoken a word since we arrested her. You need to have a word Artie, tell her that it's in her own best interests to talk to us.'

'I'll see what I can do Mr Atkinson,' whispered a still worried looking Artie.

XXXXI

Once they arrived at Copy Lane it was quickly sorted for Artie to see his sister. The pair were put into Interview Room 1 and a PC stood watch outside the door. Atkinson and Bassey also stood outside, straining to try and hear what was being said. All they could hear was the hum of an extractor fan and the quiet indecipherable buzz of conversation. No shouted accusations from Artie about him being left to worry all night and no equally voluble explanations from Maria, just a quiet murmur. All conversation stopped as soon Atkinson knocked on the door and entered the room.

'OK Artie, I'm afraid we've got to put Maria back in a cell for a while, then we need to have a little chat.' Atkinson didn't speak again until Maria had been taken from the room and Bassey had joined them, bringing with her three steaming mugs of coffee. 'So, Artie, did Maria tell you anything? Is she going to speak to us?'

'She didn't say a lot Mr Atkinson. She admitted to me that she'd attacked you and Sergeant Bassey,' Atkinson rubbed his cheek and Artie continued. 'She also said that she isn't going to answer any of your questions, no matter how many times you ask them.'

'Did she tell you why she attacked us?'

'No.'

'Come on Artie,' Bassey said. 'You were in here for ten minutes, we could hear you talking, she must have said something.'

'Honestly, she didn't give me any explanation for the attack and I've got no idea why she did it.'

'OK Artie, Sergeant Bassey and myself are just going to try and have a little chat with your sister. You sit here and drink your coffee; we won't be long.'

Once out in the corridor Atkinson almost exploded. 'He knows what's going on. I know it! He spent ten minutes talking to his sister and she told him nothing? Bollocks! He knows why she attacked us alright, but he doesn't want to say. Why doesn't he want to say?'

'Is it because … if he told us the reason for the attack it could lead us to other things, things he doesn't want us to know about?'

'Like what? I can't really see Artie being involved with the disappearance of Ben and Ruth, or the murder of Josie. Can you?'

'No, but Artie is linked to Ben. Could this all be to do with Ben's exercise book?' Atkinson looked blank. 'C'mon, think about it. Ruth disappears, probably murdered, and Ben keeps a book about it and shares its contents with Artie. Ben then tells Artie he's got new information, and puff, Ben disappears, again probably murdered. The book is given to Jan Carter for safe keeping and Josie is murdered. Jan gives us the book and Maria attacks us.'

'Hmm, but why kill Ruth in the first place? And what's the connection between Ruth and the Millers?'

'I don't know, let's go and ask Maria.'

They had Maria brought up from the cells and put into Interview Room 3 and left her to stew for thirty minutes while they went to look for Mitchell and Rogers.

XXXXII

They eventually found Mitchell and Rogers in the canteen having lunch. As they approached their table, Atkinson trouser polishing his shoes, Rogers put down his ham and cheese sandwich.

'Any success with the brother?'

'No, not yet,' Atkinson answered. 'But we're both certain that he knows something. He had ten minutes alone with his sister and then told us that she hadn't told him anything, apart from admitting to the attack. He also says she didn't tell him why she attacked us, but I don't believe that. Shirl thinks that Artie and Maria are both tied in with the disappearances of Ruth Anderson and Ben Smart, as well as the murder of Josie Rutherford.'

'Sit down then the both of you,' invited Rogers. 'And Shirley you can tell us why you think they're all linked together.'

'Well Sir,' started Bassey, sitting down. 'I think it's all to do with Ben Smart's exercise book - that's the link. Everyone who has had possession of that book has either disappeared, been murdered or been attacked.'

'But as I understand it, Miss Rutherford didn't have anything to do with the book.'

'Yes sir, you're right, but she lived with Jan Carter who did. The killer could have mistaken Josie for Jan, or thought that because she shared the house she knew where the book was.'

'And you and Martin were the next people to have the book. I see your reasoning Shirley, but why was the only true murder scene we have, such a mess? Our other supposed murder scenes were scrupulously clean.'

'Yes Sir, but might it not be that the killer didn't have time to tidy up the scene in Kenmere road? Maybe Jan came home before the clean-up could begin.'

'A good point, yes,' said Rogers. 'But Miss Carter didn't disturb anyone as far as we're aware, and if she had I'm sure that she also would be dead. You do realise, don't you, that I'm playing devil's advocate here. I quite like your theory Shirley, but we need to find the link between the Millers and Miss Anderson. So off you go, the pair of you, get it sorted.'

'Get it sorted, he said. Fucking hell Shirl does he not think we're trying?' Atkinson grumbled as they walked back to the Interview Suite. 'We've got one who won't speak at all and another one who's not really saying anything. So, we'll try rattling Maria's cage, again shall we?'

'I've got an idea,' Bassey said pulling Atkinson to a halt. 'Just continue with lots of questions about her attack on us and I'll jump in when I think she's ready.'

Atkinson looked at Bassey intrigued by what she'd just said. He nodded his agreement and continued walking.

XXXXIII

After the preliminaries with the tape recorder, Atkinson asked Maria if she wanted a solicitor. She gave her usual smile as a way of reply, Atkinson shrugged and kicked off the interview.

'Miss Miller, we know that you attacked us but we don't know why. Would you care to enlighten us about your reasons?'

Smile

'OK, would your brother be able to tell us why you attacked us?'

Smile.

'Let's go back a little bit, shall we? Why did you follow us? You must've followed us because I'm sure my address isn't public knowledge. So, why? Was your plan all along to attack us?'

Smile

The interview followed this pattern for the next fifteen minutes or so when Bassey suddenly cut in. 'What's your connection with Ruth Anderson?'

There was no smile this time. The question had taken Maria unawares. Was that a hint of fear that Bassey saw in her eyes?

'OK, interview terminated at 1:47pm,' Bassey said turning off the tape. 'Mac! Mac!' she shouted and a PC put his head around the door. 'You can take Miss Miller back to her cell now. Thanks'

After Maria had left the room Bassey looked at Atkinson. 'Interesting, eh?'

'Too right! That question threw her completely, coming out of left field like that. Totally unexpected. She wasn't prepared for any questions about Ruth. Well done Shirl. Let's go and have a word with Artie.'

'Right then Artie, does your sister have any connection to Ruth Anderson?'

Bassey saw the same look in Artie's eyes that she had seen in his sisters. What did they know?

'Come on Artie, it's time to be telling us what the hell's going on,' she said. 'Did your sister know Ruth Anderson? In fact, did you know Ruth Anderson before Ben Smart showed you his book?'

Artie sat very still and didn't say a word, he just stared at the wall behind Atkinson's head. The only sound in the room was the hum of the extractor fan. Not another one playing dumb!

'Artie, if you know anything, anything at all, it's best that you tell us.'

'Look Artie,' Atkinson said. 'If you play dumb like your sister, we'll have no choice but to arrest you as well. Tell you what, you sit there and think about it for a while, we'll be back soon.

XXXXIV

'Nothing we can do now but wait Ron, lets nip out and have a word with Fred Lowe. We said we'd let him know about Artie, and we can see if he knows anything about Maria.'

'OK, but I don't think we'll get much.'

Twenty minutes later they walked into Fred Lowe's butchers' shop, Lowe was just finishing serving a customer.

'Hello Miss Round,' Bassey said as she recognised the woman at the counter.

'Oh, it's you two. Solved it yet? Thought not. Waste of time the pair of you,' and with that Miss Round marched out of the shop.

'Nice to see someone's got faith in you,' smiled Lowe. 'Did you find Artie? Is he OK?'

'He was safe and snug at home Fred,' Atkinson answered. 'He was in a right state though. His sister didn't come home last night and he was worried sick.'

'Maria didn't come home?'

'No,' said Atkinson rubbing his cheek. 'She's turned up though, so everything's good.'

'What happened to your face Inspector? Upset the wife?'

'Just a little run in with a ne'er do well. All part and parcel of the job unfortunately.'

Lowe seemed satisfied with this explanation so Atkinson continued. 'Talking of Maria, do you know her at all Fred?'

'Not really no. I've met her .... twice I think it is. Seemed a nice girl, very pretty but a bit quiet. Some are though, aren't they?'

'Do you know anything about her and Artie's relationship?' asked Bassey. 'We know they live together but that's about it.'

'Artie used to live with his mother, around the corner in Stuart Road. In a flat above a shop, just by the lights where Stuart Road meets County Road. He was living there when he started here with me, but not so long ago he moved in with Maria. I suppose a young man in his twenties living with his mum is not the sort of image you want to portray.'

'No, I suppose not,' Atkinson agreed.

'Well, Maria's a nurse of some kind, I don't think she works on the wards, more in a clinic, I think. From what he says I gather that they're very close and always have been, look out for each other if you know what I mean? A couple of times he's had a phone call from her and had to leave early.'

'Did he ever say what the phone calls were about?'

'No, and I never asked. Family business, I suppose. Nothing to do with me. You seem very interested in Maria; I must say.'

Atkinson and Bassey stayed silent, hoping Lowe would say more.

'She didn't give you that, did she Inspector?' smiled Lowe.

'Now you know I couldn't tell you even if she had.'

Lowe looked askance at Atkinson and slowly nodded his head as if everything had suddenly become clear.

'C'mon,' Bassey said. 'We'd better get back to the station. Thanks Fred,' with this she grabbed Atkinson's arm and hurried him out onto the pavement. 'God knows what Fred's thinking now. Let's go before he starts really getting inquisitive.'

'Going back to the station will have to wait a bit, Shirl,' Atkinson said looking at his watch. 'Let's go to Stuart Road and see if we can find Artie's mother. There can't be that many shops there, can there?'

Atkinson was right, there were only two shops at the County Road end of Stuart Road. A newsagent on one side of the road and an old-fashioned electrical shop opposite. They tried the electrical shop first. The window had an underwhelming display of light bulbs, plugs and boxes of fuses - all illuminated by a string of half-hearted flashing coloured lights. Atkinson stepped inside, followed by Bassey. They found themselves in a short corridor. In front of them was a solid looking door and to the left the entrance to the shop. A man, who could have been in his sixties, looked up from his newspaper. A cigarette dangled from the corner of his mouth, the ash from which decorated his maroon cardigan. For some reason Atkinson couldn't take his eyes from the cardigan - it was buttoned up wrong.

'Can I help you?' he asked, speaking around his cigarette.

'I hope so,' Bassey answered, Atkinson's mind was obviously somewhere else. 'Is there a flat above this shop?'

'There's two. Why, who's asking?'

'Oh, sorry,' Bassey fished for her warrant card. 'I'm DS Bassey and this is DI Atkinson.'

'Dibble, as my grandson calls you.'

'Guilty as charged. Does a Mrs Miller live in one of the flats?' The man nodded. 'Which one and do you think she'll be in?'

'The top one. I saw her come in about half an hour ago, so unless she's sneaked out again without me seeing ...'

'How do we get up there? Is there a bell or anything?'

'No bell. I can let you in though,' said the man coming out from behind the counter, scattering cigarette ash on the floor. He led them back into the corridor, fumbled in his pocket and pulled out a huge bunch of keys. The cigarette never left his mouth.

XXXXV

While Bassey knocked on the door, Atkinson polished his shoes. There was the sound of a TV as a door was opened inside and someone shuffled along the hallway.

'I've told him, I don't know how many times, not to let people come up here … '

'Mrs Miller?' Bassey waved her warrant card. 'I'm DS Bassey and this is DI Anderson, can we have a few words please?'

'Police? What do you want? And it's Miss, not Mrs …. I suppose you'd better come in.'

The living room of the flat was small but cosy. There was a window on one wall that looked down on Stuart Road, a smallish artificial leather three-piece suite, a coffee table and a large TV fixed to the wall opposite the sofa. Miss Miller indicated that they should sit down and then left the room saying she was going to make tea, and they were to make themselves at home. Atkinson immediately sat and began watching the black and white film that was playing on the TV. Bassey walked across to the window, drawing back the lace curtains she could see the newsagents opposite and the junction with County Road.

'Not much of a view,' said Miss Miller, startling Bassey somewhat. 'But as Basil Fawlty said, I shouldn't be expecting to see herds of wildebeest.' She smiled and put the tray of tea she was carrying onto the coffee table. 'Help yourselves to milk and sugar.'

'Sorry to disturb you like this,' Atkinson said as he spooned sugar into a cup. 'But we'd like to talk to you about Artie and Maria.'

'Artie! Pretentious prat! His real name's Arthur, I don't know why he doesn't use it, me and Maria always call him Arthur. It's like those bloody blue lenses in his glasses. He thinks they make him look cool and mysterious. Everybody else thinks they make him look like a knob!'

Wheels began to turn in Bassey's brain – Arthur and Maria? 'Can I ask you Miss Miller, were you married to Mike Cooksey, the butcher in St John's Road?'

Atkinson stopped stirring his tea and looked at Bassey.

'Yes, yes I was. We split up when Arthur was in his last year at school, and we moved here. Just me and Arthur, the girls already had their own flat. The man was a pig! You've obviously met him,' Bassey nodded and Miss Miller continued. 'He could be as nice as pie in company, but when he was at home … He used to drink. Drink a lot I mean; probably still does I suppose. After a few he became obnoxious, throwing his weight around. Even hit me a couple of times. Our Arthur seemed to get the brunt of it though, no idea why, no idea at all. Alpha male shit?'

'Possibly,' Bassey agreed nodding, encouraging Miss Miller to continue.

'Our Maria was great though. She'd often stand between her dad and Arthur, protecting the lad. They became inseparable, the two of them. He'd follow her everywhere. I suppose he felt safe and she didn't seem to mind. Took him everywhere she did, the beach, Sniggery Woods, all over the place. You wouldn't think there was eleven years between them. In fact, he moved out of here and moved into her flat with her, when my other daughter, Jenny, moved on.'

'So, is Miller your maiden name then?' Atkinson asked.

'Yes. I started using it when I left Mike, and the kids started as well. Anyway, why do you want to talk about Arthur and Maria? Are they in trouble?'

'I'm afraid they're both down at Copy Lane police station,' explained Atkinson, touching his cheek. 'Your daughter, Maria, attacked Sergeant Bassey and myself last night.' A look of incomprehension and shock passed over Miss Miller's face. 'We don't know why she attacked us, and she's obviously under arrest. Artie though, he's just helping us with our enquiries …. at the moment.'

'Can I see them?'

'No, not just now I'm afraid, if you give the Sergeant your phone number, we'll give you a ring and let you know when you can,' Atkinson stood up. 'I'm sorry we had to bring you such bad news.'

As they walked back to the car Atkinson and Bassey looked at each other and smiled.

'Why didn't we make the connection before now?' Atkinson shook his head. 'Artie – Arthur, Arthur – Artie. It seems so obvious now.'

'So, there is a connection with Ruth Anderson. Let's go and see what Artie has to say now.'

XXXXVI

'Sorry we've been so long Artie,' Atkinson said as he settled into a seat. 'But we've received some new information.' Artie continued to stare at the wall, so Atkinson continued. 'We've been speaking to your Mum,' this got Artie's attention. 'And very interesting it was too. Why did you never tell us that you were Mike Cooksey's son? You knew Ruth, didn't you? She rented the flat from your dad. Maria probably knew her as well.' Atkinson paused, waiting for Artie to speak.

Artie sat very still and didn't say a word for two or three minutes; the only sound in the room again, was the hum of the extractor fan. Suddenly –

'I want a solicitor.'

'A solicitor?' parroted Atkinson.

'I'm not saying another word until I've seen a solicitor.'

'OK, it may take a little while, but we'll get you a solicitor. C'mon Shirl,' Atkinson said standing up. 'Let's go and see who the duty solicitor is.'

Outside in the corridor Atkinson cracked a big smile. 'If he wants a solicitor, we're onto something Shirl.' Bassey nodded. Did this mean either Artie or Maria were responsible for the disappearances of Ruth and Ben, and the murder of Josie? If so where did the other sibling fit in? Or were they adding two and two and getting five?

XXXXVII

Bassey was waiting at the front desk when a middle-aged man, looking the exact opposite of Atkinson arrived. He wore a well-cut suit, a double cuff shirt complete with cuff links and his shoes sparkled. She recognised him immediately and sighed. Keith Turtle was well known at Copy Lane. He tended to be officious, obstructive and a pain in the arse. But if she was in trouble, it was the Mutant Ninja who she would want to see walking through the door, riding to her rescue.

'Good afternoon Sergeant,' he said pleasantly, raising one eyebrow. 'I take it you're something to do with the reason I've been called? Very unusual for you to be seen at the front desk.'

'Afternoon, Keith, good to see you too, I just happened to be here if you really want to know,' more eyebrow raising. 'If you'd like to sign in and follow me.'

No more words were exchanged until they were standing outside the door to Interview Room 1, where Atkinson was waiting for them.

'Inspector - this makes me feel that you and the Sergeant here have been awaiting my arrival. Now what does that remind of? Yes, that's it, two cats on hot bricks,' Turtle smiled. He nodded at the closed door. 'My client in here? Yes? Good. You can leave it to me now, I'll give you a shout when we're ready.'

Atkinson pulled a face as they walked away from the interview room. 'Fucking hell! Why him?' he exploded. 'Why the Mutant Ninja? Why couldn't we have gotten some young lad? One who's still wet behind the ears would've been nice.'

'Not happening, Ron, not happening.'

'Let's go and have a chat with Maria, see if she screams for a solicitor,' smiled Atkinson. As Holmes would say – the game was afoot.

'Well Maria, yes we know your names Maria,' Atkinson said kicking off the interview after Bassey had started the tape. 'We also know that Miller isn't really your surname, it's your Mum's maiden name. We've been talking to your Mum, the former Mrs Cooksey.'

No smile this time.

'Yes, and she's been telling us how close you and your brother Artie are. Or should we call him Arthur?'

No smile.

'I think Arthur may want to tell us something,' Bassey chipped in. 'He's asked for a solicitor. Do you want one?'

A nod of the head.

'OK, we'll get you a duty solicitor, may take a little while,' Atkinson paused. 'Look Maria, you've got to speak to us at some point, why not start now?'

A shake of the head.

'Someone will be in in a moment to take you back to your cell, we'll talk again later.'

In the corridor Bassey looked at Atkinson and said 'At least she's expanding her repertoire. We've now got head nodding and shaking as well as smiles. I'd call that progress.'

'I have to agree with you there, not much, but progress.'

'They both know something, but what? Do you think they're trying to protect each other? If so, what have they got to hide?'

'It looks that way, let's get this solicitor organised, have a cup of coffee and then update Mitchell.'

XXXXVIII

It was a full three hours before a PC found them in the canteen. 'The Mutant Ninja – sorry, Mr Turtle, would like a word with you sir.'

Atkinson thanked him and turned to Bassey with a grin. 'We'll just finish these coffees, no rush. Let Mr Turtle wait for us for a change.'

Bassey put her cup purposely on the table. 'I agree. But I don't think we should leave it too long; we don't want him being even more of a pain than he usually is.'

Five minutes later curiosity had got the better of them and they were in the corridor outside Interview Room 1. Turtle was standing with his back to the door, as if he was guarding the contents of a bank vault. Neither detective could read his face. You had to give the man credit where credit was due. It didn't matter what a client told him, no matter how bad, grisly or gory, he always gave out an air of calmness and control. It must have given those that he represented a great confidence boost. Even those who were "bang to rights".

'I've had some discussions with my client. And, you'll be pleased to hear, he has agreed to answer your questions. I have advised him, that at the moment he's not under arrest, but it would probably be beneficial for him if he answered your questions fully and frankly. I hope that your happy with that Inspector?'

'Sounds good to me Keith. Shall we go in and see if we can find out what's been going on?'

Once the tape was running and everyone had been identified Atkinson started proceedings.

'OK then Artie, are you going to tell us what's going on, or do we have to drag it out bit by bit?'

'They had a baby! A baby no one knew anything about,' blurted Artie.

It was not where Atkinson had envisioned starting. 'Who had a baby Artie?'

'Miss Anderson and Clarke, the Headmaster.'

So, Clarke was the father of Ruth's baby. He had been hiding something. 'And how did you find out about this?'

'I was at school, and the cook asked me to take a couple of rubbish bags out to the bins.'

'You were a pupil at St Michaels?' Bassey asked.

'Yes. And as I was outside, I overheard them talking behind the bins. They didn't see me though. Miss Anderson was shouting, something about him not wanting to take responsibility.'

'And what did Mr Clarke say?'

'He said she should keep her voice down in case somebody heard them. Then Miss Anderson said that he hadn't changed and he was still just thinking about himself. That's when I snuck away before they realised, I was there.'

'OK Artie, you've obviously been bottling that up for a while,' Bassey said. 'Feel better now?' Artie nodded. 'Good, so let's start at the beginning, shall we?'

Artie nodded again and after a short pause began to speak. 'Me and Clarke never got on, never got on at all. I'd upset him in assembly one morning and he never forgave me, thought I'd made him look a fool in front of the whole school. Served the prick right. He was a right bastard at school, spying on everybody. Peeking into classrooms, things like that,' Bassey recalled the benches in the school corridors. 'Even the teachers thought he was a prat! Then she came, Miss Anderson,' Artie paused again. 'Oh, she was lovely. She was pretty and friendly and spoke to everyone in a nice way, even the nutters in the Unit liked her. Me though, I loved her. Looking back, I realise now it was just a crush, but at the time I really thought it was love. If I was walking down a corridor and I saw her I would follow her.'

'How did she feel about that Artie?' interrupted a slightly disturbed Bassey.

'Oh, she never noticed me, I kept far enough behind, not too close, but close enough so that I could pick out her scent. She always smelled of strawberries.'

'Did you tell anyone about this .... infatuation?'

'No one at school, but I did tell our Maria. She said I was just being stupid.'

'Ahh, your Maria,' Atkinson joined in. 'You're very close you two, aren't you? Can you tell us a little about your relationship?'

Artie looked at Turtle, who gave an imperceptible nod of his head. 'Well, Maria's always looked after me, ever since I was little. You've met my Dad and if you've seen her, I'm sure my Mum told you all about him. He was OK when he hadn't had a drink, but he was a right bastard when he'd had a couple. He used to take it out on me for some reason,' Artie saw the look on Atkinson's face. 'Don't ask me why, I don't know. He hit my Mum a couple of times as well, that's why she left him. Anyway, our Maria's eleven years older than me and she's always looked out for me. She stood in between me and Dad a couple of times to stop him hitting me.'

'When was this?'

'Oh, I'm not really sure, I was only little and I don't remember much about it.'

'How do you know then?'

'Our Maria told me.'

'Not your Mum?'

'No, she doesn't like to talk about Dad much. But our Maria says she used to grab me, when he started hitting me or was about to, and take me to the park or somewhere until he'd calmed down. Sobered up more like!'

'So, Maria told you all about these .... rescues?' Bassey asked. Artie nodded. 'And your mother never really mentioned them to you?' Artie shook his head. 'I suppose your very grateful to your sister for saving you from those beatings?' Artie nodded enthusiastically.

'She was your saviour, you looked up to her,' added Atkinson. Artie nodded. 'Apart from being your own private Batman ...'

'Inspector!' interjected Turtle.

'Sorry. Apart from the times Maria protected you from your father, did you spend much time together?'

'Oh yes, she used to take me everywhere with her. We'd go to the beach, the woods, the park, places like that.'

'And what had you used to get up to on these outings? A small boy and his elder, much elder sister. She wasn't taking you to meet her boyfriend, was she? So, what did you do?'

Artie looked at Turtle, who shook his head. "I think my client could do with a little break Inspector.'

Atkinson showed his agreement by standing up and gesturing to Bassey to shut off the tape.

'I think we'd better get Mr Clarke in here, don't you?' said Atkinson once they were out in the corridor.

XXXXIX

Things were getting complicated, they had Artie in Interview Room 1, Maria moved up from the cells and into Interview Room 3 and Clarke had been put into Interview Room 2. Artie and Maria had their solicitors with them and it was a nap that Clarke would be screaming for one in about five minutes. It was going to be like spinning plates – if they wanted the whole story, they couldn't let one fall.

'Hello Mr Clarke,' Atkinson said as he and Bassey sat down at the table opposite the Headmaster.

'Why have you had me brought here Inspector?' demanded Clarke.

'We just need you to help us understand a few things.'

'Did you have to bring me here to ask me these things? Could we not have done it at home?'

'Well, one of the things we want to ask you is …. why didn't you tell us that you're the father of Ruth Anderson's daughter?'

The look of shock on Clarke's face was text book. 'I want a lawyer, before I answer any questions,' he stammered as the blood continued to drain from his face.

Bingo!

'We'll organise a duty solicitor for you,' Atkinson said conversationally as he and Bassey stood up to leave. 'That's if there's any left,' he whispered to Bassey.

'OK Shirl, what have we got?' Atkinson asked as they sat in the canteen drinking more coffee.

'Well, Artie has told us that he had a crush on Ruth and that Clarke is Alice's father. He also told us that he and his sister have a very close relationship. We've got nothing from Maria yet and Clarke's not saying anything without a solicitor. We know that they're all connected in some way, but not how. So, a little more than we knew this morning, but basically, still not a lot.'

'We think that Artie and Maria know something and might be trying to protect each other. Agreed?' Bassey nodded. 'Artie's started talking, under close supervision of the Mutant Ninja, and Maria's now got a solicitor, so we can expect her to break her vow of silence.

That leaves Clarke. He's been with his solicitor long enough, let's go and see what he has to say.'

L

'Mr Clarke,' Atkinson began as he and Bassey sat down. 'You're not under arrest, but we are going to record our conversation. We do still have the option to arrest you for obstructing a police investigation, and we will do so if you don't answer our questions fully and frankly. Do you understand what I've just said?'

Clarke looked at his solicitor who nodded. Clarke also nodded.

'OK then, let's begin. When did you first meet Ruth Anderson?'

'I first met Ruth when she came to lodge with us in Oxford,' Clarke answered in almost a whisper.

'Can you please speak up for the benefit of the tape Mr Clarke?'

'Yes, yes, sorry. As I said I first met Ruth when she came to lodge with us in Oxford in 2005. At the time my wife and I provided lodgings for students at the university. Ruth had come down to read … Politics and Philosophy I believe. Anyway, all the Halls of Residence were full and she was allocated to us by the accommodations people. She arrived, with her parents, on the Sunday, just before term started. The three of us, Ruth, my wife and myself, hit it off almost immediately. She became part of the family you might say.

'My wife and I have never had children of our own, Inspector. After her accident it would have been life threatening for Anne to get pregnant. In fact, if I'm totally honest, that complete side of our marriage had been curtailed. So, I suppose we compensated by taking in students from the university. Young people who were probably away from home for the first time. And I like to think that we gave them some stability and a caring home to come back to when they were so far away from their own families.'

'Did you not think about adopting?' Bassey asked.

'We ruled that out very early on, Sergeant. What with me working and Anne being confined to a wheelchair, I don't think we would have even been considered. Plus, students were, shall I say, easier to look after. They were house trained, hopefully appreciated what we did for them and usually moved on after twelve months.'

'OK, can we get back to Ruth?' interrupted Atkinson.

'Yes, as I said she became part of the family. She accompanied me to the theatre a couple of times and we went for a drink occasionally.'

'With or without your wife?'

'Usually without, Inspector. My wife doesn't really like pubs too much, she finds the access difficult and always feels that she's in people's way.'

'So, you thought you'd give it a go with this young girl who was far from home?'

'I wouldn't put it as crudely as that Inspector. My wife actively encouraged me to look outside our marriage for .... satisfaction shall we say? Ruth was a very pleasant and attractive young lady, we got on well, so I thought why not - using your words here Inspector - why not give it a go? As it transpired Ruth was attracted towards me and became, shall we say, a very enthusiastic partner.'

'Let me get this right,' interrupted a disgusted Bassey. 'You say your wife was OK with this? Where did you go? Hotel rooms?'

'Yes, Sergeant my wife was perfectly happy with the arrangement. And no, we did not use hotels, that would have made the whole affair somewhat sleazy, don't you think?'

Sleazy! Could it sound anymore sleazy? 'So, where did you go? Don't tell me you did it at home.'

'Yes Sergeant, we did it – as you say – at home. My wife and I shared a ground floor bedroom in an extension at the back of the house. Ruth's room was upstairs and at the front. I would retire at night with my wife and when she was asleep, I would slip out of the bed and go to Ruth's room. I always made sure that I was back in my own bed before my wife woke up in the morning.' Clarke spoke as if he had nothing to apologise for.

'Bloody hell!' Atkinson exploded. 'And you don't think that's sleazy? That's right under your wife's nose! The poor woman, having to live with that.'

'Inspector,' said the solicitor, with a slight look of disgust on his face. 'We're not here to discuss my client's arrangements with his wife, no matter how .... interesting they may be.'

'You're right, let's get on. So, Mr Clarke the result of your dalliances with Ruth Anderson ended up with her being pregnant. Can you tell me what happened when she told you?'

'Well Inspector it came as quite a shock to me, as you can imagine.'

'Did you not practice safe sex?' a bewildered Bassey asked.

'No, I assumed that she was on the pill when she never mentioned using condoms.'

'You assumed!' continued a now exasperated Bassey. 'You met her parents when they dropped her off?' Clarke nodded and Bassey continued. 'They are very religious people and that girl would probably have had the strictest and tightest upbringing imaginable. She probably didn't even know what contraception was. My father had a saying – you can't keep going to the well and not expect to get wet. Very apt in this situation, don't you think Mr Clarke?'

Atkinson stepped in as Clarke was nodding his agreement. 'So, we know you were shocked, but how did the conversation go?'

'Well, I told her that I knew of a discrete little clinic which could make the problem go away.'

'And how did she react to that?' Bassey enquired sharply.

'Not very well, not very well at all I'm afraid. I explained that I was at a crucial time in my career, I was starting to apply for headships, and that a child would make life very difficult for me.'

'Let me guess. She said you were selfish and only thinking about yourself and not her and the baby.'

'Yes, yes you're right Sergeant. She said that it didn't matter what I said she was going to keep the child. I said right away that if that was her plan, she would really need to find somewhere else to live. I told her that, naturally, I would contribute to the upkeep of the child, but I couldn't have her in the house, parading her pregnancy in front of Anne. Anne is very *laissez faire* about many things but I don't think she would have stood for that. Ruth told me that she had already thought about it and had spoken to the accommodations people. It seems that there was a hostel that they used for just such circumstances and that she could move in as soon as she wanted or needed to.'

'Not an uncommon problem then,' Atkinson mused. 'And when was it she broke this news to you?'

'March, March 2006.'

'Did you stay in contact after Ruth left your house?' Bassey asked.

'No, I didn't see Ruth again until after the child was born. We ran into each other in the city centre and I persuaded her to go for a coffee. It was then that she told me that her parents were looking after the child.'

'So, let me get this clear,' Atkinson said. 'After getting Ruth pregnant, you threw her out of your house and didn't see her again until a chance encounter in Oxford city centre?'

'Yes, that's factually correct Inspector. Putting it like that, in such a stark manner, I can see how you think I'm some sort of callous brute. But perhaps I should add, that I had tried to see Ruth during the course of the pregnancy, and she'd refused to see me.'

'OK, if she obviously wanted nothing to do with you, how come you both ended up at the same school in Crosby?' Bassey asked. 'Because I don't believe in coincidence.'

'Well Sergeant, after the coffee we began to see more of each other, you could say she mellowed towards me somewhat. Over the final two years of her course we met quite often and began to draw closer together.'

'Closer together?'

'I suppose, you could say we started again with our relationship,' Atkinson rolled his eyes. 'Yes Inspector, all aspects of it.'

'So, let me see if I can fill in what happened next,' Bassey said. 'Your relationship blossomed and when you moved to Crosby, you used your position as headteacher to get Ruth a job at your school. You helped her out with the rent for her flat and bought her a few nice things?' Clarke nodded. 'I assume that Mrs Clarke knew all about this arrangement?' Clarke nodded again. 'Then Ruth decided that it would be a good idea if Alice came to live with her and be close to her father, the father she'd never met. You were dead set against this and the two of you argued. She said that you were selfish and regretted having anything to do with you. You became worried that the existence of the child would become common knowledge. You couldn't allow that to happen so you went to visit Ruth and murdered her.'

'No! I could never do that! Not to Ruth, not to anyone.'

'But her going missing quite neatly sorted out your problem,' Bassey continued. 'For someone who you were so close to, you didn't appear to be over concerned about Ruth's disappearance.'

'I'd been round to the flat a number of times over the summer to try and talk to her. I honestly believed that she had gone home to Birmingham, to stay with her parents and see the child. I just thought that she'd delayed her return to school.'

'OK Mr Clarke,' Atkinson said. 'I think we've got everything we need. You can go home, but please don't leave the district. You will hear from us again; this isn't finished yet. You may still be charged with obstructing the police.'

'Oh, one last thing,' Bassey said as Clarke was getting up to go and she was turning off the tape. 'Does your wife do amateur dramatics?'

'Amateur dramatics Sergeant?'

'Yes, because as I remember she put on one hell of a show those times we came to your house. Protecting you, I suppose.'

'No amateur dramatics Sergeant. As you say, she just wanted to protect me.'

'She did a good job. Why she bothered though I'll never understand.'

Clarke had the good grace to look at least a little embarrassed as he left the room.

LI

'Have a productive break Artie?' Atkinson asked as Bassey set off the tape recorder. There was no reply so Atkinson continued. 'So, what did you and your sister do on your little trips? It must have been something interesting, or Mr Turtle here wouldn't have jumped in quite so quickly.' He looked knowingly at Turtle.

'It didn't start right away,' Artie began. 'I don't remember when it actually did start, but it wasn't right away.'

'What didn't start Artie?' Bassey asked.

Artie hesitated before speaking in a whisper. 'The killing, she liked to kill things.'

'What things?' asked a mystified Bassey.

'Small animals,' Artie replied in a stronger voice. 'It started with small animals. We found a bird with a broken wing in Sniggery Woods. The poor thing couldn't fly. It just fluttered around in circles on the floor. She picked it up, so gently, held it and talked to it in a soft low voice, telling it how she was going to make everything better. Suddenly she smashed it against the trunk of a tree and then stamped on it. I just burst into tears. She told me to stop snivelling and that it was the best thing to have done, as it put an end to the poor animal's suffering. She explained how it would have eaten by a fox or something. Or slowly died of starvation. We had just put it out of its misery.'

'What happened then?' prompted Bassey.

'She told me to stop crying and said we should bury the bird so that foxes couldn't get at it. That could be my job, I could be in charge of the burial. So, I dug a small hole using a stick to put the body in, I covered it back up and put a little marker on the grave,' Artie stopped speaking for a couple of seconds. 'Then when it was done, she gave me a big hug and kissed my eyes. To dry up the tears she said. On our way home she said that I shouldn't say anything about what had happened, as some people wouldn't understand.'

'And you said, that was the first time,' prompted Bassey again.

'Yeah, well after that she used to look for small animals that were injured "to help them on their way" as she put it. She always did the killing and I took charge of the burial. And even though I'd stopped getting upset she still gave me a big hug and a kiss every time. But injured animals are difficult to find, they're an easy meal. So, we widened the search, well our Maria widened the search, and she started looking for any small animals to "help on their way". Animals in the woods or on the beach are quite difficult to find and she soon got fed up with just "helping" frogs. So, she moved on to other things, cats, small dogs, things like that. It was then that things changed.'

'Changed, changed how?' asked Atkinson.

Artie looked at Turtle again before he answered. 'She started cutting them up after she'd killed them. Taking out the heart and the lungs and things like that.'

'Why would she do that?'

'I don't know. I asked her and all she said was that it made her feel good, excited her in some way, that she enjoyed seeing the blood and pulling out the different bits.'

'And you continued with the burials?'

'Yes, that was my job …. to clean and tidy up when she'd finished.'

'Did anything else change?' Bassey asked, hoping she was wrong.

'No, nothing, nothing else happened,' it came out in a rush, unlike the previous answers.

Bassey knew that her fears could well be correct and pushed on. 'Are you sure about that Artie? You can tell us you know, in fact you need to tell us, tell us everything.'

Again, Artie looked at Turtle, but this time Turtle just looked confused. They were obviously going into areas that solicitor and client had not discussed.

'Can we have ten minutes or so please Inspector?'

"Fine with me Keith,' the tape was turned off and the two officers left the room.

'OK Shirl, what just happened in there?'

'Fucking hell Ron you're dense sometimes,' Atkinson still looked puzzled. 'Didn't that hugging and kissing light any fires in your brain?'

'Ohhh.'

'Yes "ohhh". This isn't just about blood lust or whatever you want to call it, it's sexual.'

'You don't think …...?'

'Yes, I do. I don't want to, but I do.'

Twenty minutes later the interview restarted. Artie was looking rather sheepish and Turtle looked a little embarrassed, well as embarrassed as a hardened duty solicitor can look.

'OK Artie,' Bassey said taking the lead. 'Let's go back to what used to happen after Maria had …. finished what she was doing. What happened next?'

Artie looked at the ceiling for a moment before he began to speak. 'Well, as I said, I'd tidy up the area. I'd bury the body and the body parts, and then I'd clean up so that there were no traces of anything.'

'And then?'

'And then …. Maria …. would give me …. a cuddle.'

'Just a cuddle?'

'Yes, just a cuddle!' Artie shouted. Turtle patted Artie's arm comfortingly.

'You were quite young when all this started Artie, what happened when you got older?'

'What do you mean, what happened?'

'Come on, you know what I mean, what happened with the cuddles? Did they stay just cuddles?'

Again, Artie looked to Turtle for reassurance before he spoke. 'No …. as I got older, they became more than cuddles.'

'More than cuddles?'

'Yes …. she started touching me, y'know, down there,' almost a whisper.

'How old were you when Maria started touching you?'

Another long pause. 'About seven or eight, I suppose.'

'I know this is going to be a difficult question for you to answer, but how long was it before it became fully sexual?'

Artie just sat and stared at the table, saying nothing.

'Come on Artie,' Atkinson said quietly, joining the conversation for the first time. 'We know it must have become sexual; these things always do. So please tell us when it started.'

A deep breath. 'I was thirteen when we did it for the first time.'

'Thirteen?' Bassey repeated. 'Was she still telling you not to say anything about what was happening?'

'You don't understand, it was love, we love each other!'

'You're brother and sister, Artie.'

'Yes, but we love each other,' Artie whispered.

'Is it still going on? Is that why you moved into the flat when your other sister moved out? So, you could be together?' Artie nodded. 'For the tape please Artie.'

'Yes.'

'Has Maria ever had a boyfriend?'

'No. No, she hasn't.'

'I think we should have another break Inspector,' said Turtle.

'An hour OK for you?' Atkinson said looking at a visibly upset Artie.

LII

When the interview resumed, Artie had recovered his composure. Atkinson decided to bring the conversation back to the original line of questioning. 'So, how long did this go on for this …. this "helping" animals?'

'She stopped when I was about thirteen.' There's that thirteen again. 'It was around the time she started working for the Blood Transfusion Service,' he shrugged. 'I suppose she saw enough blood at work.'

'What you're saying then, is that your sister liked to kill and cut up animals and it was your job to bury the bodies …. to clear away the evidence,' Atkinson said. Artie nodded. 'OK then Artie, what happened with Ruth?'

Artie took a deep breath, looked at his solicitor and began talking. 'I'd told our Maria about Miss Anderson, how I thought she was lovely and how she smelled of strawberries. Maria didn't say much, but I could tell she was upset. She didn't say anything, she didn't have to, I could tell. Then, when I heard Miss Anderson and Clarke talking about the baby, I had to tell someone, so I told our Maria. She said that I wasn't to brood on it, these things happened.'

'All too often, I'm afraid,' said Bassey.

'I left school not long after that, and when the school summer holidays started, I was looking after the shop while Mum and Dad were on holiday. Then one day, when I was shutting up, I got a phone call from our Maria. She wanted me to go to Miss Anderson's flat above the café. But to come in the back way. I didn't know what she was doing in the flat, but she seemed to be a little excited, so I went around straight away. She'd left the back gate from the jigger open and the back door to the building. As soon as I went into the flat, I knew that something wasn't right.'

'How could you tell that something was wrong?' Atkinson asked.

'I'd been to the abattoir with Dad a couple of times and I recognised that metallic smell of fresh blood. Lots of fresh blood. Our Maria was in the kitchen and Miss Anderson was lying on the floor. There was blood everywhere and her insides were stacked on the draining board. I nearly passed out. She said to me that this was just like when we were out in the woods, and I had to clean up. She didn't say what had happened and I didn't ask, not then anyway, I just went into clean up mode.'

'How did you clean it up Artie?' Bassey asked.

'I knew exactly what I needed to do. I went back to the shop and got a pile of black bin bags, some sharp knives and a cleaver,' both Atkinson and Bassey hoped this wasn't going where they suspected. 'Then I …. and then I finished what our Maria had started. I stripped to my boxers, to keep the blood off my clothes and started to cut the body up into smallish pieces.'

'What did you do with the pieces?

'I put the pieces into the bin bags. When I'd finished, I got our Maria to make a path of bin bags to the bathroom and I took a shower.'

'So, you used the bin bags to try and stop blood dripping off you and onto the floor?'

'Yes, after the shower I took the bags with the bits of body and put them in the cold store at the shop.'

'What about Maria?' Atkinson asked.

'I cleaned what blood I could see off her and sent her home to change and get rid of her clothes and the bath towel I'd used.' That's why there was no bath towel! 'What she did with them I've got no idea.'

'So, she wasn't there for the next stage of the clean-up?'

'No, that was just me.'

'Go on Artie, what happened next?' prompted Atkinson.

'Well, the kitchen was a mess so I decided that the best thing to do was give it a deep clean. When I took the bags to the shop, I got all the cleaning materials I could find, and I spent the next four or five hours scrubbing. It looked clean to me, but I'd seen CSI on the telly, and I knew there were chemicals that could show up blood stains even when the blood had been cleaned away.'

'Luminol.'

'Yeah, that's it. So, I thought I'd come back the following night and do it all again. But first I looked it up on the internet. It said that if you used an oxy bleach rather than a normal bleach it stopped the luminol working.'

Both Atkinson and Bassey knew that luminol worked by releasing oxygen which combined with any haemoglobin it came into contact with to form oxyhaemoglobin. And it was this that caused the characteristic glowing result. By using an oxy bleach, the oxygen released turned all the available haemoglobin to oxyhaemoglobin. So, when the luminol was sprayed onto a surface there was nothing for its oxygen to bond to – so no glow.

'Next day I bought more cleaning materials, to replace the ones I'd used from the shop and lots of oxy bleach. As I said, my plan was to go back that night and clean everywhere again and then bleach the fuck out of the place.'

'You must have used a lot of bleach, we could still smell it in September,' Bassey added.

'Yeah, I kept cleaning and scrubbing until I was certain that I'd removed all traces. Then I got rid of the clothes I'd been wearing by putting them in a bin bag and putting them in a bin in the jigger.'

'What did you do with the body parts?' Atkinson asked, although he thought that he already knew the answer.

'Well, in the shop we have two large waste bins, one for bones and one for other animal waste. Over the next couple of nights, I removed what flesh I could from the bones, minced it and put it back in the cold store labelled "Pork Mince". Human flesh is supposed to taste like pork, that's why it's called long pig.' Yuk!! Bassey tried to remember if she'd ever bought mince from Cooksey's butchers. 'The other bits, the lungs, brain, heart and such like I minced up and used to make faggots. What I couldn't use I put in the animal waste bin and the bones I broke up and put in the bone bin.'

'So, you're saying that the good people of Waterloo and Crosby disposed of the body for you?'

'Yes Inspector,' Artie agreed.

'Ingenious, but very grisly,' Bassey said. He was so matter of fact about it all!

'OK,' Atkinson continued. 'What did Maria have to say about what happened?'

'When I asked, she said that she'd only gone up to the flat to talk to Miss Anderson. She said she'd taken the spare keys from the hook in the shop and gone in the back way so that no one in the café saw her. Miss Anderson let her into the flat because she recognised her as the landlord's daughter.'

'What had she gone to talk about?' interrupted Bassey.

'She said the baby. Where she thought it would get her, I don't know. Anyway, it seems they started to argue and she grabbed a knife and stabbed Miss Anderson. According to our Maria, she didn't mean for her to die.'

'Why did Maria split Ruth open and take out her organs?'

'I asked her that. All she'd say was that after Miss Anderson was dead it seemed the right thing to do.'

'It seems to me,' Bassey said. 'That you both reverted to your younger selves. Maria did what she used to do to animals and you cleaned up her mess and made sure no one could find out about what she'd done.'

'What about the blood on the knife though?' asked Atkinson. 'There was a knife in the block with blood on it. The way you cleaned up it can't have been Ruth's and I'm pretty sure it wasn't yours or Maria's. So, if you did such a good clean up job how did you miss it?'

'It's Clarke's,' Artie answered.

'Clarke's?'

'Yes Inspector, Clarke's a blood donor,' Atkinson remembered the lapel badge Clarke wore, it was heart shaped. 'A week after Miss Anderson …. passed away, there was a blood doning session at St Luke's church hall and Clarke went along. It was our Maria who was his nurse for the session, she recognised him, and took a small vial of his blood. It was an easy thing to do, it seems they always take a couple vials of blood to test for Factor X, HIV and things like that. She just took an extra one and pocketed it. We put some on the knife in Miss Anderson's flat, just in case.'

'Just in case someone started investigating,' Bassey said. 'So, if we found out about the child and the argument he would be implicated. You were putting everything into place to frame him.'

'Yeah, that was the plan.'

'Well Artie,' Atkinson said. 'I'm sure Mr Turtle prepared you for this, but we're going to have to arrest for being an accessory to murder.'

Artie gave a tight-lipped smile and nodded.

LIII

'Jesus!' Bassey said when Artie had been taken down to the cells and they were alone in the interview room. 'He must be conditioned like one of Pavlov's dogs. I can't think of another way to put it, conditioned to clean up after his sister.'

'Yeah,' Atkinson agreed. 'If you've been doing it since you were five, it must almost be like second nature. He said himself that he switched into clean up mode.'

'And she was sexually grooming him as well, on top of everything else.'

'Ah Inspector, before you go,' Turtle poked his head into the room. 'My client has obviously got a lot more questions to answer. Can I ask you when you intend to question him again? I do have other clients and I think I should clear the decks and concentrate on Mr Miller for now.'

'I think we'll leave him for today now, Keith,' Atkinson answered. 'Ten in the morning OK for you?'

'That would be great, thanks,' Turtle said, withdrawing his head and closing the door.

'How does he do it?' mused Bassey. 'He must know the whole story, or at least the meat of it, if not the exact details,'

'Poor choice of words there Shirl. It's just a job, a game to him, he can't afford to get too involved or too judgemental. He has to represent his client to the best of his ability. Anyway, we don't know the full story yet, so let's go and find out.'

Maria and her solicitor, Sarah Mercer, were waiting, not quite patiently, in Interview Room 3. Maria was staring at the table top on which Mercer was drumming her elegantly manicured finger nails.

'Ah Inspector,' said Mercer as they entered the room. 'I wondered when you were going to grace us with your presence.'

Again, to Atkinson's disappointment, Mercer was another old hand. When was he going to get his young wet behind the ear's attorney? 'Sorry to have kept you, Sarah, but we've been having an interesting conversation with your client's brother ... Arthur.' Maria looked up at the mention of her brother's name. Once Bassey had sorted the tape he spoke again.

'Arthur's been telling us all about your adventures in the woods. Can you tell us about what you used to get up to, Maria?'

'Inspector, what has this got to do with the charges you've brought against my client?' Mercer asked.

'You'll see Sarah, you'll see. Well Maria? Did you get a thrill out of it? You must have got some sort of thrill, or you wouldn't have done it, would you?'

A confused Mercer looked at her client. What on earth were they talking about?

Maria said nothing for a little while. 'It started when Arthur was young,' her voice was quiet, the voice Atkinson and Bassey had heard before. 'He was about five, and for some reason Dad had a downer on him. He's eleven years younger than me, so I suppose he was a bit of a surprise. You know, not planned. Dad used to drink and when he got violent, I'd take Arthur off somewhere to get him out of the way. One day, in Sniggery Woods we found a bird with a broken wing. I thought that the poor thing was a target for other animals and would be eaten. So, I put it out of its misery.'

'How did Arthur feel about that?' Bassey asked.

'I suppose he was a bit shocked; I think he cried for a bit. I got him to bury the body. You know, to give him something to do, take his mind off it.'

'And how did it make you feel?'

'Feel?'

'Yes, feel.'

'It felt great,' Maria's pretty face contorted as she answered in a much more strident voice. The voice Atkinson had heard in his flat. 'It felt like nothing I'd ever experienced before, it was great.'

Bassey looked over at Mercer, who had a look of shock and horror on her face.

'And? There's more isn't there Maria?"

'Well,' back to the quiet voice. 'We started to look for other injured animals whenever we went out to the woods or the beach.'

'But injured animals were difficult to find, weren't they? Other animals tend to eat them, and you needed the rush didn't you Maria? So, what did you do?'

'We started putting animals that weren't injured out of their misery.'

'But they weren't in misery,' Bassey interrupted. 'They were perfectly alright. Why not admit it Maria, you did it because it gave you a rush and made you feel good. Then you conditioned Arthur to do the clearing up for you.' She could see Mercer's face becoming more and more horrified. Just wait, Queen, it gets better. Or is that worse? 'When did you start mutilating the bodies?'

'I don't remember.'

'Was the rush from the killing not enough to satisfy you and you needed to mutilate the animals to feel satisfied?'

Maria said nothing. Mercer looked aghast. Could she see where this was leading?

'What else did you get up to in the woods?'

'What do you mean?' an obviously worried Maria asked.

'Come on Maria, when we said that Arthur had told us all about your adventures in the woods. We meant all about.'

'Inspector!' Mercer almost screamed. 'I think I need to have further talks with my client.'

'Yes, I think you do. Switch the tape off Sergeant.' When the tape was off, he turned to look at Mercer as they left the room. 'I think your client has a lot she needs to tell you, take as long as you like. We'll start again in the morning. I hope you've got a strong stomach Sarah - you're going to need it.'

LIV

It was seven o'clock the following morning, Atkinson and Bassey were in the canteen drinking their first coffees of the day. Both looked like they hadn't really slept.

'You look a bit rough Shirl.'

'Thanks. You don't look so good yourself. I suppose neither of us really slept well last night. I kept going over and over things in my mind, thinking about poor old Artie.'

'Poor old Artie?'

'Yes, poor old Artie. He's just his sisters' pawn. She gets him to do whatever she wants him to. When he was small, he just did as he was told. He didn't understand what was happening to him, what his sister was doing. And to look at her and listen to her speak, you'd think that butter wouldn't melt,' Bassey paused. 'But did you notice how her voice and attitude changed when she was talking about the thrills?' Atkinson nodded. 'All that rescuing him from his father must have made him very dependent on her. I wonder how many times she really had to do that? Then getting him to bury the dead animals, slowly building up to bigger and bigger bodies. As well as slowly increasing the amount of sexual contact. I wonder when he realised that what they were doing was wrong? Why didn't he stop it happening when he got older and had more understanding? Or did he ever realise it was wrong? Was he so dependent on her? Did she plan to murder Ruth Anderson, or did it just happen?'

'A lot of questions there Shirl. Let's drink up and try to find the answers,' Atkinson said finishing his coffee and standing up.

Sarah Mercer looked even worse than Atkinson and Bassey. She had had a very late session talking to Maria, followed by a few hours of troubled sleep.

Atkinson began once the tape was running. 'Well Maria, do you want to tell us about your outings with your brother?'

'Inspector,' cut in Mercer. 'Before my client answers that question, I'd like to say that I have advised her to answer all your questions as fully as possible. I know that up until now she has been .... a little uncooperative shall we say. But she has now agreed to tell you everything.'

'Thanks Sarah. So, Maria ....?'

It was the quiet voice. 'Arthur used to come with me everywhere when he was very young. That day in the woods, when we killed the bird, he did cry. He was very upset, I don't know why, it was only a bird. To settle him down a bit I gave him a cuddle and kissed his tears away. I remember …. they were very hot and salty. I thought that was it. Done with, never going to happen again. But he had other ideas, he wanted a cuddle every time we went out and …. Then as he got older, he wanted more and more. I wanted to stop but he was so needy, and I didn't want to hurt him.'

'So, you're saying that your …. relationship with Arthur is all down to him and nothing to do with you? You just went along with it so as not to upset him?' Bassey asked.

'Yes, yes that's right.'

'That's not the story Arthur's telling us. He says that you were the instigator, that you started it all.'

'He's telling lies!' Maria shouted. 'It was all him, I just …. just …. just couldn't find a way to stop it.'

'Inspector, my client is obviously getting upset by this line of questioning. Can we have a little break please?'

'OK, we'll have half an hour,' Atkinson said looking at Bassey and gesturing towards the tape. 'We'll have some drinks brought in to you.'

LV

While Bassey was collecting coffee, Atkinson found a quiet table at the back of the canteen. What the fuck was going on? They needed to be careful where they went with their questioning of both Artie and Maria. Their incestuous relationship mustn't be allowed to overshadow the murders of three people.

'Here y'are Ron,' Bassey said putting a coffee in front of him and breaking his train of thought.

He took a deep breath before he spoke. 'What do you make of all that then Shirl?'

'Jesus Ron, what a mess! They're both blaming each other, but I believe Artie over Maria.'

'Why's that then?'

'Well …. I've not had much experience dealing with sexual abuse, and that's what this is Ron. He was only five remember. But from what I've picked up, the abuser always lays the blame on the victim. "I wouldn't have done it if they hadn't wanted me to", sob, sob.'

'I agree with you Shirl, the whole sexual thing is down to Maria. She's groomed him over the years and now he's become almost totally dependent on her. But what we've got to do is not let this …. sideshow, for want of a better word, get in the way of the main feature. The deaths of three people.'

'Yeah, but do you not think that this could have something to do with the reason Maria killed Ruth? Could she have been jealous and seen Ruth as a rival for Artie's affections? Even though it was all one sided and Ruth knew nothing about Artie's infatuation.'

'A possibility Shirl, we'll have to ask. Whether we'll get a straight answer is another matter.'

'Something Artie said has got me thinking. He said that they started having sex and Maria stopped killing things around the same time. When he was thirteen. Do you think she didn't need the killing and mutilation to get her thrills anymore? Do you think she was getting all the thrills she needed from her relationship with Artie?'

'Could well have been,' Atkinson said looking at his watch. 'Come on Shirl, they've had their thirty minutes.'

LVI

Once everyone was settled and the tape turned back on Atkinson continued questioning Maria. 'OK then Maria, can you tell us what happened when you went to see Ruth Anderson in her flat?'

'Arthur told me about her, how he fancied her and everything. He knew nothing could ever come of it and I thought it was a harmless enough infatuation. Then he came around to the flat, the one I was sharing with our Jenny, and told me about her and the headmaster and that they had a baby. He seemed very upset by it all, and in the end, I told him not to worry I would try and sort something out.'

'Sort something out?'

'I had no idea what I could do, but I had to say something to him, he was so upset. He thought he loved her and he definitely hated Clarke,' Atkinson nodded encouragingly. 'So, I decided I'd go around and see her. I lifted the spare flat keys from the hook in the shop and let myself in the back way. I knocked on the flat door and when she opened the door, she wasn't really sure who I was. I told her that Dad had sent me up to check out one of the windows which looked onto St John's Road. It looked like the double-glazing unit had blown. She said that it would be one of the kitchen windows. She wouldn't have noticed it from the inside as there were thick net curtains on the window. I followed her into the kitchen and we checked on the windows. There was obviously nothing there, but it gave me an opportunity to start talking to her. We chatted for a while about how she found living in the area, had she made any new friends, you know, things like that. Then I asked her if she'd known anyone up here before she'd moved. She said no, she hadn't known anyone before she moved.

'I don't know how, it just sort of came out, but I called her a liar. I said I knew that she knew Clarke and that they had a kiddie together. She just went berserk, started screaming at me and pushing me. I had to protect myself,' here the voice changed. It became louder and more excited, and her face took on a look of malevolence. 'So, I grabbed a knife from the draining board and stabbed her in the neck and the chest and she went down like a bag of spanners!'

'So,' Atkinson asked. 'You hadn't gone to the flat with the idea of killing Ruth Anderson?'

'No,' quiet voice again. 'I'd only gone to talk.'

'Self-defence then?' Bassey asked. Maria nodded enthusiastically. 'But, it's not as if Ruth had come at you with a weapon is it? To use your own words, she was screaming and pushing, a bit of an overreaction to stab her don't you think?'

Silence.

'OK, you admit to killing Ruth Anderson, but have you told us the real reason you went up to the flat?' Atkinson asked. 'Did you kill Ruth as a result of an argument like you say? I think you went up there with the express intention of killing her,' Maria just stared at him. 'I think you saw Ruth as a rival. A rival who could steal Arthur away from you. And where would you be if you lost Arthur? He was your little pet. He did things for you that no one else could or would do. You had too much history together to lose him to another woman.'

'It was just a teenage crush he had! There was nothing real to it!' screamed Maria, her face twisted with anger.

"But you didn't see it like that did you?' pursued Bassey. 'All you could see was the worst possible outcome, well for you anyway. Which was Arthur finding someone else. You knew the someone else wouldn't be Ruth, but that didn't mean that it wouldn't happen sometime. So, you decided to put a marker down. You thought that if you got rid of Ruth, Arthur would think twice about ever going off with someone else. That he would think if he ever found someone, he could have a normal relationship with, you would kill them as well. And it worked didn't it? Has Arthur ever had a girlfriend?' Maria shook her head. 'Thought not. So, it worked Maria. You killed a young girl who was no threat to you, and screwed up your brother's life even more than it was already.'

Maria said nothing, but Bassey could tell that she had scored a direct hit by the look on Maria's face. Maria hadn't gone to talk to Ruth about the baby, she had gone to kill her as a warning to Artie.

Atkinson let the silence linger for a while before he spoke. 'OK Maria, I think we know the real reason why you went to see Ruth. But why did you gut her like you did?'

'It's what I always did with animals,' she sneered.

'But she wasn't an animal. Did it increase the rush, the excitement of the kill?' asked Bassey sharply.

'It felt great, just like it used to,' excited voice.

'So, you called Arthur so he could do what he always did. In fact, what you'd trained him to do, tidy up your mess and get rid of the evidence. But also, so that he'd get the subliminal message you were sending him.' Maria just stared into space. 'Did you stay and help? Did you cut up Ruth's body as well, or did you leave it all to Arthur?'

'I helped with the bin bags,' quiet voice. 'But Arthur did all the cutting and chopping, I just took the bags off him, the bags with the pieces in. When he'd finished that, he cleaned me up as best as he could and sent me home to change and get rid of the clothes I was wearing.'

'Did you help with the cleaning of the flat?'

'No, Arthur did all of that by himself.'

'So, by leaving Arthur to do everything, you were in fact, hammering home your message,' said Bassey. 'Was it your idea to put Clarke's blood on the knife?' Maria nodded. 'I take it that was to frame Clarke if the worst came to the worst and the investigation was getting too close to the truth. Arthur could let slip about the argument he'd overheard and bingo, Clarke had a motive. We would then have had reason to match his blood with that on the knife, and it would have been very difficult for him to get out of that,' more nodding. 'But we didn't get anywhere near close, did we? And I bet you thought you'd got away with it.'

'Now, let's turn to Ben Smart,' Atkinson said. 'What can you tell us about his disappearance?'

Maria looked at Mercer, who shook her head and said 'Can we leave it there for a bit Inspector? My client is looking tired and I need to talk to her about what she's already said.'

'OK Sarah, we'll take a break for a while. Sergeant, the tape?' Bassey shut down the tape and left the room with Atkinson.

'Let's go and get a coffee and have a little break, and then go and talk to Artie,' said Atkinson once they were out of the room. 'Let's see what he has to say about Ben Smart.'

LVII

'OK then Artie,' said Atkinson after Bassey had turned on the tape. 'We've spoken with your sister about what happened with Ruth. What we'd like to know now is, what's the story with Ben Smart?'

Turtle nodded to Artie and he began talking. 'I recognised Ben from school as soon as I saw him. He used to run the Unit where Miss Anderson worked. He came into the shop one day, when Fred was out, to introduce himself. He'd just taken over the newsagents. He didn't recognise me, but why should he? I was never in the Unit. He never bumped into me around school and I look very different to what I did when I was sixteen.'

'You certainly do.'

'Ben and Fred became great friends and I suppose by extension I did as well, especially when it turned out we both loved crime novels. Ben introduced me to people like Luca Veste and Steve Cavanagh,' neither name meant anything to Atkinson or Bassey. 'Then one day he brought an old school exercise book to the pub with him. I nearly died of fright when he told me what was in it, but he didn't seem to notice anything. He let me have a look and I quickly made sure there was no mention of me and our Maria. As I'd shown an interest, he quickly started sharing things with me. We'd regularly meet in the pub after that and talk about what might have happened to Miss Anderson.'

'Artie,' Bassey interrupted. 'I notice that you always call Ruth, Miss Anderson. Is there any reason for that?'

'I only ever knew her as Miss Anderson, and it's always seemed wrong to call her anything else.'

'I picked up on it, did Ben?'

'If he did, he never said anything, well not to me anyway.'

Both Atkinson and Bassey were pleased with the way Artie was answering their questions. His voice was strong and confident. Obviously, the Mutant Ninja had told him that things couldn't really get any worse, but they may get a little better.

'OK, go on then Artie,' Atkinson said.

'Well, I met Ben in the pub one day and he said he'd made a breakthrough in the case, as he called it. I asked him what it was, but he said he wanted to keep it to himself for the time being, as he had to do a bit more digging. He hadn't brought the book with him so I thought he must have written it down in there, and he'd left it at home so I wouldn't be able to get a look at it before he was ready to share. I must admit I started to get a bit worried about what this new information was. I knew he couldn't have found out anything about me, or he wouldn't have told me about it, would he? But that didn't mean he hadn't found out something about our Maria. He didn't know she was my sister, and if he found that out ….'

'So, what did you do Artie?'

'I told our Maria, and she said not to worry she'd think of something.'

'After what had happened to Ruth, did that not worry you a bit?' Bassey asked.

'No, not at the time. You see, what happened with Miss Anderson was a long time ago. And she seemed to have stopped doing that sort of thing. Then, I got a phone call to go around to the newsagents, and as soon as I went in, I knew what she'd done. I could feel it and I could smell it, if you know what I mean,' Atkinson and Bassey both nodded. 'I shut the shop door and made sure it was locked and went upstairs to Ben's flat. They were there in the kitchen, she was sitting on a stool and Ben lying on the floor. I'm sorry to say, but my first thought was - how am I going to clean up the mess? Fred was on holiday, so I decided it had worked once, why not again?'

'You mean you turned Ben into mince and faggots, just like Ruth?' Artie nodded in answer to Bassey's question. 'Did Maria say what had happened?'

'She said she'd managed to sneak into the flat and was looking for the exercise book when Ben disturbed her.'

'OK, so you did the big clean up and with Fred being away you had plenty of opportunity to dispose of the evidence,' Atkinson said. 'But there was no sign of the book?'

'No, I searched the place from top to bottom, I even looked in the shop. It wasn't until you told me about Ben giving it to a friend for safe keeping that I worked out where it was.'

'That was just after you got back from Ireland wasn't it?' Bassey asked. Artie nodded. 'When I asked you about your holiday, you said it had been OK and you'd been doing the usual thing, tidying up after your sister. What did you mean by tidying up?'

'Just tidying up the tent and campsite. Our Maria never puts anything away, she's the same in the flat, dead untidy.'

'Not bodies then?' Artie shook his head. 'Was it you who cancelled the newspaper deliveries? Being tidy again?'

'Yeah, well I didn't want them piling up. I thought it was better to cancel them and just act as if Ben had gone away suddenly. It also made sure I wasn't disturbed while I was cleaning the flat.'

'I suppose Maria still had some of Clarke's blood somewhere, so you could leave a little clue?' Bassey asked.

'Yeah, she'd kept it in the freezer, I don't know why.'

'OK Artie, that's enough for now. I think we need to talk to your sister and see what she has to say.' Atkinson stood up and nodded at Bassey, who turned off the tape.

'So, it looks like it was a desperate search for the book then,' Bassey said as they sat in the canteen drinking more coffee.

'Looks that way,' Atkinson agreed.

'Do you think Ben had finally picked up on Artie always calling Ruth Miss Anderson?'

'And that was what he thought was his breakthrough? That Artie knew Ruth from school?'

'Yeah, and he didn't tell Artie because he needed to flesh things out more. And probably didn't want to spook him.'

'That worked well, didn't it?'

LVIII

As she slid the cassette into the tape Bassey glanced across the table to Sarah Mercer. She looked better and seemed much more in control now.

'Right Maria,' Atkinson said. 'Can you tell us about Ben Smart?'

'Arthur told me that Ben had made, what he called, a breakthrough in the search for what happened to Ruth Anderson,' said Maria in her quiet voice. 'We both thought that he may have written down what he'd found in his blue exercise book. So, I decided to go and see if I could find it. I went into his shop and scouted out the layout, looking for the way up to the flat. I knew I was safe doing that, as he didn't know who I was. I then waited outside until the local school finished. When a big gaggle of kids went into the shop, I followed them. I thought he'd spend all his time keeping an eye on them, making sure they weren't robbing things, and ignore me. So, I managed to sneak up the stairs by the side of the counter.

'The door to the flat was unlocked and I went inside and started to search for the book. I must have been really concentrating, because I never heard him come in. I was looking in the cupboards under the sink and the first thing I knew was when he shouted. I stood up and turned around and he was just coming for me shouting and screaming, just like Ruth had done. There was no way that I could get past him to the door. I'd found a screwdriver under the sink and it was in my hand as I turned around. I waved it at him. He just kept coming though, shouting and screaming. I told him to stand still or I'd stab him, but he ignored me and just kept coming. So, I stuck him in the guts and he just sort of looked at me shocked. I pulled the screwdriver out and stabbed him again in the side of the neck and he fell to the floor. I wasn't sure what to do next, so I phoned Arthur who came right over.'

Atkinson looked at Bassey who nodded, while they'd been interviewing Artie, Sarah Mercer had obviously been coaching Maria. Telling her how to frame her answers to put the best possible spin on them and not to get too excited when she spoke, but to stay quiet and calm. It was working so far.

'So, what happened when Arthur came?' Bassey asked.

'Before you answer that Maria,' interrupted Atkinson. 'Did you cut out Ben's organs?'

Maria nodded slowly and Atkinson continued. 'Why? Why did you do that?'

'I don't know,' still the quiet voice, remembering what Mercer had told her about getting excited. 'It just sort of …. happened.'

'OK, so what did Arthur do?'

'Well, he wasn't best pleased with me. He didn't shout or anything, but I could see he wasn't happy. He told me to go home and that he'd clear everything up. There was a coat in the cupboard that fitted me where it touched, so I put it on to cover the blood and went home.'

'Do you know what Arthur did with the body?' Bassey asked.

'He told me that he did the same as he did with Ruth.'

'OK Maria, you stay here with Sarah, I'm sure you've still got a lot to talk about. We'll be back later. Sergeant …. the tape.'

Outside the Interview Room Atkinson sucked air through his teeth. 'It looks like they're telling the same story Shirl. Let's have a ten-minute break and then talk to Artie about Josie Rutherford.'

LIX

'So, Artie,' Atkinson began, as the tape whirred into life. 'What happened with Josie Rutherford?'

Artie sat quietly for a few seconds before he began. 'Well Mr Atkinson, when we went to the Stuart pub and you told me that Ben had given the book to a friend to look after, I couldn't for the life of me think who that was. Ben didn't seem to have many friends, there was Fred and there was me. Then it hit me as I was walking back to work. Miss Carter! They seem to have been great friends at school, and she always came to look after the shop when he went away. I decided that I'd tell our Maria when I got home, I didn't want to phone her and her go off half-cocked and do something stupid.'

'Which, I think, is exactly what happened,' Bassey said.

'Yeah, I suppose so,' agreed Artie. 'When I got home, I found her in the living room, wearing one of those white plastic suits, you know, like they wear on CSI. She really put the shits up me I can tell you. I thought it was the police looking for evidence. I asked what she thought she was doing. She told me that a guy at work had put her on to them. Said they were great for when you were painting, and they were quite cheap on the internet. So, she'd bought a couple because she was going to do some decorating.'

'And you thought that was the real reason she'd bought the suits?' Bassey asked.

'Yeah, why wouldn't I believe her? Anyway, I told her about our conversation in the pub and how Miss Carter was the only one I could think of who might have the book. She said we had to find out, one way or another. She wanted to know if I knew where Miss Carter lived. I told all her that all I knew was that it was number seventy something on Kenmere Road, the other side of town. She asked me what Miss Carter looked like. I told her that she usually wore a tracky, as she was a PE teacher, and she had long blonde hair that she wore in a pony tail. She said not to worry, she'd think of something.'

'Did you start to worry then though, Artie. After what she'd done to Ben?' Bassey asked.

'I suppose I should've done, but our Maria would always do what she wanted to do, no matter what I said. She tended to act first and think later. I knew there was no way of stopping her if she'd made her mind up to do something. I just hoped no-one would get hurt …. or die this time,' Artie paused for quite a long time.

'Go on,' encouraged Bassey.

'Well, when I came home from work the next day there was no sign of our Maria's car. But that wasn't unusual, she quite often did evening sessions with the transfusion service. She got home about half eight, nine o'clock and told me what had happened.'

'And what had happened?'

'She'd gone to Kenmere Road to see if she could get into Miss Carter's house. She'd seen a blonde woman with a ponytail go into the house, and she'd somehow managed to get in as well. She didn't say how. She honestly thought it was Miss Carter, neither of us knew someone else lived there.'

'Doesn't make it any better though does it Artie?' Atkinson pointed out. 'Your sister killed and mutilated a totally innocent woman.'

'Yes, I know,' and tears began to trickle down Artie's cheeks.

'When did you find out that it wasn't Miss Carter?' Bassey asked.

'Our Maria said that when she came out and was sitting in the car, she saw another blonde go into the house,' sniffed Artie. 'This one was carrying a sports bag so she knew right away she'd got the wrong one. And that's why I didn't go and tidy up.'

'So, if Maria had killed Miss Carter, and no-one else had lived there,' filled in Bassey. 'You would have gone in and cleaned up, and there would be more mince and faggots?' Artie sniffed and nodded.

'OK Artie,' Atkinson said. 'I think we've finished with you for now. Thanks for being so forthcoming. Sergeant, can you do the tape please?'

'Do you think he'd have been so upset if Maria had actually got to Jan Carter?' Bassey asked after Artie had been taken back down to the cells.

'No, I don't think so. Everything he's done, he's done to protect his sister. Jan was seen as a threat, by both of them.'

'So, do you think that's real remorse about Josie?'

'Yes, I do. Let's have another chat with Maria, shall we? I'd like to know exactly what happened at Jan Carter's house.'

LX

The tape was rolling so Atkinson started to ask his questions. 'OK Maria, Arthur tells us you bought some Tyvek suits off the internet. Can you tell us why?'

'Tyvek suits? What's a Tyvek suit?'

'White plastic coverall type of thing,' supplied Bassey.

'Ah, those. I'd said at work that I was going to do some decorating in the flat,' answered Maria in her quiet voice. 'One of the guys said that he'd bought some plastic suits off the internet and they were great for keeping the paint off your clothes.'

'Now as I remember it, you turned up at my flat wearing one of those suits. They're good for keeping blood off your clothes as well. So, did you really buy them for decorating?'

'Yes, yes I did. I also bought a couple of big plastic ground sheet thingy's, some latex gloves, plastic overshoes and some tins of paint as well. Everything I'd need to decorate the flat.'

'OK, let's move on then,' Atkinson said. 'Tell us about your trip to Kenmere Road, to see Jan Carter.'

'Well, Arthur told me that after talking to you, he thought that Ben had given the exercise book to Miss Carter. So, I thought that it was important for us to find out if she had it. We needed to know what it said. I don't know how to break into a house so I had to think of another way to get inside. The white suits gave me the idea.'

'And what idea was that?' Bassey asked, intrigued.

'I thought I could go as a decorator.'

'Go as a decorator?'

'Yes. What I did was I put a tin of the paint I'd bought in the boot of the car and put on one of the suits. Then I drove over to Kenmere Road. Arthur wasn't sure of the number; all he could remember was it was number seventy something. So, I parked in a place where I could see all the houses in the seventies. I got there about the time the schools finished. I thought if I kept a good look out, I'd see her come home from school and go into one of the houses. Then about four o'clock I saw a blonde woman with a ponytail, wearing a white top and jogging bottoms go into one of the houses.'

'Did you see her get out of a car?' Bassey asked.

'No,' replied Maria. 'She was walking down from the top of the street.'

'So, did you not think,' continued Bassey. 'That she'd got back to Wavertree from Crosby a little quickly? And without a car?'

'No, I was concentrating on which house she went into, I suppose it never occurred to me that someone else could live there. Especially someone who looked exactly like Arthur's description.'

'OK, so what happened next?' prompted Atkinson.

'I pulled the hood up on the suit, put on a pair of the latex gloves, took the paint out of the boot and knocked on the door. I thought that anyone watching would just think that I was a decorator on a job.'

'And then,' prompted Atkinson again.

There was complete silence for a few moments before Maria spoke. 'When she opened the door, I pushed her into the vestibule and smacked her on the side of the head with the paint. She was out for the count, so I put on a pair of the overshoes and dragged her down the hall and into the kitchen. I managed to struggle and get her onto the kitchen island. I rooted around in the kitchen drawers and found some thick twine. I used it to tie her hands to the sink taps and her feet to some drawer handles at the other end of the island. She was still out, so I started to have a look for the book, but first I put the tin of paint by the front door so I wouldn't forget it.'

'But you couldn't find the book, could you Maria?' stated Atkinson. 'So, what did you do?'

Maria looked at Sarah Mercer, who nodded her head encouragingly, and she began to speak. 'I went back into the kitchen and she was starting to come around. I asked her where the book was. She said she didn't know what I was talking about. So, I thought that I needed to encourage her to remember. I found a filleting knife in a drawer and waved it in her face, telling her I'd cut her up if she didn't tell me.' Maria's voice was beginning to sound excited again.

'Excuse me Inspector,' interrupted Mercer, coughing and spluttering. 'But could I possibly have a glass of water please?'

Atkinson immediately realised what the solicitor was doing. She was trying to create some time so that her client could calm down again. He had no option though, but to agree to her request.

It was a full twenty minutes before Mercer had stopped coughing and spluttering and the interview could continue.

'OK Maria, now everyone's calm again,' began Atkinson looking knowingly in Mercer's direction. 'What happened after you started waving the knife about?'

'Well, she still wouldn't tell me anything,' back to the quiet voice. Well done Mercer. 'Kept saying she knew nothing about any exercise book. But I thought she must do; our Arthur had said he was certain that Ben Smart had given it to her. So, I pulled open her shirt and cut the front of her bra. Then I put the tip of the knife just between her boobs and pushed a little so that it drew a bit of blood. Just to show I was serious. She started screaming and saying that if she knew where the book was, she'd tell me. I still thought she was lying and I dragged the knife slowly down her body, all the way to her belly button, leaving a large gash. She screamed all the way until she finally passed out. I got a little upset then that she couldn't answer any more questions and pushed the knife right in.'

'OK, we know what you did next Maria,' Bassey interjected. 'I suppose the plan after that was to phone Arthur and get him to tidy up?' Maria nodded. 'But something stopped him from doing that didn't it? What happened?'

'I got a plastic bag from the cupboard and put the suit, gloves and overshoes in it before I left the house. I grabbed the tin of paint and some keys from by the door for Arthur, and took everything over to the car. I was just about to phone Arthur when a car pulled up outside the house, and a blonde with a ponytail got out and opened the boot and took out a sports bag. It was then that I realised that I'd got the wrong person. I thought about going back into the house, but I didn't have another suit in the car, so that was out. So, I decided to sit and wait and see what happened. I left for home when the first police car arrived.'

'What did Arthur say when you told him what had happened?' Atkinson asked.

'He wasn't happy at all, but when he calmed down, we had a good talk about what had happened. We decided that no one really knew what had happened to Ruth Anderson and Ben Smart. They were only missing, there was no evidence to say that they had …. passed on. So, we thought because there was a body this time, the police might not connect the three together, that they'd think that this one had been done by someone different.'

'Which is a possibility, I must admit, we considered,' Atkinson said. 'Well, until you paid me a visit. But I think we'll leave that until after lunch, I'm hungry. We'll get some food brought to you both in here, and start again in about an hour. Sergeant?'

'Yeah, I know, the tape.'

'Do you believe that about buying all that gear for decorating?' Bassey asked as they sat in the canteen eating the "meal of the day". It was amazing how when they made too much beef stew one day it became "meal of the day" the following day.

'Yeah, I think I do. OK it's an anti-forensics kit, but you don't buy all that on the off chance you're going to kill and eviscerate someone, do you? And she knew nothing about Jan Carter having the book when she bought it. Then again, if you're a total screwball?'

'Do you not think she is a total screwball? There's got to be something wrong with her, look at the shite she's done. Started by putting animals "out of their misery", then killing them before they were injured, then killing and eviscerating them and then moving on to people. You can't tell me that's normal behaviour.'

'No, I don't think it's normal behaviour and if this case sticks, which I'm 100% certain it will, I see her spending the rest of her life in a secure hospital like Ashworth in Maghull, or somewhere like that. But I do believe that she bought all that stuff for decorating.'

Bassey nodded and went back to trying to decide what the really chewy bits were in the stew. Then, thinking about Artie's body disposal methods, decided to push them to the side of her plate, it was probably safer.

LXI

While Bassey was outside getting some much needed fresh air, Atkinson took ten minutes to fill in Mitchell and Rogers about what they had learned. They both agreed with Atkinson that it was a good strong case, but as Mitchell had said – "a little bit of forensics wouldn't go amiss."

Back in the Interview Room 3, Bassey fitted a fresh tape, turned the machine on and nodded to Atkinson.

'OK then, Maria, I hope you enjoyed your lunch; I can't say I that did, I kept thinking about your brother.' Out of the corner of his eye he could see Bassey nodding. 'Let's go back to the night you turned up at my flat, shall we? We know that you came to look for Ben's exercise book, but talk us through it please.'

'Well, you came around to our flat looking for Arthur and you told me then that you had the book,' quiet voice. 'I thought that was why you were looking for Arthur, because it had said something in the book. When you went, I realised that I didn't have time to talk things over with him about what we should do.'

'So, that's why he didn't go into work and was in such a state when we saw him. He didn't know where you were.'

'I'd decided to follow you, and see where you went. I never thought that you might just be going back to the police station. If you'd done that, I don't know what I would have done. Or if you'd split up, who would I follow? Arthur always says that I never think things through, that I just act.'

'Lucky for you we went for a drink then,' Atkinson said.

Maria nodded. 'Yeah, I suppose it was. I followed you to the pub and parked up in the carpark, in a place I could watch for you coming out. I waited for ages, and when you did eventually come out, you both looked to be paralytic. I watched you get into the taxi together and decided, having had time to think about it, that if you split up, I'd follow you, Inspector. You're the senior officer, so I thought you'd know more than your Sergeant.' Bassey tried, and failed, to hide a look of incredulity. 'I followed the taxi to your street, I thought about running you over when you were getting out of the car. But I decided that that would cause more problems than it would solve. I did come pretty close, though didn't I?' Atkinson nodded grimly, remembering the little white car.

'Then I watched you go into the building and by the time you'd got through the front door I'd got to the bottom of the path. You just let the door swing shut behind you, but I was quick enough to stop it closing fully and squeezed inside.

'I followed you up the stairs, you made so much noise I could've banged a drum and you still wouldn't have known I was behind you. I managed to work the same trick on your flat door, Inspector. But this time I reached inside and put the snick on so I could let it shut and still be able to get in if I needed to. I went back downstairs and kept watch from the car for ten minutes. Nobody came out and no one else went in, so I made up my mind what I was going to do.

'I'd put one of those suits in the boot, what did you call them? Tyvek, that's it, so I put it on along with a pair of the gloves and went back upstairs. I pushed open the door to your flat and had a little peek inside. I was just in time to see the Sergeant here disappear into one of the rooms off the corridor. I thought she'd seen me looking, because of the speed she came back out, but she just went into the next one along. Obviously looking for the toilet. From the door I could also see straight into the living room. You were there on the couch, with your head lolling trying not to fall asleep. I let the door close and waited for five or ten * minutes. I hadn't heard anyone come out of the toilet so I risked another look inside.'

'What would you have done if a neighbour had seen you hanging around in a Tyvek suit at that time of night?' Atkinson asked.

'Pest control. I'd have said I was from pest control and that your flat had a cockroach infestation, and we come around at night because that's when the little buggers come out of hiding.'

'OK, go on,' Atkinson said, quietly impressed, but not sure it would have worked.

'Well, when I got inside, I took a quick look in the loo,' she looked at Bassey. 'And you were slumped on the seat with your head on the sink snoring your head off. So, I went down to the living room,' she looked at Atkinson. 'And you were comatose on the couch, snoring even louder. I had to decide who to deal with first, I was worried that either one of you might wake up at any time. So, to make sure it wasn't you Inspector, I whacked you on the side of the head with that wooden mallet you had in the kitchen,' Atkinson unconsciously touched his temple.

'I then went back to the loo and helped the Sergeant to the bedroom,' she looked directly at Bassey. 'Do you know, you never woke up at all? You were that drunk. Anyway, there was some thin electrical wire of some kind and tape in the kitchen. I used it to tie you to the bed and gag you. I then brought a kitchen chair into the living room and managed to get you,

Inspector, into it. Then I taped you up so that you wouldn't slide off. I found a nice sharp knife in one of the kitchen drawers, and when you woke up, I sliced your cheek. Y'know just to show I was serious.'

'I realised you were serious alright Maria,' said Atkinson touching his cheek.

'I was just about to start asking you about the book when I saw the look on your face. I knew there was someone behind me, but when I turned around, I was surprised to see it was you, Sergeant. I thought you were still passed out and tied up in the bedroom. Then you hit me with that guitar and I ended up here.'

LXII

Once Maria had been returned to her cell, Atkinson and Bassey went down to the canteen for coffee. They were sitting in silence, both thinking about what they'd been told by Artie and his sister.

'I don't think we'd ever had found out what was going on if Maria hadn't come for us,' Bassey said breaking the silence.

'Yes, I think you're right,' agreed Atkinson. 'We had nothing to go on about Ruth's disappearance and nothing about Ben's. We knew there was a link, but what? Who'd have thought it would go back to a schoolboy crush? Then poor old Josie, I think her death almost did what Maria had hoped.'

'Muddied the waters, you mean?'

'Yeah. If they hadn't been on the trail of the exercise book, and if we hadn't told Maria that we'd got it, I think we'd still be banging our heads against a wall.' Atkinson paused for a few seconds before he spoke again. 'Pity there's no forensics though, they were just too clean and tidy. CSI and the internet have got a lot to answer for in my opinion. And juries …. juries love a bit of forensics, again thanks to CSI.'

They relapsed back to silence again, drinking their coffee. It was on the walk back to Atkinson's office that Bassey spoke.

'Do you remember Miss Round, Ron?' Atkinson nodded and Bassey continued. 'How big an appetite do you think she has?'

'Looking at the size of her, about as big as a small bird, why?' he asked, not following Bassey at all.

'So, you think she should still have some of those faggots in her freezer then, you know, the ones Artie made when Fred was away?'

'Shirl you're a genius!' shouted Atkinson as light bulb went off in his head. 'Those faggots will be stuffed with Ben and his DNA. And there'll be plenty of his DNA in the flat to match it with. Come on, let's get around there and see if she's got any left.'

They obtained Miss Round's address from Fred Lowe and hurried over there. When she opened the door, Miss Round peered at them for a couple of seconds until it dawned on her who her visitors were.

'Oh, it's you two,' she said derisibly. 'Have you found out what happened to Mr Smart yet? Didn't think so! Waste of space the pair of you.'

'Miss Round,' Bassey interrupted. 'Sorry to disappoint you, but we do know what happened to Ben Smart. We just need your help to prove it. Can we come in please?'

The two officers followed a puzzled Miss Round through to her small kitchen at the back of the house. Once they were seated around the tiny kitchen table Bassey began the conversation.

'Do you remember those faggots that Artie made when Fred was on holiday, Miss Round?'

'Of course, I do. Lovely they are. I've got two defrosting on a plate in the fridge for my tea.'

'Miss Round, I'm afraid we're going to have to take those faggots away with us. As well as any others you might have in the freezer,' Bassey said.

'But why?' exclaimed Miss Round. 'They're my last two! What will I have for my tea?'

'I'm afraid you'll have to think of something else for tea. But what I can say is that you are not in any trouble at all, and that those faggots will guarantee us a conviction,' Atkinson answered.

Miss Round stood up from the table and opened the fridge, removing a plate. She grudgingly passed it to Bassey. On it sat two faggots. Bassey had just had their forensics handed to her on a plate!

LXIII

Six months later, Atkinson was sitting in his living room listening to one of his all-time favourite albums – "Dark Side of The Moon" by Pink Floyd. His father may have been the scourge of the Jehovah's Witnesses but he'd introduced his son to some superb music. He was thinking about how lucky he was to be alive, how much he had to thank Bassey for and what had happened in court that day. Maria Miller had been found guilty of the murders of Ruth Atkinson, Ben Smart and Josie Rutherford. She had been sentenced to life imprisonment with no opportunity for parole. Here, life meant life and as Atkinson had predicted, she would see out her sentence in a secure hospital. Arthur Miller had also been sentenced to life imprisonment for his part in the murders, there were though, no parole restrictions on his sentence. A good result all round, and he could finally bin his "You Can't Win Them All" file. It was a pity they couldn't have sorted it out eight years ago; Ben and Josie would still be alive.

He looked down at his hands and was surprised to see he was holding a jagged piece of wood. A piece of his broken guitar. It was the piece that had been signed by David Gilmour. Atkinson didn't remember picking it up, but now that he was holding it, he wondered what to do with it. Why had he kept it? He'd thrown the other bits away a long time ago. His phone interrupted his thoughts and he pulled it from his jacket pocket.

'Hi Shirl,' he said after glancing at the screen.

'Crows? We need to celebrate a result and raise a glass to the memory of Ben and Josie, the two we couldn't save.'

'Good idea, see you there in thirty minutes.' He cut the connection and put the phone back into his jacket pocket. He felt something at the bottom of the pocket and pulled it out, it was an old crumpled business card, it had obviously been there for quite a while. Where on earth had he got that from? He brushed off the fluff and crumbs and read what was written on the card:

James Lester

Picture Framing

07843667982

He now knew what to do with the piece of broken guitar - it would look good on his office wall. He stood up, put the piece safely on the table along with the card, turned the stereo off, rubbed his shoes on the back of his trousers and walked out of the flat. Making doubly sure that the door swung shut securely.

Afterword

On the 20th June 2019, David Gilmour of Pink Floyd auctioned 120 of his guitars for charity at Christies in New York. They raised in total $21,490,750. The Martin D35 which he played on "Wish You Were Here" contributed $1,095,000 towards that total.

Or Maybe You Can

Printed in Great Britain
by Amazon

75207065R00115